THE AFFINITIES

BY ROBERT CHARLES WILSON
from Tom Doherty Associates

———

A Hidden Place
Darwinia
Bios
The Perseids and Other Stories
The Chronoliths
Blind Lake
Spin
Axis
Julian Comstock
Mysterium
Vortex
Burning Paradise
The Affinities

THE AFFINITIES

Robert Charles Wilson

A TOM DOHERTY ASSOCIATES BOOK

NEW YORK

THE AFFINITIES

Designed by Mary A. Wirth

A Tor Book
Published by Tom Doherty Associates, LLC
175 Fifth Avenue
New York, NY 10010

www.tor-forge.com

Tor® is a registered trademark of Tom Doherty Associates, LLC.

The Library of Congress Cataloging-in-Publication Data
is available upon request.

ISBN 978-0-7653-3262-2 (hardcover)
ISBN 978-1-4668-0077-9 (e-book)

Tor books may be purchased for educational, business, or promotional use.
For information on bulk purchases, please contact the Macmillan Corporate
and Premium Sales Department at 1-800-221-7945, extension 5442,
or write to specialmarkets@macmillan.com.

First Edition: April 2015

Printed in the United States of America

0 9 8 7 6 5 4 3 2 1

PART ONE

A House on a Winter Night

When an obscure data-management company launched what it called "the Affinities" a couple of years ago, almost no one paid attention. It was a quixotic idea that seemed to gain no traction: there was no ad campaign outside of a few media outlets in a few major cities, and not much press coverage even in those markets. But something surprising was happening under the radar . . .

Invited as a special guest to a local meeting, I arrived with limited expectations. What I would find, I suspected, was a group of perfectly ordinary people who had been convinced to pay annual dues for the privilege of flattering one another, a commercial conceit of which P. T. Barnum might have been proud. But there was a real energy in the gathering—social, sexual, intellectual—that took me by surprise. It made me wonder where all this was going, and I asked one young woman what she thought the members of her Affinity might be doing in twenty or thirty years.

She laughed at the question. "Writing our memoirs, I guess," she said. "Or maybe signing our confessions."

—*The Atlantic*, feature article,
"Teleodynamics, Meir Klein, and the Rise of the Affinities"

CHAPTER 1

I made the decision when I saw the blood in the mirror. The blood was what changed my mind.

I had thought about it, of course. I had clipped the ad out of the back pages of the local entertainment paper, checked out the website, memorized the address of the local test center. I had strolled past the building earlier that afternoon, lingering at the brass-and-frosted-glass door with what I tried to pass off (not least, to myself) as idle curiosity. I pictured myself stepping into the cool, dim lobby behind the InterAlia logo and maybe changing the course of my life forever, but in the end I shrugged and walked on—a failure of courage, the better part of valor, I honestly couldn't say which.

Tempted as I was, opening that door would have seemed like a confession of my own inadequacy, a confession I wasn't prepared to make.

The sight of my own bloody face changed my mind.

I walked south from the InterAlia building, on my way to meet my ex-roommate Dex at the ferry docks: we had made plans to ride over to the Toronto Islands for an open-air concert. What I didn't know, because I had been too self-absorbed to pay attention to the news, was that a large-scale demo was going on in the city's financial district, directly between me and the lakeshore.

The sound of it reached me first. It was like the sound you hear from an open-air sports stadium when there's a game on: no discernible content, just the undulant buzz of massed human voices. A couple of blocks later, I thought: *angry* voices. Maybe a bullhorn or two in the mix. And then I turned a corner and saw it. A mass of protestors filling the street in either direction and about as easy to cross as a raging river. Bad news, because dithering at the door of the InterAlia office had already made me late.

The crowd appeared to be a mix of students and academics and labor union people, and according to their banners it was the new debt laws and a massive University of Toronto tuition hike that had brought them to the streets on a hot late-May evening. A block to the west, where the sky still smoldered with sunset, some kind of serious altercation had begun. Everyone was staring that way, and I guessed the sour tang in the air was a promissory drift of tear gas. But at that moment all I wanted was to get to the waterfront, where the air might be a degree or two cooler, and meet Dex, annoyed with me though he must already be. So I pushed east to the nearest intersection and tried to shoulder through the thick of the crowd at the crosswalk. Bad decision, and I knew it as soon as I was caught in the tidal bore of human flesh. Before I had made much progress, some new threat or obstruction forced everyone closer together.

By craning my head—I'm fairly tall—I caught a glimpse of police in riot gear advancing from the west, beating their sticks on their shields. Tear gas canisters arced into the crowd, trailing smoke, and a woman to the right of me pulled a bandanna over her nose and mouth. A yard from where I stood, a guy in a faded Propaghandi t-shirt climbed onto the roof of a parked car and tossed a Dasani bottle at the cops. I tried to turn back, but it had become impossible to make headway against the pressure of bodies.

A skirmish line of mounted police appeared at the adjoining intersection, and I began to realize it was actually possible that, worst case, I could be kettled into a mass arrest and carted off to a detention cell. (And who would I call, if that happened? My family in New York State would be shocked and angry that I had been arrested; my few friends in the city were hapless art-school types, in no position to post bail.) The crowd lurched eastward, and I tried to veer toward the nearest sidewalk. I took some elbows to the ribs but managed to reach the north side of the street. The building immediately in front of me was a café, locked and barred, but there was a set of concrete steps descending to a second storefront just below ground level—also barred, but I found a place to crouch in the overhang of the concrete stairwell.

I kept my eyes pressed shut against the drifting tear gas, so what little I saw, I saw in blurry glimpses: mostly moving legs at street level, once the face of a woman who had fallen, eyes wide and mouth in a panicked O, as she struggled to stand up. I covered my own mouth with my t-shirt and breathed in gulps as another round of tear gas drifted down from the street. The roar of voices gave way to random screams, the industrial stomp of the police line. Mounted cops passed the niche where I had hidden, a weird chorus line of horse legs.

I had begun to think I was safe when a cop in riot gear came down the steps and found me squatting in the shadows. His face was plainly visible behind the scuffed plastic faceguard of his helmet. A guy not much older than me, maybe one of the foot police who had been roughed up in the struggle. He looked almost as scared as the woman who had fallen a few minutes earlier: the same big, jittery eyes. But angry, too.

I held out my hands in a *hey, wait* gesture. "I'm not one of them," I said.

I'm not one of them. It was possibly the most cowardly thing I
could have said, though it was also perfectly true. It was practically my fucking mantra. I should have had it tattooed on my
forehead.

The cop swung his club. Maybe all he intended was a moti-
vating blow to my shoulder, but the club bounced up and hit
the left side of my face across the ridge of the cheekbone. I felt
the skin break. A hot numbness that bloomed into pain.

Even the cop seemed startled. "Get the fuck out of here," he
said. "Go!"

I stumbled up the stairs. The street was almost unrecogniz-
able. I was behind the parade line of cops, who had encircled a
body of protestors east of the intersection. The block where I
stood was empty except for a litter of paper handouts, abandoned
backpacks and banners, the still-sizzling husks of tear gas canisters, and the granular glass of broken windshields. A block to
the west, someone's car was on fire. Blood from my face had
begun to decorate my shirt in rust-red paisleys. I held my hand
against the cut, and blood like warm oil seeped through my
fingers.

I turned the nearest corner. I passed another cop, a woman,
not in riot gear, who gave me a concerned look and seemed about
to ask whether I needed help—I waved her away. I took my phone
out of my pocket and tried to call Dex, but he didn't answer. I
guessed he had written me off as a no-show. At University Avenue I stumbled into a subway entrance and caught a train, fend-
ing off expressions of concern from other passengers. All I wanted
was to be alone in some sheltered place.

The bleeding had mostly stopped by the time I made it home.
Home was a bachelor apartment on the third floor of a yellow
brick low-rise with a parking lot view. Cheap parquet floors and
a few crappy items of furniture. The most personal thing about
it was the name on the call-board in the lobby: *A. Fisk.* A for

Adam. The other A. Fisk in the family was my brother Aaron. Our mother had been a committed Bible reader with a taste for alliteration.

The bathroom mirror doubled as the door of the medicine cabinet. I fumbled out a bottle of Advil, closed the door, and stared at myself. I guessed I could get by without stitches. The cut had clotted, though it looked fairly gory. The bruise would be with me for days.

Blood on my face, my hands, my shirt. Blood pinking the water in the basin of the sink.

That was when I knew I was going to call InterAlia. What was there to lose? Book an appointment. Open that brass-and-glass door. And find what?

One more scam, most likely.

Or, just maybe, some new and different version of *them*. A *them* I could be *one of*.

They gave me an appointment for Tuesday after classes. I showed up ten minutes early.

Behind the door, past the tiled lobby of the remodeled two-story building, the local branch of InterAlia was a suite of cubicles divided by glass-brick walls. Cool air whispered from ceiling vents and a polarized window admitted amber-tinted sunlight. There was a steady in-and-out traffic of people, some in business clothes and some in street clothes. Nothing distinguished the employees from their clients but the embossed lapel badges they wore. A receptionist checked my name against an appointment list and directed me to cubicle nine: "Miriam will do your intake today."

Miriam turned out to be a thirtyish woman with a ready smile and a faint Caribbean accent. She thanked me for my interest in InterAlia and asked me how much I knew about Affinity testing.

"I read the website pretty carefully," I said. "And that article in *The Atlantic* a couple of months ago."

"Then you probably know most of what I'm going to tell you, but it's my job to make sure potential clients are aware of how we do placements and what's expected of them. Some people come in with misconceptions, and we want to correct them up front. So bear with me, and I'll try not to bore you." Smile.

I smiled back and didn't interrupt her monologue, which I figured was the verbal equivalent of those caveats in microprint at the bottom of pharmaceutical advertisements.

"First off," she said, "you need to know we can't guarantee you a placement. What we offer is a series of tests that will tell us whether you're compatible with any of the twenty-two Affinity groups. We ask for a small deposit up front, which will be refunded if you don't qualify. A little more than sixty percent of applicants ultimately do qualify, so your chances are better than even—but we still end up turning away four of every ten, so that's a real possibility. Do you understand?"

I said I did.

"We also like to remind our clients that failing to qualify isn't any kind of value judgment. We're looking for certain clusters of complex social traits, but everyone is unique. There's nothing wrong with you if you fall outside those parameters; all it means is that we're unable to provide our particular service. All right?"

All right.

"You also need to be clear on what we're offering if you *do* qualify. First off, we're not a dating service. Many people have found partners through their Affinity, but that's absolutely not a guaranteed outcome. Sometimes people come to us because they're in trouble, socially or psychologically. Such people may or may not need therapeutic attention, but that's also not the business we're in."

As she said this she glanced pointedly at the bandage I was wearing. I said, "This isn't—I mean, I don't go around getting into fights or anything. I just—"

"None of my business, Mr. Fisk. You'll be evaluated by professionals, and the tests, both physical and psychological, are completely objective. No one is standing in judgment of you."

"Right. Good."

"Should you qualify, you'll be placed in one of the twenty-two Affinities and offered an invitation to join a local group, called a tranche. Each Affinity has regional and local subdivisions— the regional groups are called sodalities, and the locals are called tranches. A tranche has a maximum of thirty members. As soon as one is filled, we initiate a new group. You might be assigned as a replacement to an existing group or as part of a new tranche—either way, there might be a waiting period before you're placed. Currently the average is two or three weeks following assessment. Got it?"

Got it.

"Assuming you're placed in a tranche, you'll find yourself in the company of people we call *polycompatible*. Some clients come in with the misconception that they'll be placed among people who are *like themselves*, but that's not the case. As a group, your tranche will most likely be physically, racially, socially, and psychologically diverse. Our evaluations look beyond race, gender, sexual preference, age, or national origin. Affinity groups aren't about excluding differences. They're about compatibilities that run deeper than superficial similarity. Among people of the same Affinity as yourself, you are statistically more likely to trust others, to be trusted, to make friends, to find partners, in general to have successful social engagements. Within your Affinity you will be misunderstood less often and you'll have an intuitive rapport with many of your tranchemates. Understood?"

Understood.

"Again, your deposit will be refunded in full if we fail to place you. But the testing requires a commitment of your time, which we *can't* refund. You'll have to attend five test sessions of at least two hours each, which we can book to suit your schedule—five consecutive evenings, once a week for five weeks, or any other sequence that suits you." She turned to the monitor on her desk and tapped a few keys. "You've already filled out the online form, so that's fine. What we need from you now, if you choose to proceed, is a valid credit or debit card and your signature on this consent form." She took a single sheet from a drawer and slid it to me. "You'll also need to show me a piece of government-issued photo ID. A nurse will take a blood sample before you leave."

"Blood sample?"

"One now, so we can commence basic DNA sequencing, and one at each session for a drug assay. Apart from bloodwork, all our tests are non-invasive—but the results will be useless if you come in under the influence of alcohol or other intoxicants, so we do have to test. Results are completely confidential, of course. Clients taking prescription medication need to make us aware of it at this point, but according to your application you don't fall into that category."

The only drugs I had been taking lately were over-the-counter painkillers, so I nodded.

"All right then. Take your time and read through the agreement carefully before you sign it. I'll step out for a cup of coffee while you do that, if you'll excuse me—would you like a cup?"

"Please," I said.

The logo at the top of the agreement form—

INTERALIA
Finding Yourself Among Others

—was the most comprehensible part of it; all else was legal boilerplate, mostly above my pay grade. But I set myself to the task of reading it. I was about finished when Miriam came back. "Any questions?"

"Just one. It says that the result of my tests becomes the property of the corporation?"

"The result, yes, but only after your name and other identifiers have been stripped from it. That lets us use the data to evaluate our client base and maybe focus our research a little better. We don't sell or share the information we collect."

So she claimed. Also, the check is in the mail and I'll pull out before I come. But I didn't really care who saw my test result. "I guess that's all right."

Miriam pushed a pen across the desk. I signed and dated the document. She smiled again.

Dex called me later that night. I saw his number and thought about letting the call go to voice mail, but picked up instead.

"Adam!" he said. "What are you doing?"

"Watching TV."

"What, like porn?"

"Some reality show."

"Yeah, I bet it's porn."

"It's a show with alligators in it. I don't watch alligator porn."

"Uh-huh. So what happened the other night?"

"I texted you about it."

"That bullshit about a demo? I almost missed the ferry, waiting for you."

"I'm lucky I didn't end up in the emergency room."

"You couldn't just take the subway?"

"I was almost there, and I was already late, so—"

"You were *already late*—that says it all, doesn't it?"

I had shared my apartment with Dex for six months last year. We took some of the same classes at Sheridan College. The roommate thing didn't work out. When he moved, he left his bong and his cat behind. He eventually came back for the bong. I gave the cat to the retired librarian in the apartment down the hall—she seemed grateful. "Thank you for your compassion."

"I could come over. We could watch a movie or something."

"I'm not in the mood."

"Come on, Adam. You owe me an evening's entertainment."

"Yeah . . . no."

"You can't be a dick twice in one week."

"I'm pretty sure I can," I said.

Of course it wasn't Dex's fault that I was moody—not that Dex would ever admit that anything was his fault.

I figured I had a couple of good reasons for applying to the Affinities and a few bad ones. The fact that my social life revolved around a guy like Dex was one of the good ones. A bad one? The idea that I could buy a better life for a couple of hundred dollars and a battery of psych tests.

But I had done my research. I wasn't totally naïve. I knew a few things about the Affinities.

I knew the service had been commercially available for four years now. I knew it had gained popularity in the last year, after *The New Yorker, The Atlantic,* and *BoingBoing* ran feature articles about it. I knew it was the brainchild of Meir Klein, an Israeli teleodynamicist who had ditched a successful academic career to work for the corporation. I knew there were twenty-two major and minor Affinity groups, each named after a letter of the Phoenician alphabet, the "big five" being Bet, Zai, Het, Semk, and Tau.

What I didn't know was how the evaluation process actually worked, apart from the generalities I had read online.

Fortunately I had a talkative tester . . . who turned out to be Miriam, the woman who had done my initial intake. She grinned like an old friend when I showed up for the first session. I recognized the smile as customer relations, but I was still grateful for it. I wondered whether Miriam was a member of an Affinity.

She escorted me to a nurse's station in the back hall of the InterAlia office, where I was relieved of another vial of blood, and then to a small evaluation room. The room was windowless and air-conditioned to a centigrade degree above chilly. It contained a teakwood desk and two chairs. On the desk was a fourteen-inch video monitor, a laptop computer, and a chunky leather headband with a couple of USB ports built into it. I said, "Do I wear that?"

"Yes. Tonight we'll use it to do some baseline measurements. You can put it on now if you like."

She helped me adjust it. The headband was heavy with electronics but surprisingly comfortable. Miriam plugged one end of a cable into the band, the other into the laptop. The monitor facing me wasn't connected to the laptop. I couldn't see whatever Miriam was looking at on the laptop's screen.

"It'll take a minute or two to initialize," she said. "Most of the information we collect is analyzed later, but it takes some heavy-duty number-crunching just to acquire the data."

I wondered if she was acquiring it now. Was our conversation part of the test? She seemed to anticipate the question: "The test hasn't started yet. Today, it's just you looking at a series of pictures on that monitor. Nothing complicated. Like I said, we're establishing a baseline."

"And the blood sample? That's for drug testing, you said?"

"Drug testing plus an assay for a range of primary and secondary metabolites. I know this must seem scattershot, Mr. Fisk, but it's all connected. That could be InterAlia's slogan, if we needed another one: *everything's connected.* A lot of modern science is concerned with understanding patterns of interaction. In heredity, that's the genome. In how DNA is expressed, we talk about the proteinome. In brain science it's what they call the connectome—how brain cells hook up and interact, singly or in groups. Meir Klein invented the word *socionome*, for the map of characteristic human interactions. But each affects the others, from DNA to protein, from protein to brain cells, from brain cells to how you react to the people you meet at work or school. To place you in an Affinity we need to look at where you are on all those different maps."

I said I understood. She consulted her laptop once more. "Okay, so we're good to go. I'll leave the room, and the monitor will show you a series of photographs, like a slide show, five seconds per slide. Twenty minutes of that, a coffee break, then twenty minutes more. You don't have to do anything but watch. Okay?"

And that was how it went. The pictures were hard to categorize. Most showed human beings, but a few were landscapes or photographs of inanimate objects, like an apple or a clock tower. The photographs of human beings were drawn from a broad cross section of cultures and ages and were gender-balanced. In most of them, people were doing undramatic things—chatting, fixing meals, working. I tried not to overanalyze either the pictures or my reaction to them.

And that was it: session one of five.

"We'll see you again tomorrow evening," Miriam said.

The next day's test used the same headset but no photographs. Instead, the monitor prompted me with displays of single words in lowercase letters: when the word appeared, all I had to do was read it aloud. A few seconds later, another word would appear. And so on. It felt awkward at first, sitting alone in a room saying things like, "Animal. Approach. Conciliation. Underwater. Song. Guilt. Vista . . ."—but before long it just seemed like a job, fairly tedious and not particularly difficult.

Miriam came back for the midpoint break, carrying a cup of

coffee. "I remembered how you liked it. One cream, one sugar, right? Or would you prefer a glass of water?"

"Coffee's great. Thank you. Can I ask you a question?"

"Of course."

"Personal question?"

"Try me."

"Do you belong to an Affinity? I mean, if you're allowed to say."

"Oh, I'm allowed. Employees can take the test for free. I did. I know my Affinity. But no, I never joined a tranche."

"Why not?"

She held up her left hand, the ring finger circled by a modest gold band. "My husband was tested too, but he didn't qualify. And I don't want to commit to a social circle he can't join. It's not an insurmountable problem—tranches organize spouse-friendly auxiliary events. But he would have been shut out of official functions. And I didn't want that. That's why the existing Affinities are a little bit skewed toward young singles, divorcees, widowers. Over time, as people meet and mate inside their own Affinity groups, we expect the imbalance to even out. It's trending that way already."

"You ever regret not joining?"

"I regret not having what so many of our clients find so useful and empowering. Sure. But I made my decision when I married my husband, and I'm happy with it."

"Which Affinity did you qualify for?"

"Now *that's* a personal question. But I'm a Tau, for what it's worth. And I take some comfort from knowing I have a place to go, if I ever need to call on people I can really trust. But let's get on with business, okay?"

The next day I got a call from Jenny Symanski.

Some people thought of Jenny as my girlfriend. I wasn't sure

I was one of those people. That wasn't a dig at Jenny. It was just that our relationship had a perpetually unsettled quality, and neither of us liked to name it.

"Hey," she said. "Is this a good time?"

She was calling from Schuyler, my home town. Schuyler is in upstate New York, and all my family were there. I had left Schuyler two years ago for a diploma program in graphic design at Sheridan College, and since then I had seen Jenny only on occasional visits home. "Good a time as any," I said.

"You sure? You sound kind of distracted."

"I kind of am. I think I told you I'm up for an internship at a local ad agency, but I haven't heard back. Classes this morning, but I'm home now, so . . ."

"I don't want to be a nuisance when there's so much else on your mind."

She was being weirdly solicitous. "Don't worry about it."

"You seem to be dealing with the situation pretty well."

"What situation? The internship? The job market sucks—what else is new?"

Long pause.

"Jenny?"

"Oh," she said. "*Shit*. Aaron didn't call you, did he?"

"No, why would Aaron call me?" Another silence. "Jen, what's up?"

"Your grandmother's in the hospital."

I sank onto the sofa. Dex and I had snagged the sofa when a neighbor put it out for the trash. The cushions were compacted and threadbare, and no matter how you shifted around you could never get comfortable. But right then I felt anesthetized. You could have pierced me with a sword. "What happened?"

"Okay, no, she's basically all right. Okay? Not dead. Not dying. Apparently she woke up in the night with pain in her chest, sweating, puking. Your dad called 911."

"Jesus, Jen—a heart attack?"

I pictured Grammy Fisk in her raggedy old flannel nightgown, white with a pink flower pattern. She loved that nightgown, but she wouldn't let any of us see her in it before nine at night or after six in the morning—and strangers *never* saw her in it. The prospect of paramedics invading her bedroom would have horrified her.

"That's what everybody thought. But I was over at your dad's house this morning and he said now the doctors are telling him it was her gallbladder."

I wasn't sure what that meant, but it sounded slightly less terrifying than a cardiac condition. "So what do they do, operate on her?"

"That's not clear. She's still in the hospital for tests, but they think she can come home tomorrow. There's something about diet and medication, I don't really remember . . ."

"I guess that's good . . ."

"Under the circumstances."

"Yeah, under the circumstances."

"I'm really sorry to be the one to tell you."

"No," I said. "No, I appreciate it."

And that was true. In some ways, it was better getting the bad news from Jenny than from Aaron. My brother didn't entirely approve of me *or* Grammy Fisk. My father had underwritten Aaron's MBA, and Aaron currently co-managed the family business. But the only one willing to pay for my graphic design courses had been Grammy Fisk, and she had done it over my father's objections.

A question occurred to me. "How did *you* find out about it?"

"Well—Aaron told me."

The Fisks and the Symanskis had been close for decades. Jenny and I had grown up together; she was always at the house. Still: "Aaron told you but not me?"

"I swear, he said he was going to call. Have you checked your phone for messages?"

I rarely had to check my phone for messages. I didn't get a lot of calls or texts, outside of a few regulars. But I checked. Sure enough, two missed calls from a familiar number. Aaron had tried to get hold of me twice. Both attempts had been yesterday evening, when I had turned off my phone for my session at InterAlia.

I called Aaron and told him I'd heard the news from Jenny. I apologized for not getting back to him sooner.

"Well, turns out it's not such an emergency after all. She's home now."

"Can I talk to her?"

"She's sleeping, and she needs her rest, so better not."

It was easy to picture Aaron standing at the ancient landline phone in the living room back home. It was hot in Toronto and probably just as hot in Schuyler. The front windows would be open, curtains dappled with the shade of the willow tree in the yard. The inside of the house would be sultry and still, because my father didn't believe in air-conditioning before the first of June.

And Aaron himself: dressed the way he always dressed when he wasn't doing business, black jeans, white shirt, no tie. Dabbing a bead of sweat from his forehead with the knuckle of his thumb.

"How are Dad and Mama Laura taking it?"

Mama Laura was our stepmother.

"Ah, you know Dad. Taking charge. He was practically giving orders to the EMT guys. But worried, of course. Mama Laura's been in the kitchen most of the day. Neighbors keep coming by with food, like somebody died. It's nice, but we're up to our asses in lasagna and baked chicken."

"What about Geddy?"

Geddy, our twelve-year-old stepbrother, Mama Laura's gift to the family. "He seems to be dealing with it," Aaron said, "but Geddy's a puzzle."

"Tell Grammy Fisk I'll be there by tomorrow morning." I would have to rent a car. But the drive was only five hours, if the border crossing didn't slow me down.

"She says not."

"Who says not?"

"Grammy Fisk. She said to tell you not to come."

"Those were her words?"

"Her words were something like, *You tell Adam not to mess up his schoolwork by running down here after me.* And she's right. She's hardy as a hen. Wait till end of term, would be my advice."

Maybe, but I would have to hear it directly from Grammy Fisk.

"You'll be paying us a visit sometime in the next couple of months anyway, right?"

"Right. Absolutely."

"All right then. I'll put Dad on. He can fill you in on what the doctors are saying."

My father spent ten minutes repeating everything he'd learned about the nature and function of the gallbladder, the sum-up being that Grammy Fisk's condition was non-trivial but far from life-threatening. By that time she was awake and able to pick up the bedroom extension. She thanked me for my concern but urged me to stay put. "I don't want you ruining the education I paid for, just because I had a bad night. Come see me when I'm feeling better. I mean that, Adam."

I could hear the fatigue in her voice, but I could hear the determination, too.

"I'll see you in a few weeks, no matter what."

"And I look forward to it," she said.

My third test session was the most uncomfortable. They strapped me under the dome of an MRI scanner for half an hour. Miriam said the scan would be combined with EEG data from my earlier sessions to help calibrate the results.

The next evening it was back to the headband, this time listening to recorded voices speak a series of bland, cryptic English sentences. *If it rains, you can use my umbrella. We saw you at the store yesterday.*

"In the end," Miriam said, "the point of all this is to locate you on the grid of the human socionome."

I took her word for it. The details were a well-kept secret. Meir Klein, who invented the test, had done basic research in social teleodynamics when he was teaching at the Israel Institute of Technology in Haifa, outlining what it would take to construct a taxonomy of human social behavior. But the meat of his work had taken place after he was hired by InterAlia, and the details were locked behind airtight nondisclosure agreements. The process by which people were assorted into the twenty-two Affinities had never been fully described or peer-reviewed. The best anyone could say was that it seemed to work. And that was good enough for me.

I liked the idea of it. I wanted it to be true. We're the most cooperative species on the planet—is there anything you own that you built entirely with your own hands, from materials you extracted from nature all by yourself? And without that network of cooperation we're as vulnerable as three-legged antelopes in lion territory. But at the same time: what a talent we have for greed, for moral indifference, for wars of conquest on every scale from kindergarten to the U.N. Who hasn't longed for a way out of that bind? It's as if we were designed for life in some storybook family, in a house where the doors are never locked and never need to be. Every half-baked utopia is a dream of that house. We want it so badly we refuse to believe it doesn't or can't exist.

Had Meir Klein found a way into that storybook house? He never made that claim, at least not explicitly. But even if all he had found was the next best thing—well, hey, it was *the next best thing*.

The final test session was four hours in front of a monitor with my body hooked up to some serious telemetry. Miriam appeared during breaks, bearing gifts of coffee and oatmeal raisin cookies.

The program running on the monitor was a series of interactive tests, using photographs, symbols, text, video, and occasional spoken words. The computer correlated my test performance with my facial expressions, eye movements, posture, blood pressure, EEG readings, and the beating of my heart.

The tests themselves were pretty simple. There was a spatial-relations test that worked like a game of Tetris. There was an animated puzzle involving a runaway train full of passengers headed for certain destruction: do you throw a switch that causes the train to change tracks, saving all the passengers but killing a couple of pedestrians who happen to be in the way, or do you let the train roll on, dooming everyone aboard it? Some of the tests seemed to touch on identifiable themes (ethnicity, gender, religion), but the majority were pretty obscure. At the end of four hours it began to seem like what was really being tested was my patience.

Then the screen went blank and Miriam popped in, smiling. "That's it!"

"That's it?"

"All done, Mr. Fisk, except for the analysis! You should get your results within a couple of weeks, maybe sooner."

She helped me peel off the headset and the telemetry patches. "Hard to believe it's over," I said.

"On the contrary," she said. "With any luck, you're just getting started."

I stepped out of the building into a hot, humid night. The last of the business crowd had gone home, abandoning the neighborhood to speeding cabs and a couple of sparsely populated coffee shops. I walked to the College Street subway station, where a homeless guy was propped against a wall with a change cup in front of him. He gave me a look that was either imploring or contemptuous. I put a dollar coin in his cup. "Bless you," he said. At least I think the word was "bless."

By the time I got back to my apartment a drilling rain had begun to fall. The short walk from the subway left me drenched, but that didn't seem like such a bad thing once I had a towel in my hand and a roof over my head. In the bathroom I looked at my cheek where the cop had clubbed me. The bruise was fading. All that was left of the gash was a pale pink line. But I dreamed of the incident that night, when the room was dark and the rain on the window sounded like the roar of massed voices.

Ten days passed.

Two interviews for a summer internship went nowhere. I finished an end-of-term project (a Flash video animation) and handed it in. I fretted about my future.

On the tenth day I opened an email from InterAlia Inc. My test results had been assessed, it said, and I had been placed in an Affinity. Not just any Affinity, but Tau, one of the big five. My test fees would be debited to my credit card, the email went on to say. And I would be hearing from a local tranche shortly.

———

I was headed to school when my phone burbled. I didn't let it go to voice mail. I picked up like a good citizen.

It was Aaron. "Things took a turn for the worse," he said. "Grammy Fisk's back in the hospital. And this time you really need to come down and see her."

CHAPTER 2

The town of Schuyler was situated at the northeastern corner of the New York State county of Onenia. "Onenia" was a corruption of the Mohawk word *onenia'shon:'a*, meaning "various rocks," and for more than a century Schuyler's primary business had been its quarries: pits carved into the fragile karst that underlay the county's unproductive farmland. Since the 1970s most of those quarries had grown unprofitable and had been shut down, left to fill with greasy brown water that rose in the spring and evaporated over the course of the long summers. As a child I had been warned never to play around the old quarries, and of course every kid I knew had gone there as often as possible, biking down county roads where grasshoppers flocked in the heat like flurries of buzzing brown snow.

On the way to my father's house I drove past trailheads I still recognized, hidden entrances to pressed-earth roads where trucks had once carted limestone to stoneworks across the state. Stone from Onenia County had helped build scores of libraries and government buildings, back when libraries and government buildings still commanded a certain respect. On Schuyler's main street there were a few remnants of that era: an old bank, gutted to house a Gap store but still wearing its limestone façade; a

Carnegie library in the Federal style, with a tiny acreage of public park to separate it from the liquor store on one side and the welfare office on the other. All dark now: I had left Toronto in an afternoon drizzle and reached Schuyler just after a rainy sunset.

Despite hard times there was still a "good" part of Schuyler, where the town's diminishing stock of prosperous families kept house: families like the Fisks, the Symanskis, the Cassidys, the Muellers. The windows of their houses glittered as if their wealth had been compressed into rectilinear slabs of golden light, and the houses seemed to promise ease, comfort, safety, all the consolations of family—though this was often false advertising.

I pulled into the driveway of my father's house and parked next to Aaron's Lexus and behind my father's Lincoln Navigator. The same comforting light spilled out of the house's windows, painting the rain-slick leaves of the willow in the yard. But no one was happy inside. The family crowded around as I came through the door: my father, my brother, my stepmother Laura. Twelve-year-old Geddy stood behind Mama Laura, and when I approached him he offered his hand with a solemnity that might have been funny under other circumstances. I noticed his hair had been cut into a military-style buzz, probably as a result of my father's crusades to make Geddy "more masculine." I had been the subject of my father's attention often enough that I recognized the symptoms.

"We waited dinner for you," Mama Laura said. "Come in and wash up. Geddy'll take your suitcase up to your room, won't you, Geddy?"

Geddy seemed pleased to take charge of the duffel bag into which I had thrown a couple of changes of clothes. "Thanks," I said.

"Don't be too long," my father said. He hadn't changed since the last time I'd seen him. Same crisp blue shirt, same crumpled black tie loose around the collar. He was a tall man, but not fat. People said I looked like him, and I guessed I did, but the only time I saw the resemblance was when I was tired or angry. As if some perpetual discontent had left its mark on his face.

At the table we didn't talk about Grammy Fisk—at least not right away. We had had the essentials of that conversation already, by phone. A second health crisis had awakened Granny Fisk in the small hours of the night, one that had nothing to do with her gallbladder. This time, Grammy Fisk hadn't apologized for the trouble she was putting everyone to, hadn't insisted on getting dressed before the EMT guys showed up. She had woken up unable to move or feel the right side of her body; she was blind in one eye; her speech was slurred and indistinct; and she could communicate nothing but a groaning, awful terror.

By the time she reached Onenia County Hospital she had lost consciousness. Scans revealed massive intracranial bleeding—a stroke, in other words. She had been comatose for the last two days, and while my father couldn't bring himself to say it ("Prospects don't look so good" was the closest he could come), she wasn't expected to recover. The hospital had promised to call if there was any change in her condition; we would all drive there in the morning to keep vigil by her bed.

"Not that she seems to notice," my father added. "I don't think she knows we're even there, to tell the truth."

Mama Laura had prepared a huge meal, including sweet potatoes in brown sugar and roast chicken, but no one had much appetite, least of all me. We watched each other pick at our plates. At forty-two, ten years younger than my father, Mama Laura still had the timid demeanor she had brought to the family when she married him: an instinctive caution that showed in her body language and in her face, always turned a shy quarter-angle away. Concealed under this deference was a genuine love of the work that embedded her in the family. We could have afforded all kinds of help, but Mama Laura refused to consider hiring a maid or a cook. It was not that she thought of herself as a servant. She expected to be appreciated for what she did. But it was also her way of demonstrating her right to be among us. She fed us and cleaned our house, and that entitled her to a certain non-negotiable minimum of respect, both for herself and for her son Geddy. Tonight she gazed forlornly at the platters of untouched food on the table, though she had taken little of it herself.

"All that trouble in the South China Sea," my father said, "and the Persian Gulf. It's not doing our business any good. Or this town."

That was his idea of something neutral to talk about. He aimed his remarks at my older brother, Aaron. Aaron sat next to me, shoulders squared, knife and fork poised over his plate—Aaron's appetite seemed relatively intact. And as always, he knew what was expected of him. "The Chinese," he said, nodding, "the fucking Saudis . . ."

The dynamic was so familiar I hardly had to listen to the rest of it: my father's opinions, amplified by my brother. Not that Aaron was faking it. He shared my father's conviction that America was a fallen Eden and that what lay beyond its gates was a wilderness of veniality, poverty, and low cunning. Mama Laura spoke up once, to ask me if I wanted more mashed potatoes. I thanked her, but no.

"How are your courses coming?" she asked during a lull.

"Not bad."

"I can't imagine how that works. I mean graphic design school. Do you draw a lot of pictures?"

"There's a little more to it than that."

"I'm sure there must be."

Aaron and my father exchanged impatient glances and went back to the subject of the Middle East, the skyrocketing price of oil. I looked at Geddy, who was sitting across from me, but Geddy's attention was entirely focused on his plate, where he was rearranging his food without eating much of it. He looked tired. His face was bloated. He was easily frightened, and his best defense, now as ever, was to retreat into himself. Grammy Fisk had always been kind to Geddy, as she had always been kind to me—what would Geddy do without her? His mother would look after him, but who would *understand* him?

We all turned in after the living room clock chimed eleven. I slept in the room that had been mine for years. I raised the sash of the window an inch or so. The rain had come through Onenia County with a cold front on its heels, and the breeze that lifted the hem of the curtain was fresh and moist. Every sound was familiar: the front-yard willow tossing in the wind, rainwater gushing from the downspouts, the four-cornered echo of a known space. It was the rest of the house that felt hollowed-out, heartless.

In the morning we went to visit Grammy Fisk.

We camped out in the visitor's lounge and took turns spending time with her. I went into the room after my father and Aaron left it.

Grammy Fisk was unresponsive, and a doctor had told us as diplomatically as possible that there was very little higher brain function going on, but it was still possible—or so we told ourselves and pretended to believe—that she might be aware of our presence. I doubted it as soon as I saw her. Grammy Fisk wasn't in that room. It was her body on the bed all right, intubated and monitored, her cheeks sunken where her dentures had been removed (an indignity she would never have tolerated), but she was gone. Just plain gone. When I took her hand it felt inert, like something made out of pipe cleaners and papier-mâché.

Still, I thanked her for everything she had given me. Which was much. Not least, the idea that I might not be entirely alone in the world.

Jenny Symanski arrived at the hospital late in the afternoon. We hugged, but there was time for only a few words before Jenny spent a few minutes of her own with Grammy Fisk. While we waited, Mama Laura hinted that it would be all right if I took Jenny out to dinner. The rest of the family would make shift with the hospital commissary, but she thought Jenny deserved something a little classier now that I was back in town. And I agreed.

We took my car. I drove Jenny away from the hospital, past the outlet malls and down the old main street of Schuyler, to what had been our hangout for years, a Chinese restaurant called Smiling Dragon. Green linoleum floors, a desperately unhealthy ficus in the window, no pretensions.

Jenny's dad had been my father's friend and drinking partner for more than thirty years. Both had started out with a modest family grubstake, and both had achieved modest fortunes by Onenia County standards. Jenny's dad owned a vast acreage of hardscrabble farmland north of town, which he had developed into housing tracts and strip malls during Schuyler's better days; my father had turned the hardware store he inherited into a statewide chain of Fisk's Farm Supply outlets. The families had grown up together. I had spent a lot of time at Jenny's place when we were younger, until her mother's alcoholism made my presence there uncomfortable; after that, Jenny had become an honorary Fisk.

Jenny and I talked about Grammy Fisk over egg rolls. "She was always the family beatnik," I said. "She showed me her high school yearbook one time. Class of fifty-seven. Some school in Allentown." Which was where my grandfather had found her, a few years later, tending a booth at the Allentown Fair. "She was pretty amazing looking, actually. Long black hair, lots of attitude. She dropped out of state college and spent a couple of years doing the bohemian thing—big into folk music, at least until she got married, and even then she would sometimes sneak out to shows with her old girlfriends. There were all these ticket stubs tucked into her photo album."

"Seriously? She never mentioned any of that to me."

For obvious reasons. My grandfather had venerated Barry Goldwater, and there had never been a word of dissent from Grammy Fisk. By the time my father was born, her Charlie Parker and Bob Dylan records had gone into permanent storage. But she saw things the other Fisks were blind to. If the world was a puzzle, she was drawn to the pieces that didn't fit. "You know how she was."

"Yeah."

Jenny was five-foot-three in stocking feet and dressed as if she wanted to be ignored: jeans and a cotton shirt and blond hair tied back so tightly it hurt to look at. A mouth that gave out smiles like party favors but had been made somber by Grammy Fisk's illness. She cocked her head at me. "How are you really doing, up there in Canada? And what happened to your face?"

I told her about the incident at the demo. At the end she said, "So are you a cop-hating lefty now?"

"Honestly? What I remember about that cop is how he looked. Pissed off, obviously, you know, all wound up, but also scared. Like what he did to me was something he might not be proud of. Maybe something he wouldn't mention when he went home to his wife."

"Or maybe he was just an asshole."

"Maybe."

"He had a choice. He could have told you to move on."

"Sure, but the situation was pushing him hard in one direction. Which made me think about how fucked up and really arbitrary it is, the way we conduct ourselves with other people.

There has to be a better way." And because this was Jenny, to whom I could say almost anything, I told her I had taken the Affinity test.

After a pause she said, "Those Affinity groups . . . they're what, some kind of dating service?"

"No, no, nothing like that." I explained about Meir Klein and InterAlia. "Basically, I was tired of not having anybody to talk to except a couple of guys from my classes at Sheridan."

"So they sort of design a social circle for you?"

"Not exactly, but yeah, you end up with a bunch of new friends."

"Uh-huh. And it really works?"

"Supposedly. I don't know yet."

"Well, well, well." Which was classic Jenny. It meant, *I don't like what I'm hearing but I'm not prepared to argue about it.* "Maybe *I* should join one of those groups."

"There might not be any in Schuyler just yet."

"Mm. Bad luck for you, then. When you move back home."

"Which won't be anytime soon."

Her eyebrows went up. "But I thought—"

"What?"

"With Grammy Fisk and all—"

"I'll be here a few days more, but I can't stay much longer than that. I need to set up a summer internship, for one thing."

"But Grammy Fisk was paying your tuition."

Because my father had refused to. He didn't approve of what he called my "artistic side," and he considered any degree that wasn't an MBA a concession to limp-wristed liberalism. But Grammy Fisk had fought him on that one. She couldn't dictate how he spent his money, but she had money of her own, and she had been determined to spend it on my education, even if that caused trouble in the family—which it *needn't*, she inevitably added, if my father would take a step back and allow her to do her youngest grandson this simple favor. What was wrong with Adam setting out on a career of his own, even if it *did* involve drawing pictures?

Jenny put her hand over mine. "I've been at the house. I hear the talk. I don't know what arrangements Grammy Fisk might have made. But she's not legally competent anymore. She signed a power of attorney after the gallbladder thing. Your dad's in charge now."

I drove Jenny home. Visiting hours were over and Grammy Fisk had been left alone with the night nurses and the cleaning staff at Onenia General. Jenny's house, a dozen streets away from my father's, was dark except for a single light in the office above the garage. Ed Symanski must have been awake in there, doing his accounts, maybe reading or watching Netflix. Jenny's mom was probably asleep. "Drunk by eight, dead drunk by ten," as Jenny had described her. But that didn't preclude the possibility of night events: unprovoked midnight arguments, objects thrown against walls. "You can sleep over at our house tonight," I said. I knew she had been doing so for the last few days, on the grounds that the Fisks needed a hand with their family crisis.

She shook her head. "I have to be here sometimes. My dad can't handle it all by himself. But thanks." And we shared a half-hearted kiss.

Back at the house I checked my phone for messages and found an email from a name I didn't recognize: Lisa Wei.

> Hi Adam. My name is Lisa and I'm hosting the next Tau get-together. You'll be invited in a general mailing, but since you're new I wanted to introduce myself and make the invitation personal. The time is two Saturdays from

now. Show up at 4 if you want to help set up, 6 if you want dinner, 8 if you just want to socialize. The tranche house is close to the Rosedale subway station and details will be in the mailing. Anyhow, please come!!! The first meet-up always seems intimidating but it's really not, take my word for it. Can't wait to meet you!

It was nice, and under other circumstances I would have welcomed it. But given the question mark hovering over my future, I had to send a noncommittal response.

I grieved for Grammy Fisk in my sleep that night. I couldn't grieve by daylight because she wasn't dead. But in my dream the loss was complete. I woke up calling her name. No one heard me, fortunately, and the sound of the wind at the window was lonely but oddly comforting, and eventually I was able to drift back to sleep.

Grammy Fisk's presence had operated in the family the way carbon rods function in a nuclear reactor: she damped down a potentially explosive force and turned it to useful work. Without her, we were bound to reach critical mass. The unstable radioactive core was, of course, my father.

But most of my week in Schuyler passed relatively quietly. Each day began with a trek to the hospital, some visits longer than others because my father was getting briefings about options for Grammy Fisk's extended care, either in a dedicated facility or at home (an option he ruled out pretty quickly). The sessions by Grammy Fisk's bedside grew more brief as the reality of her situation began to sink in.

She never registered our presence in any meaningful way. Her eyes were motionless behind the papyrus of her eyelids. Still, I talked to her. I told her about school, I shared my ambivalence about Jenny and our future, I even mentioned the Affinity I'd joined. These were the kinds of things I had once discussed with her and with no one else. Sitting beside her vacant body, I was able to imagine her responses. She spoke to me the only way she could, through the medium of memory and longing.

I also made a point of spending time with my stepbrother, Geddy. Grammy Fisk would have approved, but I didn't need to be pushed. I liked Geddy. At twelve, he was chubby and quiet and easily intimidated and more bookish than he liked to let on, all of which reminded me of how I had been at his age. (Except for the chubbiness: I had been one of those kids who needs to be encouraged to eat.) On the Wednesday before I left, Geddy took me up to his room to see the posters Mama Laura had grudgingly allowed him to tack up on the wall.

Geddy would probably have placed on the high-functioning end of the autistic spectrum, had he ever been diagnosed. His serial obsessions (which included kites, architecture, LEGO, stories about heroic animals, and the band My Chemical Romance) were what he preferred to talk about, which was why my father had banned all these subjects as dinner table conversation. The posters Geddy had been allowed to put up were a picture of Rockefeller Center ("It was designed by the architect Raymond Hood. He also did the Tribune Tower in Chicago.") and a concert photo of Gerard Way. A small wooden bookcase housed his subscription copies of *Popular Mechanics*, the only magazine my father let him read, and a few ancient Albert Payson Terhune novels, also donated by my father. In one corner was the meticulously tidy desk on which Geddy did his homework. He owned a laptop for school purposes, but he was allowed Internet access only an hour a day and under supervision. He cherished an old click-wheel iPod, which neither my father nor Mama Laura had yet learned how to police for forbidden files, loaded with slightly out-of-date goth and emo bands.

At one point Geddy said he wished he had more bookcases

and more books to put on them. I guessed he was getting a little tired of Terhune's collies. But he didn't have unguarded access to downloads, and I knew from experience how difficult it was to buy and keep paperbacks without my father's surveillance. "Geddy," I said. "You want to see something?"

He shrugged and stared, which meant *yes*.

The house had an old-fashioned attic, with a ladder you tugged down from the ceiling of the third-floor hallway. The attic was the family's memory hole, rarely visited. We waited until the coast was clear, then clambered up the ladder. The attic was where I kept books during my adolescence, hidden in the far corner of the room, where the roof slanted down to the floor, under a layer of exposed pink fiberglass insulation.

The books I stashed there had never been discovered, and Geddy's eyes widened when he saw them. Their spines were curved and in some cases broken—they were mostly used books from a secondhand shop on Main, now closed—but the colors were bright, the covers intact. Nothing special, mostly science fiction and mysteries straight out of the fifty-cent bin. But Geddy gave me an awed look. "Can I see them?"

"See them, read them—whatever you want, bro."

"But they're yours!"

"I'm finished with them. You can have them if you want."

"Really?"

"Sure. Just don't get caught. But if you do, it's okay to blame me. I'm the one who brought them into the house."

It was as if I had offered him a cache of jewels. It was funny but sad, the gratitude that came brimming out of his eyes. *They're just old books*, I wanted to say. But that would have been disingenuous. There were some good stories in there. Stories big enough to hide inside. And I imagined Geddy needed all the hiding places he could find.

The family achieved critical mass the night before I left.

That afternoon, driving back from the hospital with Aaron while the rest of the family rode in my father's big-ass Navigator, I had raised the subject of the family's finances. I was under no illusion that my brother had my best interests at heart. Aaron was five years older than me, more athletic, better-looking, arguably smarter, and a vastly better exemplar of what my father considered the family's core values. He could also be a colossal dick. But I needed to know what was going on, and I thought I might get a slightly more objective answer from Aaron than I would by asking my father.

"The thing is," I said, "I'm going to need to know about tuition and expenses for next year. I have arrangements to make." *Or not make.*

"You'll have to talk to Dad about that. But this isn't a good time for him. So be considerate, Adam. You're not the only one who loved Grammy Fisk. Dad didn't always see eye-to-eye with her, but she's his mother. And basically, he's lost her. It would pretty callous to start talking about money at this point."

"I know. Obviously. But—"

"And it's not just that. The business is looking a little shaky these days. We've got the crisis in the Gulf pushing gas prices up, which means cartage costs are killing us. Farms aren't upgrading equipment, and we've got chain stores undercutting us everywhere. I mean, it's fucking ruthless out there. We'll survive, I think, but we're on real slim margins. As for the family, if Grammy has to go into a full-time care facility, that's going to be a gigantic expense."

I told him I knew all that and understood it. I just needed a heads-up on my own future.

"Well, true," he admitted. "And it would help clarify things for Jenny, too."

"Jenny?"

"Yeah, Jenny. Sooner or later you're gonna need to fish or cut bait, Adam. No offense."

Jenny and I had been friends since grade school, but we weren't engaged, though Aaron and my father may have drawn their own conclusions. I was far from sure I wanted to marry Jenny, and I wasn't sure Jenny wanted to marry me. In fact we had avoided the subject as if it were radioactive.

And I resented Aaron for pressing me on it. But it was true that Jenny had an interest in knowing what was in store. "Then I should talk to the old man tonight," I said.

"Okay . . . but cut him some slack, is all I'm saying. You might not like what you hear, but he'll be honest with you, give him that."

I gave him that.

But in the end it wasn't my financial problems that pushed us into a meltdown, it was Geddy—or my father's contempt for him.

The weather had been warm and sunny for a couple of days now, and Aaron had proposed a family barbecue as a therapeutic change from hospital cafeteria meals. So my father stoked the grill, lofting clouds of fragrant hydrocarbons over the grassy plain of the backyard, and Mama Laura brought out slabs of raw ground beef from the kitchen on a plastic platter. Geddy, in his bathing suit, had been running through the sprinkler as it watered the lawn. My father watched him with a somber expression. And when Geddy came running over to check the progress of the hamburgers, my father said, "Laura, look at the boy. Look at your son there."

Mama Laura turned to see. "What about him? Come here, Geddy. I'll fix you a burger soon as they're ready."

"He's almost thirteen years old. Pardon my French, but it looks like he's growing himself a fine pair of boobs. Is that normal?"

Geddy had an amazing ability to go stone-faced and silent when confronted with criticism, but he was self-conscious about his weight and this one took him by surprise. His face turned red, then white. I saw the tendons stand up in his neck as his jaw clenched. Impressively, he managed not to cry.

Mama Laura winced. "He's a little portly but it's just baby fat."

"You should get his hormones checked. See if he's normal."

I said, "Of course he's *normal*."

My father shot me a hostile glare. Aaron, across the patio table from me, rolled his eyes: *Oh fuck, here it comes.*

"Is that your diagnosis?" my father asked. "What happened, did you get a medical degree without me knowing about it?"

For most of my life I had revered or feared my father, depending on his moods or mine. Even after I grew out of the fear, I never argued with him. It had never seemed worth the trouble. And Grammy Fisk had always been there to rein him back when he stepped out of bounds. He would never have said what he just said had Grammy been at the table with us.

"Get on inside," Mama Laura told Geddy in a tight voice. "Put on a shirt for supper. Something short-sleeved out of your closet. Go on now. Go."

Geddy hurried into the house, shoulders hunched.

My father dug a spatula under a beef patty and turned it. "Thank you for your opinion," he said to me. "Not that I asked for it."

"You humiliated him."

"You think I hurt his feelings?"

"You think you *didn't*?"

"And do you imagine that boy can go through life without getting his feelings hurt once in a while? He needs toughening up if he's ever going to make it through school. I guess you think you're protecting him—"

"I guess I'm thinking I shouldn't have to."

"What you *have* to do is show some respect. We need to get that straight, if you're coming back to Schuyler."

And I said, "Am I coming back to Schuyler?"

"Aaron told me you talked to him about this. You know the situation, Adam. Your grandmother had some money, and that worked out to your benefit—and that's fine, but whatever Grammy had tucked in the bank needs to help with her expenses now. I know we've disagreed on certain things, you and I, but I also know you're not selfish enough to want that money for yourself. So I'm afraid you're homeward bound, unless you can make some other arrangement on your own hook. And you're welcome here and always will be. But that doesn't entitle you to pass judgment on me. Not when I'm setting the table you're eating from. Which is what we need to do right now. Laura, pass out the paper plates. Everybody line up! Aaron, get the corn out of the boiler."

Mama Laura, who had sat through all this with an inscrutable expression and her small fists clenched, said, "Shouldn't we wait for Geddy?"

"Once he's in his room it can be hard to pry him out," my father said.

So I offered to go get him.

I found Geddy on his bed with his face buried in a pillow. He sat up and wiped his eyes when I came in. I helped him change into jeans and a fresh shirt. Then I took him out to the KFC on Main Street. I figured that way we could eat without choking on the food.

At the restaurant I told Geddy a secret: my father had asked the same question (*Is that normal?*) about me. More than once.

I had never carried the kind of extra weight Geddy did, and boob-droop had not been among my otherwise comprehensive suite of adolescent concerns. But there had been plenty of *is-this-normal* moments when I was growing up. My incessant reading of books, my disinterest in high school sports. My father had never quite accused me of being (to use his word of preference) "queer," but that inference had never been far away. I was not, as it happened, queer (at least, not in the sense he intended), but neither was I what he believed or expected any son of his should be. And for him, that was a distinction without a difference.

"Did he hate you?" Geddy asked.

"He doesn't hate either of us. He just doesn't understand us. People like us make him uncomfortable."

"Is that a thing?"

"What?"

"People like us. Are there people like us?"

"Well, yeah. Of course there are," I said.

And Geddy beamed at me. It was a little heartbreaking, how badly he wanted it to be true.

I left Schuyler the same night. Only Jenny Symanski (and Geddy, of course) seemed genuinely sorry to see me go. Jenny wrapped her arms around me and we exchanged a kiss, sincere enough that Mama Laura blushed and looked away.

And I had to admit, it was nice to be reminded how Jenny felt and tasted. There were years of familiarity folded into that hug. Jenny and I had made love (for the first time, for both of us) when we were fifteen, fooling around in Jenny's bedroom on a hot August Saturday morning when her parents were out at an estate sale. Our lovemaking that day and afterward had been driven more by curiosity than passion, but it was a curiosity we could never quite satisfy. There were times—especially during the interminable Fisk-Symanski dinners our families used to hold—when Jenny would catch my eye across the table and communicate a lust so intense that my resulting boner required serious stealth measures to conceal.

We couldn't keep that kind of relationship secret forever, and my father complicated the whole thing by approving of it, at least up to a point. I think he felt it established my heterosexual bona fides. And he liked the idea of marrying his spare son to a Symanski, as if the families were royal lineages. It was Grammy Fisk who took me aside and quietly made sure I grasped the basics of safe sex: "If you marry that girl, it ought to be because you want to, not because you have to."

"I'm so sorry about your tuition," Jenny whispered as we hugged. "But if you do have to come back to Schuyler, it won't all be bad. I'll make sure of that."

"Thanks," I said. And that was all I said.

Because I had no intention of coming back. Not if I could help it.

CHAPTER 3

I saw the tranche house for the first time on a clear, hot evening at the end of August. Because it would come to mean so much to me—because I learned and forgot and gained and lost so much in that building—I'm tempted to say it seemed special from the moment I first glimpsed it.

But it didn't. It was one house on a street of many houses, not very different from the rest. It was large, but all these houses were large. It was sixty or seventy years old, as most of these houses were. Its garden was lush with marigolds, coleus, and a chorus line of hostas. A maple tree littered the front lawn with winged seeds the color of aged paper. I walked past the house three times before I worked up the courage to knock at the door. Which opened almost before my knuckles grazed it.

"You're Adam!"

"Yeah, I—"

"I'm *so* glad you could make it. Come in! Everyone else is here already. Whole tribe. Buffet in the dining room. I'll take you there. Don't be shy! I'm Lisa Wei."

The same Lisa Wei who had sent the email invitation. Maybe

because of the tone of her message, I had imagined someone my age. In fact she appeared to be around sixty—about as old as the house she lived in. She was a little over five feet tall, and she squinted up at me through lenses that looked like they should have been fitted to a telescope. She couldn't have weighed much: I imagined she couldn't go out in a windstorm without an anchor. But she was a small explosion of smiles and gestures. The first person she introduced me to was her partner, Loretta Sitter.

Loretta owned the house, but she and Lisa had lived here for more than thirty years. "We're that rare thing," Lisa said, "a Tau *couple*. We decided we'd take the test together, and if we didn't place in the same Affinity we'd forfeit the fee and forget about it. But it turned out we're both Taus. Isn't that great?"

I said it was pretty great. Loretta was a little younger than Lisa and taller, her long, dark hair just beginning to go white. She pulled me into a hug, then stood back and said, "You look like you have something on your mind, Adam Fisk."

I would eventually get accustomed to this kind of shoot-from-the-hip psychoanalysis, but I was new here, and it startled me. Something on my mind? I had quit my courses at Sheridan College, given notice to my landlord, and would probably be back in Schuyler, tail between my legs, before the week was out. But I didn't want to say so. "Well," Loretta said before I could answer, "whatever it is, forget about it for a couple of hours. You're among friends."

Thirty people made a tranche. It was rumored that Meir Klein and InterAlia set it up that way after the model of Neolithic tribes—thirty people supposedly being an ideal number for a social unit: big enough to get things done, small enough to be governable, and containing as many familiar faces as the average human psyche can easily sort out.

Maybe so. I met twenty-three strangers that night. (Some tranche members were away on vacation or otherwise too busy to attend.) Twenty-three faces and names were too many for my

post-Neolithic brain to absorb all at once, but some were memorable. Some of the faces would become intimately familiar to
me, and some of the names would eventually show up in newspaper headlines.

Lisa Wei led me to a long table in the dining room. "You're
late for the best stuff," she said, "just pickings left," but I wasn't
even remotely hungry; I took a lukewarm egg roll. She introduced me to a couple of stragglers also grazing at the table. "What
I can do," Lisa said, "is show you through the house and you can
meet folks as we go, how about that?"

I was grateful to her for making me feel slightly less ridiculous. It wasn't just that I was nervous about meeting strangers:
I felt like an imposter. I was a Tau, but I'd probably be back in
the States before the next scheduled tranche meeting, and I was
uneasy about making friends I couldn't keep. But as I trailed this
small, effusive woman through her big, cheerful house, I began
to feel genuinely welcome. Every room seemed to frame a mood,
contemplative or whimsical or practical, and the people I met
and whose names I struggled unsuccessfully to remember seemed
perfectly suited to the house. When I was introduced to them
they smiled and shook my hand and looked at me curiously while
I tried not to let on that I was a one-timer bound for an Affinity-
less quarry town in upstate New York. It made me bashful.

But I began to forget about that. I dropped into a half dozen
interesting discussions. No one resented my presence, and when
I added a few words people paid attention. I spent a few minutes listening to a guy with a faint Hungarian accent debating
Affinity politics with a couple of other Taus in a downstairs
room. The talk was too lively to interrupt, but Lisa took my arm
and whispered, "That's Damian. Damian Levay. He teaches law
at the University of Toronto. Very bright, very ambitious. He's
written a book or two."

He looked pretty young for a tenured professor, but he talked
liked someone accustomed to an audience. He had issues with

the way InterAlia exercised control over Affinity tranches and sodalities. "If being a Tau is a legitimate identity, aren't we entitled to self-determination? I mean, InterAlia may own the algorithms, but it doesn't own *us*."

Lisa smiled as she interrupted him: " 'When in the course of human events . . .' "

"Don't laugh," he said. "A declaration of independence might be exactly what we need."

"If not precisely a *revolution*."

Damian looked at me and gave Lisa a quizzical glance. She mouthed something back at him—it might have been the word "newb." I introduced myself and shook his hand.

As we walked away Lisa said, "Damian's been with us for more than a year now. He's one to watch. Pay attention to that one, Adam."

A kind of happy exhaustion eventually set in. I made more friends over the course of an evening than I had made in the last six months, and every connection seemed both authentic and potentially important—the escalation from hi-my-name-is to near-intimacy was dizzying. Even the conversations I overheard in passing tugged at my attention: I kept wanting to say *yes, exactly!* or *me too!* Eye contact felt like a burst of exchanged data. Maybe too much so. I wasn't used to it. Could anyone *get* used to it?

I had lost track of Lisa, but when she found me again she said, "You look like your head is swimming. I'm sure it is—I remember the feeling. Handed around like a new toy. It's great, but if you need to get away for a few minutes—"

She showed me a room in the basement, furnished with a leather sofa and a big-screen TV. The only person in the room was a young woman who appeared to have Down syndrome. She wore a blue sweatshirt and drawstring pants, and she was watching *SpongeBob SquarePants* with the sound off.

"This is Tonya," Lisa said. "Everyone calls her Tonya G. Her mother is Renata Goldstein—you met her upstairs. Tonya's not actually a Tau, but we make room for her at the tranche gatherings. Because we like her. Right, Tonya?"

Tonya hollered out, "Yes!"

"Hey," I said. "Enjoying the show?"

"Yes!"

"Can you hear it?"

She turned her head and fixed her eyes on me. "No! Can *you*?"

"Mm . . . no."

"Watch it with me?"

Lisa gave me a *you-don't-have-to-do-this* look, but I waved her off. "Sure, I'll watch it with you. Some of it, anyway."

"All right."

Lisa patted my shoulder. "I'll let Renata know you're down here. She'll check in in a little while. But Tonya will understand if you want to get back to the party—right, Tonya?"

Tonya nodded emphatically.

So we watched *SpongeBob* with the sound off. It wasn't clear to me why Tonya preferred to see it in silence, but she rejected an offer to turn up the volume. And it was still funny this way. Tonya seemed startled when I laughed, but she inevitably followed with a big peal of laughter of her own. After a while I started making up my own dialogue for the characters, doing crazy voices, which she liked. "You're joking!"

"I'm a joker," I admitted.

"What's your name?"

"Adam."

"Adam's a joker!"

Among other things.

The credits were rolling when I noticed that someone had come into the room. A woman, maybe my age, leaning against the doorframe, watching us. South Asian features. Close-cropped dark hair. A Chinese dragon tattooed in three colors around the meat of her upper arm. She wore a sleeveless blouse and faded blue jeans. A belt with a purple metallic buckle.

"Getting late, Tonya," she announced. "Your mom's upstairs saying good-bye. I think you'd better go find her."

"Okay," Tonya said.

"Say good-bye to Adam first."

"Good-bye, Adam Joker!"

"Bye, Tonya SpongeBobWatcher."

Tonya ran from the room giggling. Her summoner stayed behind. I said, "You know my name, but—"

"Oh, sorry. I'm Amanda. Amanda Mehta." She put out her hand. I stood up and took it. "You're Adam. Lisa told me you were down here keeping Tonya company. Sorry, I couldn't resist having a look at the new guy."

I wasn't sure how to answer that, given that I'd probably never see Amanda Mehta again. I just smiled.

"Lisa said she already showed you around. But I bet you didn't see the roof."

"The roof?"

"Come on." She tugged my hand. "I'll show you. And maybe you can tell me what's bothering you."

"I'm sorry?"

"Just come with me. Come on!"

What could I do but follow?

"What makes you think something's bothering me?"

Amanda didn't answer, just gave me a hold-your-horses look. She led me to one of bedrooms on the third floor, where a dormer window looked south over a wooded ravine. The window opened onto the part of the roof that connected the house to the garage. She climbed out deftly—obviously, she had done this before—then turned back and said, "You won't fall. If you're careful."

So I stepped out onto the shingles. The slope was gentle enough that there was no real danger, but we were high enough to see across the backyard and over the ravine to the city—condo towers on Bloor Street, the headstone apartment slabs of the Cabbagetown district.

"Safest thing is to lie down," Amanda said.

She stretched out with her head butting the low sill of the window. I did the same. "You know the house pretty well," I said.

"I lived here for a few months."

"Are you related to Lisa or—" I had forgotten the name of Lisa's partner.

"Loretta. No, but they put me up when I didn't have anywhere else to go. I finally got my own place last May."

"They put you up because you're a Tau?"

"Well, yeah. I'm not the only one they've helped out, and they liked having me here. Loretta inherited this place back in the eighties. The house is too big for them, really, so they're always putting people up. It's a place to go when you don't have anywhere else to go. If you're in the tranche. Or at least a Tau."

"Must be nice."

She gave me a searching look. "Of course it's nice."

"I think—"

"No, hush, be quiet a minute. Listen. I love the way it sounds out here. Don't you?"

I would have said there was nothing to hear. But there was, once I paid attention. The tidal bass note of the city, the massed noise of air-conditioner compressors, car engines, high-rise ventilator fans. Plus animal sounds from the ravine and human voices from this or the neighboring house. Homely sounds that hovered over the dark backyard like phantom lights.

"And the way it feels," Amanda said. "Late August, you know, even on a hot day you get that little chill after dark. The leaves on the trees sound different in the wind." A wind came up as if she had commanded it. "This corner of the roof is completely private. No one can see you. But you can see the city."

"That's why you like it here?"

"One reason." She unzipped a pocket on her vest and took out a glass pipe, unzipped another pocket, and extracted a tiny plastic bag. "Do you smoke?"

"Not often."

"But you *have* smoked."

"Sure." In high school, in the back of a friend's beat-up Ford Taurus, out at the quarry, and occasionally with Dex, my erstwhile roommate—more than occasionally if you count secondhand smoke.

She used her fingernails to pick apart a nugget of weed and fill the bowl. "So do you want to smoke *now*?"

"Lisa and, um, Loretta don't mind?"

"They don't like people smoking anything indoors, but if they weren't so busy they might have joined us out here."

I didn't want to disappoint her. And how many chances would I have to smoke weed on the roof of a Rosedale mansion? So I took the pipe and the lighter and even managed to hold down a toke without coughing. At which point, in the ordinary course of things, I would have succumbed to my usual cannabis-induced self-consciousness; but for whatever reason I remained reasonably coherent—though the night seemed to inflate like a party balloon and the chorus of crickets became operatic in its complexity.

"So," she said, "you want to talk about what's bothering you?"

"Why does everyone say that? How do you know something's bothering me?"

"You spent a half-hour watching TV with Tonya, for one thing."

"I like Tonya."

"Of course you do. She's a sweetie. But she's not a Tau."

"You're reading a lot into—"

"It's also your body language, how you react when you shake hands with somebody, things like that."

"You must have been watching me pretty closely."

"It's just tranche telepathy. I mean, that's what people call it. It isn't really telepathy, obviously. We read each other better than ordinary people. So we can tell you're worried about something. You don't have to tell me about it, but we're tranchemates. Maybe I can help."

I felt a little tingle when she called me her tranchemate, though it was the first time I had heard the word. Did she know that about me, too? Something in her smile suggested she did. We had quite a complex little silent conversation going on, in fact.

So I gave her a quick summary of the family curse. I told her about Grammy Fisk's stroke, my awkward relationship with my father, the tuition money. I told her I had dropped out of my Sheridan courses and given notice at my apartment—I had to be out by the end of the month. No money and nowhere to go but back home. I had been curious about tonight's meeting but I was embarrassed to admit that I'd never be back.

"Not worth worrying about, Adam. You're a Tau, you're welcome even for one night. But the thing about going back home— I gather you'd prefer to stay in Toronto?"

Before I came here for school I hadn't given the city a second thought. I had wanted to study in New York City, but my father was convinced that even a brief exposure to Manhattan would turn me into a gay-marrying Democrat-voting liberal, and not even Grammy Fisk could overcome his objections. He had agreed to Toronto because he imagined Canada to be a well-mannered country, suspiciously socialistic but hardly radical. I had agreed because Sheridan offered world-class graphics and media curricula. Did I want to stay here? Sure. But no job, no work permit, no crib. She said, "You're studying graphic design?"

"Was, before I dropped out."

"So you should talk to Walter."

"Who?"

"Walter Kohler. Lisa must have introduced you. Big guy? Six foot, two hundred fifty pounds, in his forties, wears a suit?"

I vaguely recalled such a person. He had smiled and shaken my hand, that was all.

Amanda tucked away her pipe and baggie. "Really, you need to talk to him."

"Do I?"

"Walter used to work for one of the big ad agencies in town, but he's starting his own business—come on, we'll go see him."

"What, *now?*"

"Of course now. Come on!" She practically vaulted back inside the dormer window. I was a little reluctant to leave the roof—it was a good place to be stoned: safe, scenic, undemanding—but I staggered after her.

Kohler was in the game room in the basement, knocking balls around a pool table for his own amusement. He was big enough that the cue looked small in his hands. Amanda re-introduced me and, mortifyingly, told him I was looking for a job.

"Actually I'm not," I said. "I mean, I *can't*. I have a student work permit, but I'm not a student anymore. I don't even have a visa." I explained again about my family situation.

"Finished three years at Sheridan?" Kohler asked.

"Yeah, but—"

"Tell me what courses you took."

I listed them.

"Okay," he said. "Promising. What kind of grades were you pulling down?"

I told him.

"Sounds like someone you could use," suggested Amanda.

Kohler said, "What I'm setting up is basically a media-access and marketing business. People come to us, we give them what they want at whatever price point they can afford—TV, Internet, direct mail, anything from a full-court integrated ad campaign to a guy handing out leaflets on a street corner. So yeah, Amanda's right, I'm looking to hire folks with the appropriate skills. If you're up to speed on CSS and JavaScript, I can start you next week."

"That's amazingly generous, and it's tempting, but like I said, I don't have a valid work permit—"

"I have a legal guy who can expedite the paperwork. And I'm willing to advance you your salary until you're authorized. Do you want to talk about salary?"

He cited numbers that seemed ridiculously generous. I nodded and said, "But, wait—I would love to do this but I'm kind of—"

"He's new," Amanda said, as if this explained something.

"I'd have to find a place to stay—"

"*Lisa!*" Kohler roared. He was a big man. Big chest cavity. He could roar pretty impressively. I tried not to flinch. "*Loretta!* Amanda, are the Sob Sisters upstairs?"

Lisa Wei came into the room before she could answer. "Keep your voice down, Walter; I'm sure they can hear you in Vancouver. What is it?"

"Homeless waif. A loose Tau."

"Really?" Lisa took my hand and gave me a motherly look. Or what I imagined was a motherly look. I didn't remember my own mother very clearly. "Well, then, you have to stay with us! There are a couple of rooms you can choose from. Tonight isn't too soon, you know, if you don't have anywhere to go."

"My lease is good to the end of the month, but—"

"Then you can move in anytime. Welcome home, Adam! I'll tell Loretta we have a new roomer."

The next sound I heard was Amanda, laughing at the expression on my face.

———

"We call them the Sob Sisters," Amanda said, "because they don't mind if you cry on their shoulders. You don't need to worry about imposing. Lisa and Loretta love having company. Tau company, anyway. So maybe I'll see you next time, Adam."

"Are you leaving?"

"Soon. It's pretty late. I need to say my good-byes." She hugged me and walked away.

But that was fine. A small miracle had taken place: somehow, over the course of a few hours, I had internalized the idea that I was *among family*—not the messy *modus vivendi* my Schuyler relations had arrived at, but family in a better and truer sense of the word. And for another forty-five minutes I drifted through the thinning crowd with a sheepish and slightly stoned grin on my face, striking up conversations that inevitably seemed to begin and end in mid-sentence. "Newbie euphoria," someone called it. Fine. Yes. Exactly.

I caught a last glimpse of Amanda Mehta as she left the house. Dismayingly, she was on the arm of someone I hadn't been introduced to. A big guy—*huge*, actually—with a shaved head and black Maori-style tattoos all over his face.

"Is that her boyfriend?" I asked Lisa Wei, who had come to stand beside me, looking at the end of the evening like a slightly tattered apple doll.

"That's Trevor Holst. Amanda's roommate."

Lisa registered my questioning look but wouldn't say more. Amanda waved to the room as the door was closing—at everyone, but I chose to take it personally.

"I should have thanked her," I said.

"Thank her next time."

"And, I mean, you, too. And Loretta. And Walter. For, well, *everything.*"

"You'd do the same in our place," Lisa said calmly. "And sooner or later, you will."

CHAPTER 4

The first big storm of the winter announced itself on a Friday in December. For two days a low-pressure cell rotated over the city like a millstone, grinding clouds into snow. All weekend, those of us who lived in the house and a handful of our tranchemates took turns excavating the driveway. Lisa and Loretta could have afforded a removal service, but we wouldn't let them pay for labor any able-bodied Tau could perform. By Monday morning the streets were mostly passable and I was able to get to work; at the end of the day I made my way home under streetlights that bled a muddy orange glow, the color of pill bottles and chronic depression.

But I wasn't depressed, just tired. Tired enough to slow down for the familiar quarter-mile walk from the subway; tired enough to be, as Amanda liked to say, *in the moment*, thinking about nothing in particular and paying casual attention to the street, the sidewalk, the few flakes of snow silting from a cloud-locked sky. I cataloged the cars parked by curbside, some still cloaked in the white burqas of the weekend blizzard. Which is how I happened to notice a Toyota Venza idling in the curb zone not far from the house. The skin of snow adhering to it suggested it had been in place for at least an hour. Much of its glass was opaque with condensation, but the moisture had been swiped from the side windows and windshield. Which meant I could see the shape of the car's sole occupant: a man in a navy-blue parka who quickly turned away when he saw me looking.

There was nothing very unusual about this, but the long shadows of the streetlights gave it a film-noir ambience, a hint of mystery, enough so that I mentioned it to Lisa when I came into the house and found her in the kitchen fixing a *paella de marisco* so fragrant I wished I had something better in store for my own dinner than ramen and bagged salad. "There's enough for three," she said, tranche telepathy operating at optimum sensitivity, but I shook my head and asked whether she knew anybody who drove a green Venza.

She put her spoon on the counter and gave me her full attention. "Why do you ask?"

Which caused my own tranche telepathy to emit a cautionary buzz. "Because it's outside idling, and the guy at the wheel looks," I tried to make this light-hearted, *"furtive."*

"Oh. I see." Lisa exchanged a look with Loretta, who had come in from the next room with her finger marking her place in a hardcover novel.

"What? Is it somebody you know?"

"Adam, did you happen to notice the license number?"

"No—why would I notice the license number?"

Like two gray-feathered birds of distinct species cohabiting a single telephone wire, Lisa and Loretta frowned in concert. Lisa, ordinarily the voluble one, seemed reluctant to speak. Loretta, who seldom opened her mouth unless a word seemed urgent, said, "I'll call Trevor. Should we tell Mouse?"

"Maybe not," Lisa said. "I mean, until we're *sure* . . ."

"Sure of what?" I asked. "What's this all about? What did I miss?"

"I'll let Trevor explain," said Lisa.

———

I had learned some basic truths about what it meant to be a Tau in the three and a half months since I moved into the tranche house. One of those truths was *Taus don't gossip.*

Much. We were human beings; we talked about each other. But given how much time we spent together, I had heard very little malicious talk—and none that was *really* malicious. Our boundaries were pretty carefully respected, in other words, which was why I didn't know a whole lot about Mouse, the woman who lived in the basement.

Lisa and Loretta currently had three tenants including me, all Taus. One was a middle-aged used-bookstore owner with an income so sporadic that the money he saved by boarding here made the difference, some months, between eating and going hungry. I liked him, but we weren't especially close. The third tenant was Mouse. She was maybe thirty years old, and Mouse was a name she had given herself; I knew her by no other.

But she wasn't "mousy" in the ordinary sense of the word. She said she had taken the name because she was shy and liked enclosed spaces. (She had chosen her basement room over a more comfortable third-floor bedroom.) She was so obviously working her way through some deeply personal crisis that I had been careful not to ask about it. I had seen her in close conversation with Loretta several times, but they generally clammed up when I passed by. Which was fine: it was really none of my business.

Nor was this. While Lisa got on the phone to Trevor Holst, I set about fixing myself dinner. Lisa and Loretta were generous with living space but they weren't running a boarding house, and apart from a few planned communal meals it was pot luck and fend for yourself. Although I was allotted a few square inches of the big kitchen refrigerator, I was saving money for a bar fridge of my own. More space for palak paneer and freezer bags of homemade chili. All I heard of Lisa's conversation was the worried tone of her voice.

She handed me the phone as I forked the last noodle into my mouth. "Talk to Trevor," she instructed me.

Back at the end of August, when I saw Trevor leaving the tranche party with Amanda, I had guessed they were lovers. (And I had felt a pang of jealousy so unjustifiable that I was instantly ashamed of it.)

But I was wrong about their relationship. In my first month in the tranche I learned that (a) Amanda was as interested in me as I was in her, and (b) Trevor wasn't just her roommate, he was her gay roommate. Trev himself had detected my surge of jealousy and thought it was wonderfully funny, and I eventually managed to see the humor in it too.

Which wasn't *too* difficult, because I liked Trev. I liked everybody in the tranche, of course, but I felt a more immediate connection to some, and Trev was in that category. Not that we were much alike. He worked by day as a freelance physical trainer and on weekends as a bouncer at a Queen Street dance club, and his facial tattoos, which he called *kirituhi*, reflected his Maori ancestry on his mother's side. In fact he was so many things I was not that our friendship felt almost supernatural, as if each of us had befriended a creature from Narnia or Middle Earth. All we really had in common, beyond our Tauness, was our love for Amanda Mehta.

So I took the phone. "What's up? Something about Mouse?"

"Yeah," he said. "And we might need your help. Are you okay with that?"

"Sure, yeah." Of course I was. He didn't really have to ask, and I didn't really have to answer.

"So take your phone up to the second-story bedroom facing the street."

Lisa and Loretta's bedroom. "Why?"

"It's kind of urgent, so just do it and I'll explain as we go."

I hurried upstairs.

Lisa and Loretta's room was a shady cave of deep-pile broadloom and Egyptian cotton sheets dominated by an oak-frame four-post bed. The window facing the street was as old as the house, single-paned and frosted with ice. Drafty, but they had never replaced it with something more modern—I guessed they preferred snuggling under the comforter on winter nights.

"You can see the street?"

I used my sleeve to scrub away a lacework of frost. "Yeah, I can see the street."

"The car still there?"

The Venza was still idling under the streetlight, yes.

"Send me a picture."

Trev liked to mock the out-of-date Samsung smartphone I carried around, but it was good enough to capture a shot of the street, even on a dark winter evening.

"Huh," Trevor said. "That's pretty sure his car . . ."

"*Whose* car?"

"It belongs to a guy named Bobby Botero, and I need to have a talk with him."

I perched on the edge of the bed as Trev told me the story of Bobby and Mouse.

Mouse had been working in the human resources department of the Ontario Ministry of Labour when she first met Bobby Botero. Mouse's parents had died within six weeks of each other the previous year, and her only other close family member—an older sister—lived in Calgary, more than a thousand miles away. Uneasy with strangers and slow to make friends, Mouse had been understandably lonely. Her loneliness caused her to resort to the digital crapshoot of eHarmony, which had come up serial snake eyes, until the online dating service placed her in the hands of Bobby Botero.

Botero impressed her on their first evening out by ordering chilled lobster salad and yuzu aioli at a restaurant called Auberge des Pêches. He was everything her other dates had not been: tall, confident, adequately groomed. The reason he was so well received at Auberge des Pêches was that he ran the city's most successful restaurant-supply business: the plates from which they spooned their chocolate ganache and *croustade aux pommes* had come from Bobby's east-end warehouse. Clearly this was a man who knew what he was doing.

What he was doing was seducing her into a hasty marriage. Only after six months of aggressive courtship and a lightly attended exchange of vows did Mouse finally begin to sense the presence of a deeper, truer, darker Bobby Botero. Bobby, it turned out, liked to be in control. Mouse was expected to phone him at least twice daily when he was in his Danforth Avenue office, keeping him posted on her whereabouts. Eventually he convinced her to quit her job at the Ministry of Labour and take a secretarial job at Botero Food Service Supplies, where she prepared and filed invoices within shouting distance of his office door. Early in her tenure he fired a male accountant for "getting too friendly" with her, which was how he characterized what Mouse had perceived as harmless flirting. Bobby had no social life, and Mouse began to suspect she would never have any real friends of her own . . . unless she counted Bobby as a friend, which, increasingly, she did not.

"You'll need to borrow Lisa's car," Trev said into my ear. "What we're going to do, the two of us, is box in Bobby's vehicle, make it so he can't just drive off. Then I'll have a word with him."

"Okay, wait," I said, liking this less by the minute.

"Just go get in the car."

Mouse's marriage to Bobby lasted as long as it took for a few of
his secrets to float up from obscurity. A furtive phone call to
Mouse from Bobby's aunt Caprice revealed the existence of not
one but two ex-wives, both of whom had at various times caused
restraining orders to be placed on Bobby, and both of whom,
when Mouse eventually contacted them, shared similar stories:
unwarranted jealousy and tight surveillance escalating to verbal
and physical abuse. Mouse saw a grim future hurtling toward
her like an ICBM.

And there was the matter of Bobby's business. Botero Food
Service Supplies was a self-evidently successful enterprise: goods
flowed from the warehouse in a reliable stream and invoices were
paid promptly and in full. But from her position at the account
desk it seemed to Mouse that something was—well, *off*.

"Because it isn't entirely a legitimate business," Trev explained
as I shrugged into a jacket and borrowed the keys to Lisa's five-
year-old Accord. "Botero uses it to launder money for some local guys with a trade in stolen vehicles and connections to the
'Ndrangheta—the Calabrian Mafia."

"Mouse figured this out?"

"Mouse noticed some irregularities in the invoices, but she
found solid evidence in Botero's desk one afternoon when he was
out talking to a corporate buyer. And there's more to it than
that."

This was what I learned on the way from the back door to
the carriage-house garage where Lisa's Accord and Loretta's ancient Volvo brooded together in wintry silence:

Mouse had asked for a divorce. Bobby refused her request and
threatened her with a beating or worse if she so much as glanced
at a passing trial lawyer. He explained that he himself was thor-
oughly lawyered-up, and if she insisted on starting proceedings
she would come out of it with nothing to show but an aching

hollow where her self-respect used to be. And, he insisted, he *loved* her, and he wanted to prevent her from making a terrible mistake.

Mouse bowed her head and meekly agreed. The next day she left work at noon, drove home, packed a few essentials, and moved to a motel room on the Queensway strip. She emptied a bank account she had never told Bobby she possessed and sold to a pawnbroker the few items of gold and silver she had inherited from her mother.

Over the course of the next six months Mouse managed to find herself a new clerical job, moved into an apartment in the basement of a midtown row house, humanized that space with a selection of funky thrift-shop furniture, and saved as much as she could from her weekly paycheck. As soon as she had built up a useful surplus she did two more things: consulted a divorce lawyer and signed up for Affinity testing.

Before long she was a registered Tau with a pending application for divorce. Bobby was well-lawyered, but the law left little room for maneuver; in the end he chose not to contest the proceeding. Mouse had brought very little personal property to the marriage and wanted nothing from Bobby, which made it easier.

"You in the car?"

"Yes," I said. "But, Trev—"

"Good. I'll let you know when I'm at the corner, then you pull out of the garage. Come at Botero's car from behind, park up close to his bumper. I'll be right behind you, and I'll cut him off from the front."

"What happens then?"

"Then I have a conversation with him. That's all."

———

Mouse, though shy by nature, thrived in her Tau tranche. She had almost convinced herself that her bad marriage was behind her when a series of envelopes without return addresses began arriving in the mail. Sometimes the envelopes contained brief hand-scrawled messages. WHORE was a repeat favorite, as was SICK FILTHY CUNT. Sometimes the envelopes contained photographs of Mouse taken without her knowledge: Mouse coming home from work in a yellow summer frock, Mouse dressed up for a tranche party, Mouse fidgeting in the line outside the restroom at a local movie theater.

There was not enough evidence linking these threats to Bobby Botero for the police to get involved, and although Mouse's lawyer applied for a generic restraining order, Mouse wasn't convinced that it would change Botero's behavior. He was obviously nursing a massive grudge, and Mouse knew he was capable of engineering acts of vengeance beyond her power to avoid.

She moved across town, which was how she ended up attached to our tranche. She requested and obtained a transfer from the Ministry office where she worked to a location closer to downtown. She invested in industrial-strength locks for her doors and windows and signed up for a free tae kwon do class at the local community center. And when, despite these precautions, the letters began to arrive again (CUNT, WHORE, FILTH), she accepted Lisa and Loretta's invitation to move into the Rosedale house, where she wouldn't be alone.

"And now he showed up again."

"Again," Trev confirmed. "But this time it's different."

"How so?"

"This time Mouse has friends on her side. Us, plus everyone in her old tranche, plus all the local Taus we've ever networked with."

"Strength in numbers."

"Yeah, and more than numbers: experience, skills, connections."

"Even so, you really think it's a good idea to get up in the face of a guy with Mafia connections?"

"Well, that's the interesting part. Like I said, Mouse has friends in two Tau tranches, and the Tau network in this city is pretty big. For instance, there's a woman, a Tau, lives out in Scarborough, who works for a cleaning service called Daily Maid. And ever since he split up with Mouse, Botero has been a Daily Maid customer. The upshot is that we managed to acquire copies of the contents of the backup drives of Botero's home computers. Including some very ineptly encrypted financial records, which indicate that Botero has been inflating expenses and skimming some of the cash he launders for his mob friends. He puts this down as 'transaction expenses,' but it's a blatant skim. That's our leverage."

"You're still talking about confronting somebody with money and dangerous friends and an obviously unstable, uh, personality—"

"I'm not *talking* about it, I'm *doing* it. Or I will be in about sixty seconds. Get on out here, Adam."

We can't live in fear of this guy forever, Trevor said at some point in our conversation, and I thought, *We?* But he was right. Mouse was a Tau, and one intimidated Tau was one too many.

The street was slick with snow and the Accord chunked into anti-lock mode as I left the driveway. Botero's car was still parked where I had seen it. Probably he was waiting for Mouse to come home, either for reconnaissance or to frighten her by advertising his presence. When I pulled in behind him, almost kissing his bumper with the grille of the Accord, he gave me a sour look in his rearview mirror. His brake lights lit up as he started the Venza's engine and put it in gear.

But Trev came up fast in his Subaru, cutting off Botero and making it impossible for him to move. The Venza's brake lights went dark. A moment later, Botero opened the driver-side door.

He was tall, lean guy. He got out of the car like a flick knife unfolding. He wore a Canada Goose jacket over a logger shirt and faded jeans, a blue-collar-guy-made-good look. His jaw was thrust forward, his mouth bent into a perfect bell curve.

Trevor left his car at the same time. Not as tall as Botero, but broader across the chest, big arms, sure of himself.

"You need to get out of my way," Botero said.

"I'd be happy to do that," Trevor said. "Soon as we have a talk about Mouse."

"I don't know anybody named Mouse."

"I think you do. I think you know a lot of people. Like Jimmy Bianchi? Carl Giordano?"

The names meant nothing to me, but they could only have been Botero's mob connections. Botero's breath hissed into the cold air like steam from a defective radiator. "If you know those names, you know you're playing out of your league."

"If you continue to harass Mouse, there will be consequences."

"And if you continue to harass *me*, there will *sure as fuck* be consequences. You're a member of that club she joined, right? The League of Losers or whatever. Do you really think that entitles you to stand between a man and his wife?"

"I don't want to have to go to Mr. Giordano about this."

"Oh, *that's* your threat? You're going to tell on me? As if Bianchi or Giordano gives a flying fuck about what I do regarding my family?"

"They might give a flying fuck about the five grand you siphon out of their pockets every six months."

Botero did a pretty good job of concealing his shock. But there was no ignoring the gulp of air that hitched in his throat.

Meanwhile, neither Trevor nor Botero saw what I saw: a police cruiser had turned onto the street and was moving toward us with a slow deliberation.

Botero said, "I have no idea what you're talking about. And if you go to Giordano or anybody else with this bullshit story, you will be fucked beyond belief."

"All you need to do is stay away from Mouse. Just forget she ever existed. Do that, and Giordano won't hear a word from me. He especially won't see a copy of that Excel spreadsheet you have on your Mac, the one with all the notations you made. Ten grand a year for, what, seven years now? Eight?"

The police car pulled abreast of the Venza. A bored-looking cop rolled down the side window. "Is there a problem here?"

Botero was still working on recovering his composure. "No," Trevor said, "no problem."

"You know, you can't park here—not at that angle."

"Just getting ready to leave." Trev headed back to his car.

"And you," the cop said. "You're blocking a hydrant. Move along, Mr. Botero."

Botero went wide-eyed again. "What, do I know you?"

"No, sir, not personally. Move along, please. And if you're talking to Carl Giordano, tell him hello."

Tipped off by Lisa about Botero's presence, Mouse had bought herself dinner at a downtown restaurant while she waited for the all-clear.

Trev and I were in the living room when she got home. She didn't say thank you. She didn't have to. She stood on her toes and gave each of us a solemn peck on the cheek.

I met the cop again a few days later, at a multi-tranche Christmas party. His name was Dave Santos, and he belonged to a North York tranche. It was Lisa who had called him to the scene to back up Trevor. We shook hands and smiled. He didn't need my thanks, any more than I needed Mouse's. It was a Tau thing.

CHAPTER 5

At the end of February, not unexpectedly and after a long decline, Grammy Fisk died.

Aaron called and told me the news. (I hadn't spoken to Jenny Symanski since the week after Christmas, when I had told her as delicately as possible that I would be moving in with Amanda Mehta.) "Funeral's Wednesday," my brother said. "If you want to come."

"Of course I'll come. We can be there by Tuesday afternoon."

"We?"

"Amanda and I."

"You want to bring your girlfriend?"

"Is there a reason I shouldn't?"

He sighed. "Do what you want, Adam. You always have."

So we drove to Schuyler and rented a room at the Motel 6. We could have stayed at the family house, but Mama Laura wouldn't have approved of us sharing a room, and I didn't want to expose Amanda to more of my father's attention that was strictly necessary. But there was no way to dodge the family dinner the night before the memorial ceremony.

The family was polite and Amanda was studiously gracious. "I'm so sorry for your loss" was the first thing she said when we came into the house, shedding our winter coats. Mama Laura hugged her; Aaron shook her hand; Geddy was awkward in the presence of strangers but gave her a forced smile and a "Hello, pleased to meet you" that sounded unrehearsed. My father nodded curtly from across the room, our first hint that trouble might be brewing.

We sat down to dinner. Mama Laura had baked a ham the size of a dinosaur thigh, plus peas and candied yams, food to ward off the sound of a cold wind scratching willow branches against the mullions of the dining room window. We made careful conversation. Aaron talked about the work he was doing for the county Republican Party. I talked about my job at Kohler Media, the job that had rescued me from Schuyler, though I didn't describe it that way. We all talked about the story that had dominated the news for two days: the explosions in Riyadh and Jeddah, the mine or missile that had sunk a gushing Sinopec tanker in the Straits of Hormuz. Gas prices were already spiking, and there were lines at some stations: would I be okay for the drive back? (I said I'd manage.)

My father was silent through most of this, but he had been giving Amanda a series of long, cool looks. Now he said, "The Persian Gulf, that's your neck of the woods, no?"

Amanda smiled. "No, not really."

"No? Oh, that's right—you're Indian. Indian from India, correct?"

"I was born in Bramalea, actually."

"What part of India's that?"

"It's a suburb of Toronto. But my grandfather was from Gujarat."

"And what's that a suburb of?"

"It's a state, in the west of India."

Amanda's grandfather had immigrated in the 1960s and

married a Canadian woman. Amanda's father had raised her in a secular household, though the family still celebrated some Hindu festivals—I had helped them light candles for diwali. My own father was putting on his redneck act, probably hoping to draw Amanda into an argument that would make her appear shrill or condescending. His racism was selective: he did business with Indian wholesalers, and a sales rep named Banerjee had been a dinner guest on occasion. "Dad's been to India," I said. "That trade show, what was it, 2009?"

"Twenty-ten," my father said levelly, his eyes still on Amanda. "Mumbai, right?"

"As I recall."

Amanda's smile looked more genuine that it could possibly have been. "And how did you find Mumbai, Mr. Fisk?"

"It was outside the airport." He unclenched a little and added, "Hot. Crowded. Real bad traffic."

"I've never been," Amanda said. "I'd like to visit someday."

Mama Laura asked about Amanda's family, and Amanda gave her the short version: her father was an architect, close to retirement but still doing design and consultation for a Toronto firm. Her mother was an engineer for a forestry company. Her older brother was a physician, currently living in Vancouver. I had been invited often to her family's house in Bramalea, and I had been received with a graciousness that made my father's attitude all the more infuriating.

"And you?" Mama Laura said. "Adam tells us you work at a restaurant of some kind?"

"A vegetarian café," Amanda said, at which Aaron smiled and my father repressed a derisive snort.

Amanda had taken the job when she dropped out of the University of Toronto. She'd been taking pre-law courses at the urging of her family, excelled at research but hated the career prospects. She liked to say she was being educated by Tau: she had learned more from a couple of tranche meetings than she had in six months at school. Tau would find a place for her, she liked to say. And maybe that was true. One of our tranchemates, Damian Levay, was trying to set up an all-Tau investment fund, and Amanda was keen to work with him. I imagined she wouldn't be serving kale and spirulina much longer.

"And you met Adam through that, uh, interest group?"

"Affinity group," Amanda said. "Yes."

"People say it's, you know—"

"I'm not insulted by what people say."

"A *cult*," Mama Laura finished in an apologetic whisper.

"It's not a cult. There's no doctrine, no creed, no leader. Nothing we have to believe in or swear allegiance to."

"It costs money, though, doesn't it?" my father asked.

"For evaluation, plus an annual membership fee."

"Like a cult because it breaks up families, too."

"I don't believe that's the case, Mr. Fisk."

Amanda put a hand on my knee to let me know she wasn't rattled.

"Well," he said, "all I know is, I hear things. People develop a loyalty to these Affinity groups."

"They do," Amanda said. "But not for any sinister reason. The whole point is that it's a group of people you can trust, who trust you."

"That's all?"

"Think about it this way. Everything human beings do—everything worthwhile—depends on cooperation. We cooperate better than any other species. But cooperation can get derailed pretty easily. People lie, people cheat, people misunderstand each other. So we learn to be wary and mistrustful. Once burned, twice shy, no?"

"Happens in business often enough."

"Sure. It happens to everyone, and it slows you down, it costs you time and money, it leaves you cynical."

"That's just human nature, Miss Mehta."

"But an Affinity group is a place where that logic doesn't apply. It's a place where you don't have to watch your back. Where people like you, for sensible reasons. A place where—"

"Where everybody knows your name?" Geddy asked. Followed by his own goofy rendition of the old *Cheers* theme song.

Amanda returned his grin. "Yeah, like that," she said, laughing. "But in real life."

"Can't replace family," my father said, looking pointedly in my direction.

"Some of the people in our tranche come from pretty unpleasant families, Mr. Fisk. Some of them *need* a replacement."

"Do we seem that bad to you?"

"I don't mean *this* family. Is that a blueberry pie, Mrs. Fisk?"

"Boysenberry," Mama Laura said, beaming.

"It looks great."

"Bless you for saying so. I think we're about ready for dessert and coffee, now that you mention it."

"Dessert," Geddy agreed, nodding.

After the meal we adjourned to the living room. And the conversation turned to the subject of Grammy Fisk. We told our favorite stories and shared the poignant business of missing her. Amanda had nothing to contribute, but she listened attentively and put an arm around Mama Laura when she started to cry.

Displays of emotion made Geddy uneasy, and he excused himself early and went up to his room. A little while later a sound echoed down the stairs, a brassy hoot that made me think of geese heading south in autumn. "Oh, Lord, Geddy's saxophone," Mama Laura said. "It's way too late for him to be practicing."

"Geddy took up an instrument?"

"For band, at school. Yes. And not just the instrument! He brought Grammy Fisk's old record player down out of the attic and set it up in his room. Plus maybe a hundred or so of her dusty old records."

It was getting on time to leave, so I headed up to Geddy's room to say good night and investigate his newfound interest. Geddy's enthusiasms tended to monopolize his conversation and most of his waking thoughts, and when he opened his door I saw this was no exception. Grammy Fisk's fifty-year-old turntable and receiver covered most of the free space on his desk. The cloth-grille speakers were set up at the foot of his bed, and Grammy Fisk's record collection (mostly old jazz, folk, rock) snaked along the floorboards under the window.

Geddy put down his sax and waved me in. He told me about the instrument—a Yamaha alto sax, secondhand from Schuyler's only pawn shop—and about the music he'd been listening to. Forget My Chemical Romance, he was all about horns and reeds now. His favorite saxophone player was Paul Desmond. ("Because of his tone. He plays a real pure note. Only a little vibrato. He doesn't fancy up the sound. I want to learn to play a pure note like that.") Geddy was daunted by the difficulty of the instrument, but he honked out a scale for me, and I thought I could hear what he was aiming at. Years later I would admire his skill, but what I heard that night was more ambition than talent.

He grimaced when a high C went sour. "I'm just learning."

"Yeah, but I can tell you're getting better at it."

He gave me a tight smile that was both a thank-you for the compliment and an acknowledgment that I couldn't possibly know what I was talking about.

"I guess it's a way of remembering Grammy Fisk, too—all this," I said.

He thought about it. "Maybe."

"There might be some crying at the memorial service tomorrow. Are you okay with that?"

He shrugged.

"I'll be there if you need me."

"Amanda is nice," Geddy said.

"Thanks."

"Is it true, what she said about the Affinity groups?"

"Yeah, I think so."

"Maybe I'll join one. When I'm older."

I didn't know whether there was an Affinity he would qualify for, but I hoped so.

In the morning Aaron drove me to a family meeting prior to the memorial service. I was a pallbearer, and a deacon at the Methodist church explained what was expected of us: how to support the weight of the coffin, where the hearse would be waiting. After the briefing Aaron drove me back to the motel so I could take Amanda to the service. And while we were alone in the car he raised the subject of Jenny Symanski: ten earnest minutes of how-could-you-do-this and she-deserves-better.

"I mean," Aaron said, "what's she supposed to do now? Pretty girl like that, smart but no college, parents both drinking, the family business drying up in this shitty economy, and no marriage prospects because for most of her adult life she's been waiting for you to grow a pair and ask her. What the fuck is she supposed to do?"

I didn't have an answer.

Jenny was at the funeral, of course.

I was up front with the immediate family, in a church crowded with my father's business associates and his buddies from the local Republican committee. Snow melted snow from shoes and boots puddled on the oaken floorboards and made the air humid. Psalm 23, a hymn, the eulogy, a benediction, and I couldn't help wondering what Grammy Fisk would have made of all this. ("I don't know where you go when you die," she had once confided in me. "I don't think you go anywhere at all except the grave.") After the memorial service we got in our cars and trailed the hearse to Schuyler's big nondenominational cemetery, where a machine had gouged a perfectly rectangular hole into the frozen earth. It was a gray end-of-winter day, a few flakes of snow riding on a wet wind. We stood in silence as the coffin was lowered. *Blessed are the dead. They will rest from their labors.* Mama Laura leaned into my father's shoulder, weeping quietly. My father stood immobile, his features locked into a sculpture expressing, somehow, both anger and loss. Geddy stood with his head down, probably pretending he was somewhere else.

Jenny stood on the far side of the grave with her father and mother. Jenny's mother had surfaced, though not completely or for long, from her alcoholic submersion. Her father wore a suit that must have been ten or fifteen years old, and he stared at his feet while we said the Lord's Prayer. They bookended Jenny, who avoided my eyes—or maybe it was Amanda, standing next to me, she didn't want to look at.

The pastor finished his *go forth with God's peace* and we adjourned to the reception hall for finger sandwiches and Kool-Aid in Dixie cups. When I saw Jenny I started toward her but her parents, thin-lipped and sweating, took her arm and steered her away.

She looked back at me once, her expression unreadable.

What I wanted to say to her was this:

Like you, Jenny, I always figured there must be a place in the world for me. You know what I mean. Walking down some street on a winter night so cold your footsteps on the snowy sidewalk sound like glass being ground to sand, yellow light leaking from the windows of the houses of strangers, you catch a glimpse of some sublimely ordinary moment—a girl setting a table, a woman washing dishes, a man turning the pages of a newspaper—and you get the idea you could walk through the door of that house into a brand-new life, that the people inside would recognize and welcome you and you would realize it was a place you had always known and never really left. Like we talked about on Birch Street that one time, remember? The night of the big snowstorm, walking home in the dark after band practice.

The thing is, Jenny, *there really is a door like that.* There really is a house full of kind and generous voices. It exists, and I was lucky enough to find it. And that's why I can't come home and marry you.

I know you think it's bullshit. I know you think I bought a sales pitch, swallowed a line, joined a cult. You think I gave myself to Tau the way people give themselves to Scientology or Mormonism or the Communist Party. But Tau isn't like that.

It's a bright window on a cold night, Jenny. It's shelter from the storm. It's everything we envied from the enclosure of our loneliness. It's what we tried and failed to find in each other's arms.

These were the words I couldn't say.

During the hour-long reception my father circulated through the crowd, acknowledging business acquaintances and shaking their hands and the hands of their spouses and children. It was only when we stepped out into another flurry of wet snow that he allowed himself to indulge his grief.

Because he was both stoic and fanatically private, the signs would have been easy to miss. But I saw him turn and look back at the cemetery, where Grammy Fisk's burial place had become invisible among the ranks of Schuyler's dead; I saw him mouth something inaudible and swipe the palms of his hands across his eyes. My father talked about his childhood so seldom that it was almost impossible to imagine him having had one—but he had, and Grammy Fisk would have been the heart of it. He had buried his mother today, and with her a little of himself.

We headed back to our cars. I helped Amanda into the passenger seat, then walked over to where my father was still standing. We weren't a touchy-feely family—Grammy Fisk and Mama Laura had doled out all the hugs any of us ever got—but I was moved to put my hand on his arm. I felt the gnarled density of muscle under his winter jacket. The smell of him was poignantly familiar: the aftershave he habitually used, the greasy black polish he swabbed on his shoes. Melting snow had plaited his hair across his scalp.

He gave me a startled look, then pushed my hand away. "I don't need your sympathy," he said. "And I don't want it. Why don't you just take your Arab girlfriend and go back to wherever it is you call home?"

So I said good-bye to Mama Laura and Geddy and Aaron, and we drove out of Schuyler late that night. The roads were slick with snow and there were line-ups at every gas station that was open, but we managed to fill up at a truck stop on I-90. "The craziness of the world," Amanda said as we pulled back onto the interstate. "You know?"

Warring nations, paranoid politics, my fucking family. I knew all about it.

"Before I was a Tau," she said, "it just seemed so overwhelming. Salute the flag. Praise God. Honor your father and your mother. These big *abstractions*—God and country and family. They used to have power over me, as if they were real and important. But they're not. They're just words people use to control you. It's bullshit. I don't need a family or a country or a church. I have my tranche."

I said, "We have each other."

"We have *more* than each other. We have Tau. Which is what makes it okay to admit that your dad is a racist asshole."

The wind was blowing rags of snow across the highway, and I had to slow down. "Well, he's more than just—"

"I know, it's complex. It's *always* complex, out there in the world. But the truth can't hurt us anymore and we don't have to hide from it. Your dad is many things, and one of them is—"

"A racist asshole?

"You disagree?"

No. The evidence was abundant, and I had seen much more of it than Amanda had.

She said, "How does that make you feel?"

"I guess, ashamed. Embarrassed."

"Ashamed of what?"

"Do I have to say it? Ashamed of being his son. Of being a Fisk."

"But you're *not* a Fisk! That's the point. You don't belong to those people. Their sins aren't on you. That house is not your home, and Fisk is just your name."

I drove a while more. The highway was mostly empty, just a couple of semi trailers on the northern horizon, and when the sky cleared I could see a few chilly stars.

"You know I'm right," she said. It wasn't a question. "You're one of us."

After we crossed the border Amanda took the wheel and I checked my phone for voice mail.

There was a single message, from Lisa Wei.

"Trevor is in the hospital," she said. "Call me as soon as you can."

———

By the time we reached the city limits I had woken Lisa with a callback and managed to get the whole story.

Trev was in a hospital called Sunnybrook, north and east of downtown, and we drove there directly and shared a nervous breakfast in the cafeteria while we waited for visiting hours. Then we made our way to his room.

As early as we were, we weren't the first to arrive. Damian Levay was already there, standing at Trev's bedside and saying something quiet and urgent. Trev spotted us and broke into a grin, or what would have been a grin if not for the hardware attached to his face.

Damian Levay was the closest thing our tranche had to a leader, though none of us would have used that word. He was an early adopter, a Tau almost since the first assessments were offered three years ago. He was also lawyer, and in that capacity he had helped Taus all over the city, adjusting his fees to suit his clients' income. He was full of ideas about the purpose and future of Affinity groups, and Amanda thought he was brilliant. What he had been discussing with Trev was probably the subject of Bobby Botero: it was Botero who had put Trev in the hospital.

Trev's plan for defending Mouse had been ironclad, except for one thing: it presumed Botero would not continue to harass Mouse if it meant putting himself and his business in mortal danger.

What we had not reckoned on was Botero's obsessive rage, which was beyond all rational constraint. Botero had no doubt wiped his computer drives, tidied up his financial loose ends, and convinced himself he could talk his way of any trouble with his 'Ndrangheta clients. He had then undertaken a more circumspect surveillance of Lisa and Loretta's house, and yesterday, after he had seen L & L leave on a shopping expedition and he was sure Mouse was alone, he had come to the door with an aluminum baseball bat in his hand. When Mouse refused to let him in, he shattered a ground-floor window, climbed inside, and began a systematic room-by-room search for her.

Mouse, meanwhile, barricaded herself in her basement room and phoned Trev, who in turn called Dave Santos, the Tau cop who had helped us out in December. Both of them hurried to the house, but Trev was the first to arrive.

Mouse still had her phone, and she told Trev that Bobby was in the basement hammering on the locked door of her room. Trev had no weapon, but he let himself in and hurried down the stairs. In exchange for this act of heroism he took a blow across the face that broke his nose and dislocated his jaw, but he was far enough inside Botero's swing radius that when he fell he took Botero down with him. Botero was strong, but so was Trev, and the lessons he had learned as a club bouncer served him well even as he was dazed and blinded by the blood flowing into his eyes.

They were still wrestling when Dave Santos crept down the stairs with his handgun drawn. Botero dropped his bat, and at that point it was all over except for the police car that took Bobby away to be booked and the ambulance that carried Trev to the hospital.

Trev's jaw was supported by a wire brace that made it difficult for him to speak, and the bandages across his face were rusty-brown with blood. His eyes seemed a little vague—he was probably on industrial-strength painkillers—but he was more or less alert. He took a pad and pen from the bedside table and wrote,

THIS WILL ONLY ENHANCE MY RUGGED BEAUTY

—which caused Amanda to laugh and leak a tear.

"We've been talking about what happened at the house," Damian said. "Trev's going to need to sign a statement. With any luck, Botero is headed to prison for a stretch. The only possible complication is what you guys did—stealing his drives and threatening to expose him. We don't want that coming out in court. Hopefully, neither Botero nor his lawyer will want to expose his mob connections. So we're probably okay, but it could have been cleaner."

We had acted carelessly, in other words, and Trev had paid for it. "I understand," I said contritely. "What we did about Mouse and Botero—we need to stop doing things like that."

Damian startled me by laughing.

"*Stop* it? Fuck no! We have to learn to do it *better*."

PART TWO

A Theory of Everyone

In the early decades of this century we saw the world's financial elites become increasingly divorced from national loyalties. The wealthy learned to think of themselves as essentially stateless—citizens of the Republic of Net Worth—while the rest of us clung to our old-fashioned patriotism. Now the masses (or some fraction of them) have discovered their own post-national system of loyalty. They would rather tithe to their sodalities than pay taxes, and they love their tranchemates just a little bit more than they love their neighbors. If this trend seems harmless, give it time. Politicians should be worried. So should activists. And so should the stateless, wealthy one-percenters, whose continuing influence over the legislative process is no longer assured.

—*Mother Jones*, online article, "Why the Affinities Matter"

One thing the church has traditionally offered, and secular society has not, is fellowship: a body of shared values and a time and place at which congregants commune for worship. This is not the essence of faith, but it is faith's essential scaffolding. But the new secular communities—the Affinity groups—are beginning to make inroads into faith's monopoly on fellowship. Statistics have demonstrated a falling-away from traditional doxastic communities commensurate with the rise of the Affinities. And so we must ask ourselves: Is this a benign social technology, or is it something more sinister—a counter-fellowship, a church stripped of all divinity, a congregation with nothing to worship but itself?

—*Christianity Today*, online article, "Fellowship Without Faith"

In the debate over whether the Affinities are making people happy, we risk losing sight of the fact that the Affinities are making people money.

—Barrons.com, "The Benefits of Membership"

CHAPTER 6

This happened seven years later, in southern British Columbia, on a two-lane road connecting a resort town called Perry's Point to the Okanagan Highway. Three of us in a borrowed car, heading for Vancouver. Damian Levay was driving. Amanda sat up front, next to him. I sat in back, watching pine boughs whip past the rain-fogged windows.

Wet blacktop, a winding road, steep grades. Amanda had twice asked Damian to slow down, but he had eased off the accelerator only marginally. He was carrying several gigs of contraband data in his shirt pocket, and he knew there were people who would have liked to relieve him of it. So we came around a curve in fading daylight at an unwise speed, and when the headlights picked out a yellow Toyota parked on the verge Damian swerved to avoid it. It was a fraction of a second later that he saw the woman and the child crossing in front of us.

The rear of the car flailed as he braked, and although he avoided hitting either of them he risked sliding into a skid that would sweep them both down a steep embankment. So he stepped off the brake and twisted the wheel, which sent us hurtling into the forested slope to the left of the road. I caught a freeze-frame glimpse of the woman's face, inches from the window as we passed: big eyes, pale skin, a cascade of dark, wet hair. Damian braked again and managed to bleed off a little momentum before the car sideswiped a lodgepole pine hard enough to pop the airbags.

The next thing I was aware of was the smell of hot fabric and talcum powder. My face throbbed and my right shoulder felt as if I had tackled a concrete block. I opened my eyes and looked for Amanda.

She was up front, startled but not hurt. She looked to her left and said, "Damian?"

Damian was splayed over the steering wheel. He raised his head when she called his name. There was blood around his nose and mouth. "M'okay," he said.

Amanda leaned in and switched off the engine. Her door was jammed against the trunk of the tree we had hit. She looked back at me. "Adam, help me get him out."

I managed to climb out of the car into the drenching rain. I opened the driver's door, hooked Damian's left arm over my shoulder, and lifted him out. He found his feet but had to brace himself against the hood. He put his hand to his head and said, "Dizzy."

Amanda scooted out after him, and since the car seemed in no danger of bursting into flame—the only obvious damage was a trashed side panel—we helped Damian lie down across the backseat.

"He wasn't driving," Amanda said tersely.

"What?"

"Listen. We'll have highway cops here pretty soon. If Damian gets caught up in any kind of litigation, it'll make us vulnerable. So I'll clean him up, and when the police or EMS get here I'll say I was at the wheel. You back me up, okay?"

Damian had the future of the entire Tau Affinity—maybe the future of all the Affinities—in his pocket (literally!), and he'd had a couple of drinks with Meir Klein, which could complicate matters if the cops assayed his blood alcohol. "Okay," I said. "But I was driving, not you."

She thought about it a moment and nodded. Amanda had a couple of DUIs on her record from her pre-Tau days. I had a clean record, I hadn't been drinking, and of the three of us my work was the least critical. "Fine," she said. "And maybe you should go talk to that woman we almost hit."

So I walked back to the yellow Toyota. The woman was sitting inside, the door open. She watched as I approached, her skinny arms crossed and her lips pressed tight. The child was in back, a pair of solemn eyes under a drooping orange rain hat. The girl was dressed for the weather, but the mom, if she was the girl's mom, wore a brown woolen sweater that looked like the hide of a sodden Airedale. I asked if everyone was all right.

She eyed me coolly. "More or less," she said. "Felt the breeze when you went past. But no damage done."

"That's great."

"I called CAA before you came around the bend. I think my transmission's fucked up. That's why we stopped. Been here twenty minutes. You got somebody hurt back there? I already dialed 911."

"No, we're okay."

"You sure? You keep rubbing your shoulder."

"Sprained it, maybe." I looked down at her feet. "But you're bleeding."

She followed my eyes. Then she hiked up one leg of her jeans, revealing a bloody gash along her calf. "Jesus, I didn't even feel it. I mean when you went past it felt like the car maybe just brushed my leg, but I guess something caught it . . ."

Probably the rear bumper. It had lost a lug where it met the wheel well, and the edge stuck out from the frame. "You need to put pressure on that," I said.

She rummaged in her purse for a pack of Kleenex. I watched her face while she dabbed at the blood. I wanted to judge her sincerity, though it was impossible to read the motives of a non-Tau the way I could read a Tau. Of course, the woman could have been a Tau herself . . . but my intuition said not.

The injury to her leg wasn't anywhere near serious, but it might be grounds for an insurance claim if she sensed an opportunity to exact a settlement. "Don't worry," she said, apparently reading me more acutely than I was reading her, "it wasn't your fault. Though you guys took the curve at a pretty good clip."

"My name's Adam Fisk."

"I'm Rachel. Rachel Ragland. In the back, that's Suze."

"Hi, Suze."

Suze was maybe six or seven years old, as blond as her mother was dark. She ducked away from the window, shy but smiling.

Rachel said, "Is your driver really okay?"

I looked back to where Amanda was tending Damian. "Just a bump. But I was the one driving."

"No you weren't."

"Yeah, actually, I was."

"Uh-huh. So is that what I'm supposed to tell the cops—that you were the one driving?"

"Well, yeah. Because I *was*."

Rachel rolled her eyes. "Okay then," she said. "That's what we'll tell them."

Damian's nose had bled prodigiously—he looked like he was wearing a rust-colored goatee—but he was sitting up by the time I got back to the car. "The EMS guys will probably take me in for observation if they think I have a concussion—"

"They will, and you might."

"—and I don't want this stuck in some hospital locker." He gave Amanda the thumb drive containing Meir Klein's data, and she tucked it into her purse.

Amanda turned to me. "So what's the deal with the other vehicle?"

I told her about Rachel Ragland.

"You think she'll be a problem?"

"Doesn't look like it."

"You think she has an Affinity?"

Sometimes you can tell. Some people liked to advertise their affiliation, and InterAlia had licensed the rights to market lapel pins, tattoos, t-shirts. Rachel displayed none of those obvious signs, and I was pretty sure she wasn't a Tau, either tested or potential, but beyond that I couldn't say.

"Worse luck for us," Amanda said.

"Not necessarily. She seems reasonable. She has a daughter."

"Proves nothing."

Amanda distrusted outsiders. And maybe that was wise, given what Meir Klein had told us. Given the future we were facing.

Klein, of course, was the man who invented the Affinities.

More than a decade ago he had traded a successful academic career in neuroscience and teleodynamics for a contract with InterAlia Inc. At the time InterAlia had been a struggling commercial data-mining business with offices in Camden, New Jersey, using evolutionary algorithms to focus marketing strategies and reclaim "untapped commercial margins" for its corporate clients. Three years after hiring Klein, InterAlia opened its first Affinity-testing centers in Los Angeles, Seattle, Taos, and Manhattan.

The business had taken off slowly, but by the time I took my test the Affinities had become a significant component of InterAlia's revenue stream; a year after that, Meir Klein's division dwarfed everything else in InterAlia's portfolio. And Klein, whose deal with InterAlia had included a generous block of shares in the company's stock, had become quietly wealthy.

But a little more than a year ago Klein had severed all connections with InterAlia and dropped out of sight. No public explanation was forthcoming, but the *Wall Street Journal* reported that he had signed a heavily lawyered nondisclosure agreement and promised his former employers to conduct no further research on the human socionome that would compete with their interests. Most of us assumed he had simply retired. Which made it a big surprise when Damian received a hand-delivered invitation to a meeting, signed by Meir Klein himself.

We had been attending the annual All-Affinities North American Potlatch, held this year in Vancouver: more than fifty thousand delegates from tranches across the continent crammed into the city's convention center and nearby hotels. The note delivered to Damian's hotel room had been arch and cryptic—*It is urgently important that we meet to discuss the future of Tau*—but it was on Klein's letterhead, it included a phone number, and after a quick call Damian was convinced it really was Klein who had sent it.

If Meir Klein wanted to talk to a prominent Tau, it was reasonable that he would have chosen Damian. The Affinities had no official hierarchy, and under the rules laid down by InterAlia all tranches were created equal; the national sodalities existed solely to organize social events and maintain centralized websites and mailing lists. Like every other Affinity, Tau had no president, no board of directors, and no governing body apart from the policy wonks at InterAlia itself. But the Affinities were all about cooperation and organization. And more than any other Tau on the continent, Damian had been a tireless organizer. He had come into the Affinity as a successful business-affairs lawyer, and he had soon begun setting up financial plans for other Taus: pensions, investment portfolios, trusts. His reputation gradually spread from our tranche to the Toronto Tau network and from there to the entire national sodality, and before long he had hired a small army of accountants and financial experts (all Taus) to handle the huge volume of work. Out of that had emerged TauBourse, the first publicly-traded Affinity-based corporate entity. It was also the first Affinity-based business to face a legal challenge from InterAlia, which had become alarmed at the prospect of others deriving profits, even indirectly, from an institution to which InterAlia owned intellectual property rights.

The litigation was still ongoing. Damian viewed it as a bid by InterAlia for closer control of the Affinities, a prospect that had always worried him, and a few months ago he had started a much less well-publicized project: an effort to systematically debrief Taus about their membership tests, with the goal of reverse-engineering the process. Basically, he wanted to crack the neural and analytical code that identified Taus. Which *was* an explicit trespass on InterAlia's intellectual property, which is why we kept it quiet. But given how much we all meant to each other, it was inconceivable that we could leave these tools locked behind a wall of corporate law. The test protocols were the keys to our identity. They were how we had discovered ourselves as a proto-ethnicity. Unless we controlled them, how could we know they wouldn't be altered or mismanaged?

Klein hadn't said what he wanted to talk about, but Damian guessed it had something to do with the Tau codes. What was unclear was whether Klein wanted to scold us, warn us, threaten us, or help us.

Some of each, as it turned out.

The address Klein had given us was a three-story mansion dressed up as a rustic cabin. It was big enough to sleep busloads, but as far as I could tell it was occupied only by Klein and his staff. It was impossible to know how many employees Klein had, but a best guess was "many"—there was the guy who met our car (who looked like an ex-Marine crammed into khakis and a flannel shirt), the guy staking out the entrance hall (likewise), and the woman who offered us canapés on a silver tray after escorting us to a room with a glass wall overlooking the pristine shores of Lake Sanina. No doubt there were others unseen.

A few minutes after we settled onto the sofa, Klein shuffled into the room. Klein was in his late sixties, and what was intimidating about him was his intellect and his reputation, not his physical presence. He wore a white shirt open at the collar and blue jeans cinched over his hips with an expensive leather belt. His head was shaved, his face weathered and finely wrinkled. He made no objection to my presence or Amanda's—knowing Tau dynamics as well as he did, he had probably expected Damian to show up with company—but he more or less ignored us once we'd been introduced.

There was no superfluous chitchat. He settled into a chair and looked at Damian solemnly. He said, "I undertook my life's work more than thirty years ago. At the time we had only begun to apply computer modeling to the discipline of cognitive and social teleodynamics. I cannot tell you how exciting it was, to stand on the verge of a vast new range of human knowledge . . ."

And so on. It was as if he had mistaken Damian for a biographer. But he wasn't telling us anything we didn't already know. When Klein paused to sip water from a bottle, Damian said, "Your invitation—that is, I have to wonder—"

Klein cocked his head. "You're asking me to hurry up and get to the point?"

"Sir, it's a privilege to be here. I just want to make sure I'm not *missing* the point."

"And I want to make sure you understand it. All right. We can circle back to the details. The crux of the matter is this."

He took a handkerchief from the pocket of his shirt and blew his nose into it, long and loudly. I thought of the way Amanda looked when she tried to suppress a laugh. I was careful not to look at her now, because I was almost certain she had that expression on her face.

Klein examined the handkerchief, folded it, and tucked it back in his pocket. "My latest models suggest we're at the opening of an unprecedented revolution in human social dynamics. The revolution is technologically driven, and the Affinities are in the vanguard of it. We traditionally conduct the Affinity tests with mainframe computers and complex analytical algorithms, but today you can build the majority of those functions onto a single microprocessor. Throw in a half dozen sensors and a video device and you can run the application on any tablet computer or smartphone. InterAlia knows this, and it terrifies them. Affinity testing for pennies on the dollar! It would completely democratize the process. It would also put InterAlia out of business."

"The process *should* be democratized," Damian said. "But as long as InterAlia owns the protocols—"

"InterAlia owns proprietary rights to the algorithms and the methodology, but that's merely a legal barrier. You remember what people used to say? Information wants to be free. As soon as the test parameters and sorting algorithms are publically available, InterAlia's legal standing becomes almost irrelevant. Bluntly, their copyrights and so forth won't be worth shit."

His faint accent made the word sound like "zhit."

"You think that might happen?"

Klein seemed surprised by the question. "Oh, I *guarantee* it will happen! Because, you see, I mean to *make* it happen!"

And having delivered this declaration, he invited us to dinner.

At the table Klein became more obviously human. The food was impeccably presented, delivered by poised and professional servants, but Klein ate like someone who lived alone. His chief utensils were fork and fingers, and by the end of the salad course there was an oil-drenched endive clinging to his shirt collar. As he ate he reminisced about his youth, hanging out on Dizengoff Street in Tel Aviv, "back when a secular Jew in Israel was a relatively uncomplicated thing to be." He elicited a few stories from Damian in return. I had rarely heard Damian talk about his pre-Tau life, but he offered some tales from his days at the University of Toronto. What was really going on, of course, was that the two men were sizing each other up.

Amanda was brave enough to ask Klein whether he had ever applied his own test to himself—did he have an Affinity of his own?

He smiled at the question. "No."

"You were never curious?"

"Often curious, but I was afraid the knowledge would create a bias. I wanted to remain objective. And at some point it began to seem like a potential conflict of interest, to whatever extent I was capable of influencing InterAlia's policies. Now, of course, it's far too late."

"Too late to test yourself? Why? There's no age limit, is there?"

"Because I have cancer," Klein said flatly. "And it's not the kind that can be cured. Multiple metastases. If I were to join a tranche, Miss Mehta, I would only make a hospice of it. And I don't want to do that."

We sat out an awkward silence. Amanda said, "I'm sorry—"

"Please don't insult me by apologizing."

"And . . . I can only speak for my own Affinity, but any Tau tranche would welcome you, any time and under any circumstances. We aren't squeamish about helping each other. Even under extreme circumstances. In fact we're pretty good at it."

"Of course I know that," Klein said softly. "Thank you, but it's not what I want."

A servant took away our plates and came back with four cut-glass bowls, each containing a perfectly formed globe of lemon sorbet with a finger cookie standing in it like the mast of a sailing ship. We stared at them.

Damian tried to steer the conversation back to business. "You must know that if you release the Affinity protocols, there are going to be unpredictable consequences."

"On the contrary, the consequences are far from unpredictable. *I have predicted them.* But we can talk about it in the morning. I'm tired. You brought what you need for an overnight visit? Then please spend the rest of the evening any way you like. Whatever you need, ask the staff. When you're ready, they'll show you your rooms."

That night one of Klein's assistants escorted us to our bedrooms, three rooms side by side along a spacious corridor. But we only needed two.

I slept alone. Amanda, as had been her custom lately, slept with Damian.

In the morning the three of us rendezvoused in Klein's large kitchen. He had left instructions for the staff to fix us anything we wanted for breakfast, or we could raid the refrigerator and do our own cooking if we preferred. So we improvised eggs and toast and coffee, after which Damian went for a walk down by the lake. From the big window of the main room Amanda and I caught glimpses of him by the boathouse along the dock, watching the sky in case it started to rain.

Amanda sat where the window framed her. One of the servants told us Klein would be available in an hour or so, and was there anything she could do for us in the meantime?

I asked her to bring me paper and a pencil. "Plain paper, not lined."

"Making notes?" Amanda asked.

"Sketching."

The assistant came back with paper and a selection of sharpened pencils and a clipboard.

"Sketching what?"

"You, if it's okay."

She smiled. "It's been a while since you did that."

I mumbled something about the light, which really was striking: the clinical fluorescence of the house lights versus the brooding gray clouds behind the window. But yes, it had been a while. The pleasure in this case was in capturing the contrast between Amanda and the turmoil of cloud that framed her, doing it without color, just gray tones. I think she liked the attention, but her eyes kept straying to the window. To Damian where he stood on the dock, waiting and thinking.

The fact was, we both loved Damian. But only Amanda was fucking him.

"Will you show it to me when you're done?"

I said I would. But not *until* it was done. Grammy Fisk had always laughed at how jealously I guarded my work: the wary look, the cupped hand blocking the paper as she passed. She didn't understand that I couldn't share a drawing until I had finished it. Until then, it was mine and *only* mine.

Meir Klein joined Damian down at the dock. We saw them talking as they followed the path back to the house, Damian lagging to accommodate Klein's careful, plodding steps. They came in through a nearby door, and Damian steered Klein into the room where we sat—I think he wanted to make sure Amanda and I heard at least some of what he said.

Puzzlingly, it sounded like a lecture on entomology. Klein was talking about "eusociality," the ability of some insect species to act cooperatively. Hive insects like bees and ants were the classic example. By comparison, human beings seem like pretty feeble cooperators: we compete with each other, occasionally kill each other when scant resources are at stake. But that's only part of the story. In fact we collaborate even more effectively than insects (who conduct their own wars and mortal combats), and our genius for collaboration has made us uniquely successful as a species. Insect hierarchies are rigid and formal; human hierarchies are fluid and an individual can participate in more than one. The more flexible and layered these multiplex hierarchies, the more successful a human culture tends to be. Cooperation everywhere, built so deeply into our nature that it's almost invisible: all we see are the deplorable exceptions, crime and corruption and oppression.

Literacy, the printing press, high-speed travel, and instantaneous communication: all these technologies had expanded and enhanced the human genius for cooperation, Klein said. "And now we confront a technology that *directly* addresses human eusociality."

The Affinities, I assumed he meant. But he meant much more than that.

"The Affinities were the first application to emerge from the science of social teleodynamics. But recent modeling suggests that the Affinities are only one of many possible forms of enhanced human collaboration—that there exists an entire untapped phase space of potential social networks."

Klein paused for breath, and Damian took the opportunity to ask, "Is that a bad thing?"

"Not intrinsically, but there are two potential problems. One fundamental, one practical.

"The fundamental problem is that cooperation is a blade with two edges. Sometimes we collaborate in order to give our own group an advantage over others. Think of it as predatory collaboration. Predatory collaboration can also be technologically enhanced, which means short-term gain for some but a net loss of collaborative efficiency. It can also lead to a kind of arms race, in which predatory collaboration becomes a requisite for any group's survival. In that case, the results can be bloody.

"The practical problem is that we're opening the door to a cascade, a torrent, a tsunami of cultural and economic and political change. No one is prepared for this! Existing institutions could fail massively. Wholly novel loyalties and systems of loyalty may arise. And without constraints, we could be looking at a state of perpetual war between competing sodalities."

Tranche warfare, I thought, but the joke didn't seem funny.

"Worse," Klein said, "this comes at a critical juncture in human history. You know the problems we face, from climate change to economic inequality to world hunger. Problems that are easy to name but almost impossible to address, because they require a kind of global collaborative response our species hasn't yet mastered. InterAlia sold the Affinities as a commercial product, a way of making friends, like a dating service or a social club. But they were always more than that. Designedly so. Because they concentrate human collaborative potential, they are a potential avenue to the kind of work that might redeem this battered planet. But they can only become that if they remain structurally sound, within the framework I created for InterAlia."

"If you publish your research," Damian said, "aren't you tearing down that framework?"

"On the contrary, I hope to preserve it." Klein had begun to pace, as if some kind of crackling energy had percolated through his frail body. "The crisis is *already* inevitable. The corporate model of the Affinities is failing. I was the first to do this work, but other social dynamicists are following a similar path. Much more would already have been published if not for InterAlia's attempts to suppress it. So, listen: my plan is this. I mean to release my own key research within the next six months. From what I've seen in journals and on the Internet, much of the knowledge will by that time already be an open secret. Inter-

Alia believes it can contain the leaks that have already occurred, but InterAlia is mistaken. Either way, I want you to have the best available data in advance of its release. By *you*, of course I mean the Tau Affinity."

Damian blinked. I suspected he was having a hard time processing all this. I knew I was. "Why Tau?"

"Without InterAlia each Affinity must become self-governing, and some particular Affinity will have to assume the role of *primus inter pares*—first among equals."

"You think Tau can do that?"

"Already you've done more for yourselves than any other Affinity. You've generated sturdy, complex systems of mutual support. You've created institutions like TauBourse. Your members have made statistically unprecedented gains in productivity and net wealth, and these benefits have been distributed more or less equitably across the membership. Tau is a template for what the Affinities can become—what they *must* become, if they're to survive the approaching crisis."

It was Amanda who spoke up: "But what exactly are we supposed to *do*?"

"Master your own Affinity, and you become a model for the others. I can help you do that. Beyond that, you'll have to make your own choices about how to proceed."

I went on sketching as Klein talked, almost as a nervous reflex. Amanda was no longer posing, and that made her a more interesting subject.

The first crude outline had emphasized the contrast of her thoughtful eyes and her veiled smile, like a dappling of cloud and sun. There was a playfulness in her that was both deeply attractive and deeply Tau: the playfulness that comes of liberation from convention and misunderstanding. We had never been exclusive lovers, and although we inevitably cycled back to each

other we had spent plenty of time in other beds. It was one of
the small miracles Tau made possible. Our tranche wasn't utopia, there had been episodes of jealousy among members, and I
wasn't a complete stranger to that emotion myself—but as Taus
we knew how to comfort and distract one another when we
needed comfort and distraction. I was only trivially (and, I told
myself, *temporarily*) disappointed that Amanda and Damian had
become lovers.

And I wasn't surprised. My relationship with Amanda was all
art and *eros*, but Damian engaged an aspect of herself she seldom showed me: her deep political commitment to Tau. For
Amanda, Tau wasn't only an identity, it was a cause. She had
fled her birth family with all its dour immigrant aspirations to
respectability, but her sense of duty was only repressed, not really rejected. She had reassigned it to her Affinity.

And Damian shared that intensity of purpose. She was drawn
to him as if to a flame, and it was undeniable that he burned
pretty brightly. He was one of the circle of motivated and scary-
smart Taus who had turned Tau into a financial powerhouse,
lifted Taus out of poverty, and bootstrapped Tau businesses
across the continent. He was a sodality rep now, which meant
he associated with like-minded Taus from every part of the
world. He didn't have a rank or title—we weren't like Hets, who
loved formal hierarchies—but he had become one of the handful of North American Taus who could speak on behalf of us
all. When Damian began to devote himself to working full-time
for Tau he had recruited assistants from his own and local
tranches, and Amanda had leapt at the opportunity to work
alongside him. And so had I, though my motives may not have
been quite so pure.

So my sketch of Amanda against the window became a sketch
of Amanda paying rapt attention to Damian and Meir Klein. I
had to take some of the light out of her face and deepen the shadows, which made it a better drawing but a less satisfying one.

She looked past the border of the page uneasily, almost as if the clouds had moved indoors. Suddenly I wanted the earlier version back, but there was no retrieving it. When I blurred the lines to soften them it was as if she began to disappear.

In the end Klein gave us a memory key containing a few megabytes of data, which Damian accepted with due gravity.

Then Klein took a call from his lawyers. Apparently InterAlia had accused him of a breach of confidentiality regarding some remarks he had made at a conference in Shanghai last year. Klein's legal team was coming up to the house for a conference, so we were promptly and formally dismissed. He would be in touch again soon, he said.

He said good-bye to us at the driveway. He shook my hand and Amanda's and beamed at us benevolently, but I was startled by how small he suddenly seemed, surrounded by servants but without real family or friends.

I gave my drawing to Amanda as we were driving away. She looked at it and smiled abstractedly and put it in her lap.

An ambulance arrived at the scene along with a couple of Traffic Services vehicles. We told our story, Rachel Ragland told hers. The EMS guys insisted on taking Damian in for observation, over his protests. As they slid him into the ambulance on a wholly unnecessary stretcher, Amanda offered to ride along to the hospital in Kelowna.

"No, stay with the car," Damian said. "Stay with Adam." Klein's data was safe in her purse.

So we shared an umbrella as we waited for the tow truck. Amanda had already put in a call to someone from a tranche in Kelowna who would meet us at the garage. She was leaning into my arm when she spotted my drawing: it had blown out of the car onto the verge of the road. She kneeled over it and tried to peel the sodden paper from the tarmac, uselessly. It tore in her hand. She looked at me guiltily. "It's ruined! I'm so sorry."

"It's all right," I said. "It wasn't very good."

CHAPTER 7

The week-long Pan-Affinity conference drew to a close, but Damian asked me and Amanda to stay in the city and help him organize the analysis of Klein's data. We divided the work into two parts: Amanda's job was to round up Taus who were qualified to make sense of the mathematics, while my job was to assemble a team who could look at ways to turn the Affinity test protocols into a hardware/software application that could be detached from InterAlia's corporate control.

For the last few days of the conference we worked out of our rooms at the Hilton. Damian had come back from the hospital with a diagnosis of a minor concussion and a Technicolor bruise on his forehead, but he insisted on keeping his remaining commitments: a couple of roundtable discussions plus a series of private meetings with representatives of the American sodality. One of his roundtables concerned the problem of forming and stabilizing tranches in countries where the Affinities were prohibited by law (including China and most nominally Islamic nations), but where clandestine testing was already being performed—a question that mirrored the larger one nobody wanted to ask: What would happen if InterAlia went belly-up?

On Sunday night the week-long event officially ended and the

delegates dispersed, as did the demonstrators who had been making a nuisance of themselves outside the convention center. The
picketers represented a variety of groups including evangelicals
and right-wingers, but the faction most heavily represented was
NOTA (None of the Above), a kind of social club for people who
had been rejected by the Affinities or disapproved of them on
principle. In the United States, NOTA had already launched a
series of class-action suits against InterAlia for what it was
calling "category discrimination."

After the convention the Hilton began to seem both eerily
empty and absurdly expensive. We relocated to a cheaper hotel
while we set up an office in a three-story commercial building
owned by a local Tau—rent-free, because parts of the building
were under renovation, which meant we learned to live with the
sound of hammering and the squeal of power saws.

We had been there less than a week when I got a call from
Rachel Ragland. Something had happened, she was worried, and
she wanted to talk to me about it.

Leaving a Tau-specific environment in which you've been im-
mersed for days is like coming up from a deep-water dive: best
done in stages, if you want to avoid the bends. But I didn't have
that luxury when I went to meet Rachel.

I had told Amanda about the call, and she had summoned
Damian, who rolled his eyes. "She wants money, of course. She'll
probably threaten to go to the police."

"I asked her about that. Pretty bluntly. She says she already
told the police I was driving and that she hadn't been hurt, and
that was the end of it. Or would have been. Except yesterday
two guys showed up at her door."

"What do you mean—cops?"

"They said they were insurance investigators. They wanted
to hear about the accident. She says she stuck to her story."

"But?"

"But the ID they showed her looked dodgy, and she thinks there was something off about them."

"Something *off*?"

"I think she meant they seemed threatening. They scared her. And since she lied to them on my behalf, she feels like I owe her an explanation."

"Which is the one thing you can't give her."

"I agreed to meet her for lunch."

Amanda said, "You couldn't just tell her to fuck off? Because Damian's right, it's probably some kind of shakedown. She'll ask for money, bet on it."

"I didn't tell her to fuck off." For some reason I thought of Rachel's daughter Suze, owl-eyed and rain-drenched in the back-seat of her car. "But if she asks for money, I will."

So I drove to the restaurant Rachel had suggested, a chain steakhouse in a Burnaby strip mall, and a bored waiter steered me to her table. Which was good, because I might not have rec-ognized her. Her hair, which had looked black in the rain, was actually a deep coppery red. It framed her round face, brown eyes, small nose, and a pursed mouth that showed her upper front teeth when she smiled. "Adam Fisk," she said.

"Just Adam."

"And I'm Rachel."

"I remember. Where's Suze?"

"In school, but thank you for asking. I hope I didn't drag you away from anything important?"

I had been more or less confined to a room with six other Taus—IT types and electronics engineers—for days now. But I couldn't complain. "Just work," I said.

"Mm. Well, I work three days a week at the food bank on Hastings Street. But today's not one of those days."

So we stared at our menus and discussed the comparative vir-tues of the salad plate and the club sandwich and wondered what else we ought to say. After we ordered I said, "You had some people come visit you?"

"Yeah. Like I said, two guys with IDs I didn't trust. Kind of pretending to be nice—at least at first—but you could tell they were only pretending."

"What did they look like?"

She shrugged. "Hard to describe. White guys in suits. Short hair. Maybe Russian or Eastern European–looking, if that means anything. Something about the cheekbones. But no accent, so I don't know. One was a little chunky, the other was taller and looked like he worked out."

"And they asked about your accident?"

"They seemed to know the details already, which is why I thought they were legitimate. I told them about the transmission. Actually the car's still in the garage. Until I can bail it out. Expensive repairs." I wondered if this was the point at which she would ask for money. "I got suspicious when they kept asking about what they called 'the other vehicle.' *Your car.*"

"What about it?"

"Well, they asked who was driving. Wanted a description."

"And you told them—?"

"I said I there were three people in the car, two guys and a woman, and the younger guy was driving. Same as I told the cops. But these guys kept asking the same questions over and over. Was I hurt? No. Was I sure? Yes. Was I frightened? No. And so on. Like they thought I was being uncooperative. Which admittedly I kind of was. They weren't very good at hiding their pissed-offness." The waiter put down glasses of ice water and Rachel took a long gulp. "So I asked them to leave."

"Which they did?"

"More or less peacefully. They didn't make any threats. But I still felt threatened. So I called you." Her expression hardened. "Since I stuck to the story about you driving, I feel like you owe me something."

"Owe you what exactly?" I refrained from saying, *How much?*

"Well, for starters, an explanation! Who *were* those guys? What did they want? Am I in some kind of danger? I mean, I've got Suze to worry about. For that matter, who are *you?*"

"To be honest, I don't know how much of that I can answer. I have no idea who those guys were."

"Okay. I guess I believe that. But you don't seem real *surprised* by any of this."

And suddenly I wasn't sure what to say. I was coming out of a long Tau immersion. Had she been a Tau, I would have just explained. But she wasn't. I could neither trust her nor be sure she would understand anything I told her. Still, it was true she had done me a favor, and not just me; she had helped protect Damian, and by implication our entire Affinity. I said, "I'm a Tau—"

She rolled her eyes. "And I'm a Pisces. So what?"

"All the people in the car were Taus."

"You're saying this is some kind of Affinity thing? I knew the convention was in town, but—"

"My friend is involved in a legal wrangle with a major corporation. Their lawyers probably have investigators in the field looking for something they can use as leverage. Now, I'm not saying that's who came to your house. I honestly *don't know* who came to your house."

"But it's a possibility?"

"It's a possibility. Did they ask anything that struck you as particularly odd?"

"They asked if I knew where you were coming from, the day of the accident."

We had been coming from Meir Klein's country house. InterAlia knew where Klein lived. Maybe someone had connected the dots.

———

We talked through lunch. Rachel asked a few questions about the Affinities, I asked a few questions about Rachel. She was fairly voluble now that she had relaxed, and I liked the way she stroked the air with her right hand as she talked, index finger and middle finger pressed together as if she were holding an invisible cigarette. The waiter cleared our dessert dishes. We ordered coffee. Another twenty minutes and we were still talking. And enjoying it.

So I went home with her. Though I knew it was probably a bad idea.

Affinity members tend to be endogamous: they're more likely to form sexual relationships within their Affinity than outside of it. When it comes to long-term commitments, that's true of *all* the Affinities. But some Affinities—Delts and Kafs, most notoriously—have a penchant for short-term liaisons outside the group. Taus fall somewhere in the middle of that range. Trevor Holst, for instance, hadn't lived with anyone but another Tau since he joined our tranche, but he treated the annual convention as an all-you-can-eat sexual buffet, pun not entirely unintended. Wherever some Kaf was organizing a hotel-room orgy, there you would find Trev.

I told myself I wasn't like that. Since I joined my tranche my single long-term partner had been Amanda, and all my dalliances had been Taus. If for no other reason than that it made life easier. No mixed signals, fewer hurt feelings.

But Rachel had attracted my attention, suddenly and deeply and in a way I didn't entirely understand. And by the time we left the restaurant, both of us knew it. She had come by bus, and I asked her if she wanted a ride home. She said she did.

I wasn't sure what was beginning, only that I was willing to let it begin.

———

"So you have somebody?" she asked. "Back in Tau-land?"

She had invited me into her basement apartment in New Westminster. Rachel was a single mother on a shoestring income and had furnished the place accordingly. Cotton throw rugs over scuffed linoleum, a thrift-shop sofa, three overflowing laundry baskets occupying the space between a video panel and a bookcase stocked with secondhand paperback bestsellers. The tablet computer on the coffee table was a couple of years out of date and there was a burn mark on the plastic frame.

She caught me looking. "Okay, it's a mess."

"No, it's fine." I liked the personal touches she had added—the paisley silk scarf draped over a lampshade, a magazine photo of the Great Barrier Reef tacked to the wall. There was a small kitchen, a bedroom for Suze, Rachel's bedroom.

"So answer the question. Are you seeing anybody?"

"Yes. Or—it's complicated. Sort of yes."

"Uh-huh."

"You want me to explain that?"

"Actually, no. But thank you for offering. My last steady guy was Suze's dad. He took a job as a rigger on an Alberta oil pipeline about the time I got pregnant. He was kind of absentminded, though. Forgot to leave a forwarding address. How long have you been a Tau?"

"Seven years."

"Doesn't it get boring, hanging around with people who're just like you?"

"That's not how it works. Have you been tested?"

She laughed. "Fuck no!"

"Why not?"

"I doubt there's a group that would have me."

"Why do you say that?"

She shrugged off the question and scooted closer. "So what are you here for, Adam Fisk?"

"I guess I want to get to know you."

"Oh? I thought maybe you wanted to fuck me."

My mouth went dry. "Well . . . that, too."

"Then maybe you should *do* it."

She leaned in to kiss me. It wasn't a tentative kiss. I liked the way she tasted. I moved to put my arms around her, but she pushed me away. She unbuckled my belt, unzipped me, knelt down.

I was seconds away from an orgasm when she stood up, took my hand, led me to her bedroom, pushed me onto the bed. She tugged off her blouse and stepped out of her jeans. Nothing under them but a pair of cotton dollar-store briefs, which I yanked down. She straddled me, and we locked into an urgent rhythm, Rachel moving to some music I couldn't hear, eyes wide open— her eyes were my entire field of vision, her hair a curtain that sealed us from the world. When it was impossible to do anything else, we came hastily and greedily and simultaneously.

After we caught our breath she said, "How long has it been?"

"What do you mean?"

"Since you did it with somebody who isn't a Tau."

"Honestly? A few years."

"Who was it? I mean the last one who wasn't in your Affinity." Jenny Symanski. "Just a girl I knew."

"Like me." She kissed me again. "Now I'm a girl you know."

She got up, left the room, came back with a joint and a lighter. I liked the way she moved, unselfconsciously naked, fluid, her body more wave than particle. The bed creaked when she climbed back in. We shared the joint: some generic weed Amanda would have turned up her nose at, but it did the trick. We settled into a measured second round.

The next thing I noticed was the fading light from the bedroom window. Because this was a basement apartment the window was high in the wall but low to the street. Sunset turned the curtains scarlet. We listened to the sound of footsteps passing on the sidewalk outside. Strangers coming home from work. Shadows of unfamiliar lives. The murmur of voices. "Might rain tonight," Rachel said sleepily.

"I wish I could stay, but—"

"I know. It's okay. I have to go get Suze." Suze was at her grandmother's, where she often went after school.

"Need a drive?"

"Easier to bus it, but thank you for asking." She cleared her throat. "So . . . is this just a happy afternoon, or can I call you?"

She meant it casually but I heard a hitch of tension in her voice.

"Of course you can call me. More likely I'll call you first."

"That's a nice thing to say. Are all Taus as nice as you?"

"In their way. Uh, maybe not *quite* as nice."

I used the bathroom before I left. There was a row of brown prescription bottles on the shelf over the toilet. I resisted the temptation to read the labels, and I congratulated myself for respecting her privacy. Or maybe I just didn't want to know what was wrong with her.

I stopped by the building where we worked to pick up some papers and to see if there was anyone I could recruit for dinner company. I ran into Amanda, who was hurrying down the hallway. She noticed me, stopped, did a double take, and drew an instant conclusion about where I'd been and what I'd done. I couldn't help it: I blushed.

"Well," she said. *"Well."*

"I, uh—"

"Uh *yeah*. So I guess she didn't ask for money, huh? Or *did* she?"

"That's not fair. And no, she didn't. Where are you rushing off to?"

"Meeting. With Damian. You're invited."

We joined him in one of the building's newly renovated

conference rooms, nothing inside but a trestle table, a dozen folding chairs, and a faint haze of plaster dust. Just the three of us. If Damian had any thoughts about what might have happened between Rachel and me, he didn't bother to share them. He had bigger issues.

Meir Klein was dead.

Klein had died in his big house in the Okanagan Valley. "Staff found him," Damian said, "when he didn't get up this morning."

"His cancer," Amanda whispered.

"Actually, no. According the police, he died of a ligature injury."

In other words he had been strangled. Or had strangled himself: maybe an autoerotic strangulation gone wrong, unlikely as that sounded given Klein's fragile physical condition. The evidence was ambiguous, the coroner was performing an autopsy, but until the report was finalized, the police were betting on foul play.

Amanda knocked on the door of my hotel room a few minutes after midnight, and it didn't take Tau telepathy to figure out what she wanted. She pressed herself hard against me. "Now fuck me," she whispered, "like you fucked your tether."

I didn't like the word "tether." It was what some Taus called the lovers they took outside of the Affinity. It was a term of contempt, like *shiksa* or *shegetz*. As in, *Don't let that tether of yours drag you down.* But this was Amanda. It was not in my power to refuse her. Which is to say, I didn't want to refuse her. And she knew it. "Let me shower first," I said.

"No," she said. "*Now.* While the smell of her is still on you."

CHAPTER 8

Amanda and I met Damian at the office the next morning, an hour before the research teams arrived, early enough that the light of dawn through the east-facing windows made the motes of plaster dust in the air sparkle like diamonds. Amanda slumped in the nearest chair, her eyes still bruised with sleep. Damian stood at the head of the table, looking grim. "I've been talking to some contacts in the Vancouver Police Force," he said. "The RCMP is investigating Klein's death, not the cops, but I managed to learn a few things. Almost certainly homicide. A couple of hard drives are missing from Klein's office. So we can assume that whoever killed him knew he was in possession of valuable data."

"InterAlia's data," Amanda said.

"You're picturing some goon ransacking the place and murdering Klein on orders from corporate headquarters. And maybe that's a reasonable assumption, but unless someone was unforgivably clumsy there won't be any evidence linking the murder to InterAlia. What we have to ask ourselves is, if InterAlia *is* behind this, what's their next move? Especially if the drives they stole contain anything that would connect Klein to *us*."

I said, "Somebody wants to keep Klein's data from going

public, they have money to spend on hired thieves, and they're apparently willing to kill for what they want. If they suspect Klein passed us the data, we're the next logical target."

"Maybe. But only as long they figure they have something to gain by intimidating us."

"So if they're going to act," Amanda said, "they have to act soon."

"Right. So we need to be able to protect ourselves. We have two teams here, twenty people in the building during daylight hours if you include the three of us, and any or all of us could be targeted. How do we afford protection to twenty people, either here or when they're moving freely around the city?"

"Warn them, obviously," I said. "House them in one place, even the ones who live here in the city. And we need help. People who know how to do real-world security."

Damian nodded. "I'll get on T-Net this morning and set it up."

T-Net was the hidden webspace where sodality reps interacted with each other. A tech guy had once tried to tell me how it worked. All I remembered was that the explanation involved words like "serial/parallel encryption" and "onion routing." Basically, it was a space where sodality-level Taus could exchange information with minimal risk of surveillance. Through T-net, Damian could put out the word that he needed volunteers with security and military experience who lived in the area or could get to Vancouver on short notice.

"Okay," I said. "But are we the only ones at risk?"

"What do you mean?"

Amanda said, "He's thinking of the guys who questioned his new tether, Rachel Ragland."

"I doubt she's in any danger," Damian said. "They've talked to her already, they didn't learn anything."

"Depends on whether they know I've been seeing her."

"Well, that's easily fixed," Amanda said. "Stop seeing her."

Damian said, "The guys who came to see her, did she describe them?"

"Only vaguely."

"Do you think you could get a better description from her?"

"I don't know. I could try. Why? Do you think they're the same people who went after Klein?"

"Could be. It would help if we could give our security guys some faces to look out for."

"You mean, like a sketch?"

"Yeah," Damian said. "Like a sketch."

I said I would get on it.

The first of our new security team showed up that afternoon, a local guy named Gordo MacDonald. Gordo was ex-military, Princess Patricia's Canadian Light Infantry, chest like a rain barrel, abs so defined you could count them through his t-shirt. Shaved head and one glittering gold earring. I would have flinched when we shook hands, but *the look* passed between us. The Tau look: a wry curvature of the mouth, something indefinable about the eyes, but it was as if all the threat went out of his face. He gave me a sheepish grin, and I gave him one back. "Hey, bro," he said.

I wasn't a *hey bro* kind of guy, but I said, "Hey."

Gordo told Damian he wanted to start by walking through the building, get to know the layout, "make sure the bad guys don't have a place to hide."

Amanda touched my arm after Damian and Gordo left the room. "I wanted to say, I wasn't just being bitchy this morning. About Rachel Ragland, I mean. It's none of my business whether you keep on seeing her. It's just, I can't help thinking, a single mom on social assistance, she's bound to need more than you can give her. A couple of months of great sex and then you're gone—is that good for her? Does she need that?"

"I told her what the situation is."

"You told her, but did she hear you? You've been living in Tauland. It's different out there. People lie. Not just to each other but to themselves. People get hurt."

"I know that. And I don't intend to hurt her."

"It may not matter what you *intend*. You're treating her like a Tau, and she's not."

And that was true. But I needed to see her at least once more. If only to make a forensic sketch.

So when Rachel suggested we get together Saturday afternoon, I said sure. She had a whole day planned, she said. We could drive to Stanley Park with Suze. Walk the seawall. Drop off Suze at her grandmother's, then have the evening to ourselves. Go out for dinner and drinks, maybe. If I was free?

I said I was free.

When I pulled up to the low-rise building in New Westminster, Rachel came out of the lobby with a big backpack over her shoulder and Suze clinging to her left hand. Rachel was wearing shorts and a yellow blouse and a Canucks cap to keep the sun out of her eyes. Suze was decked out in a summer dress and pink plastic Barbie sunglasses.

"Remember me?" I said to Suze when she climbed in the backseat.

"No!"

"From the forest," Rachel prompted her. "When our car broke down."

I told her my name was Adam. Suze gave me a solemn look, then said she was pleased to meet me.

The car's sound system had been playing the news from a US netcast, but the announcer's voice was so solemn and the news so ominous (the India-Pakistan conflict had heated up again) that I turned it off as soon as we pulled into traffic. Suze immediately began to sing the chorus (and only the chorus) of a song from an old kids' movie: "*Chiddy* chiddy *bang* bang I-love-*you!* *Chiddy* chiddy *bang* bang I-love-*you!*"

"It's 'chitty,'" Rachel told her. "Not 'chiddy.'"

"CHIDDY chiddy BANG bang! I LOVE YOU!"

"Have it your own way. A little quieter, though, okay?"

Suze grudgingly moderated her chiddies. An hour later we were at the seawall, watching cargo ships glide like iron ballerinas across the water of English Bay. The water was too cold for swimming, but Suze seemed more interested in digging in the sand and chasing gulls. Rachel and I settled into a patch of packed sand in the shade of a sea-bleached drift log. She opened her backpack and took out a selection of plastic-wrapped Wonder Bread sandwiches and a thermos of lemonade. I reached into my own pack and produced a sketchbook and a pencil. She said, "What's that? You draw?"

"Now and then."

"Is that what you do for a living?"

"No. I thought about it once, but you go where life takes you. I'm more of a management consultant these days."

She gave one of her quick, full-throated laughs. "That sounds like a money-for-bullshit job. No offense."

"None taken. Those two men who visited you, you think you could describe them to me?"

"What, so you can draw them?"

I nodded.

"Are they so dangerous you need to know what they look like? No, don't answer that. Are you, like, a police sketch artist or something?"

"To be honest, I've never tried to draw a face from a description. I'd like to try. But we don't have to if you don't want to."

"Oh, I think we *do* have to. Since you brought your pencil and paper and all. Afterward, maybe you can draw a picture of me?"

"I'd like to. Once we get this out of the way."

She shrugged. "What do I do?"

"Start by picking one of the two men. Don't think about what he looked like, just think about something he did. Like, smile or not smile. Blink. Pick his teeth."

She squinted her eyes. "The taller guy. His head . . ."

"What about it?"

"He kept cocking it to the left, like a dog hearing a whistle. Head shaped like a rectangle. Like a loaf of bread with eyes and a mouth."

I made some tentative lines, more to encourage her than to accomplish anything. "Hair?"

"Bald as a bottle cap. I don't think he *shaved* it bald, I think it was just *bald* bald. Narrow eyes, close together. His mouth, when he tried to smile, you could see his clenched teeth. White teeth. He's got a good dental-care plan, whoever he is."

"What do you mean, when he tried to smile?"

"He smiled like he was faking it. He had one of those mouths that opens like a puppet's jaw, like on a real crude hinge. Wide. Kind of bracketed, the lines at the side of it, not a curvy smile, kind of inorganic, like a robot smile."

It turned out I wasn't especially good at translating any of this to paper, but before too long I had scribbled and erased my way to something Rachel called, "Cartoony, but I guess I'd recognize him from that. Sure."

The second guy—shorter, rounder, pig-eyed—took less time. I had just finished when Suze came bounding up, demanding to see what I'd done. I showed her. Her eyes went wide. "Who are *they?*"

"Nobody in particular," I said.

"Draw me!"

"I think your mother wants to go first."

"Oh, no," Rachel said. "Go ahead and make a picture of her. I need to stretch my legs."

She went off to find a public washroom and smoke a joint. Drawing Suze was fun, though she kept jumping up to see how the picture was coming along. It was pretty good for a rough sketch, I thought. I captured her sandy knees poking out from the hem of her dress, her cautious eyes and wary smile. When it was done I gave it to her. She inspected it critically. "Can I color it?"

"If you like. It's all yours."

She nodded, tucked the drawing into her mother's backpack, and rose to return to the holes she had been making in the beach (because they filled up with seawater, she said, and there were tiny shells in them, along with cigarette butts and bits of charcoal from the nearby barbecue pit). Then she seemed to remember something. She turned back and said, "Thank you for making a picture of me."

"You're very welcome."

When Rachel came back she posed on the drift log, riding it sidesaddle. I produced a quick sketch but a good one; good enough that I was almost reluctant to hand it over to her. She said, "Well, this is bullshit, Adam. I mean, it's great. But you prettied me up."

What I had done was pay attention to the way doubt and mischief took turns with the curve of her lips. "Or maybe you're just pretty."

"More bullshit." But she grinned. "Time flies. We should collect Suze and take her to my mom's. She'll be wanting dinner soon."

A few hours in the parking lot had left the car sun-warmed and smelling of sand and ozone. Suze insisted on holding the picture I had drawn of her, and she sang *chiddy chiddy bang bang* to the hum of the wheels on corduroy blacktop as we crossed the Lions Gate Bridge.

———

Rachel's mother struck me as a wearier, more cynical version of Rachel. She had suffered a minor stroke a couple of years back and lived in a public housing complex with two Corgis and a budgerigar named Saint Francis. She didn't say much—the stroke had left her slightly aphasic—but she surveyed me with unmistakable suspicion, and I did my best to appear small and harmless. "TV dinners?" Suze asked. Her grandmother nodded. "Yay," Suze said.

Rachel kissed her mom and promised to pick up Suze by noon tomorrow. Then we were on our own. Rachel wanted to have dinner at a New West bar she liked. It was a working-class bar that smelled of stale hops and was dim as a dungeon, but the tables were reasonably clean and the staff called Rachel by name. We ordered steaks from the grill, and I asked for a beer. "Usual?" the waitress asked Rachel, and she nodded. "Usual" turned out to be a rum-and-Coke. She went through a couple of them while we waited for the food, then ordered another. She eyed the beer I was nursing and said, "You drink like you're afraid of it."

"I'm not much of a drinker."

"Yeah, I heard that. About Taus. Big potheads, but not heavy drinkers."

Sociologists had been taking long, interested looks at the Affinities for years now. The studies were generally accurate, but the public's misunderstanding of them had generated all kinds of stereotypes. "That's true," I said. "Statistically. But in the real world all it means is that the numbers are a little skewed. We have our share of drinkers. A couple of months ago, in my tranche, we helped a guy get into rehab for his alcohol habit."

"Ah, *rehab*. Where rich people go, because prison's so darned uncomfortable."

The bigger Affinities ran their own rehab and therapy services. It had nothing to do with being rich, but it had a lot to do with being treated by people whose Affinity you shared. Nobody can help a Tau like another Tau. "It's not always about the money. What else do you know about us?"

"There's a lot of LGBT people, I've heard."

"A few percentage points over the general population."

"And you all sleep together."

"Not true."

"Maybe not as much as Eyns or Delts. I know a woman who joined the Delts. More like her *vagina* joined the Delts. We used to be pretty friendly, but she started to ignore me once she found a bunch of fuck friends to play with."

The steaks arrived from the kitchen, and they were big and unpretentious and reasonably tender. Rachel continued drinking at a steady pace. I did not, which seemed to make her unhappy. I was a bush league drinker; I didn't like being drunk, I didn't drink gracefully. So I ordered serial rounds of chips and salsa to keep the waitress happy while some local band began to set up on the tiny stage across the room. The bass player struck an open E that rattled the cutlery.

"You're going back to Toronto in a few weeks," Rachel said.

I had told her that the first time we had lunch. "Right."

"So I guess that means we're just, we're . . . not anything, really. The famous two slips. I mean ships. I keep thinking, I'll never know him better than I do right now."

"It is what it is," I said. "I like you, Rachel. I don't want to mislead you."

"You like me all right, but I'm not a Tau."

"I didn't say that."

The heat or the alcohol was making her sweat. She ran the back of her hand over her forehead. "You don't have to. They used to say, 'All the good ones are gay.' Or 'All the good ones are married.' Well, sometimes the good ones just have an Affinity to go home to."

"It's nice you think I'm one of the good ones."

"Maybe I *shouldn't.*"

The band launched into a full-tilt cover of some old Tom Petty tune, and suddenly Rachel and I were shouting to each other as if we were separated by an abyss. I suggested it was time to start for home.

"Hey," she said, "no! We're just getting started! It's fucking early! Or maybe that's what you had in mind—some *early fucking.*"

"Come on, Rachel."

"I want to hear the music! Then we'll go. You can keep it in your pants until then."

She began to sing along, loudly and inexactly, to "I Won't Back Down." I leaned back in my chair and surveyed the room. A guy at the bar, a tall dude with long pale hair and narrow, angry eyes, had been giving Rachel covert glances for the last hour, and now he was just staring.

Rachel looked where I was looking. She leaned toward me and yelled, "That's just Carlos!"

"Carlos?"

"Old friend of mine! We had a thing for a while! He gets protective!"

Great, I thought. Carlos. Then I thought: What if the guy staring at us hadn't been Carlos? What if it had been one of the insurance adjustors from the drawings? It was possible I was endangering her simply by being with her. "Okay, Rachel. Let's leave Carlos to his business and go home."

She gave me a contemptuous, drunken smile. "Are you afraid of him?"

"Yeah. I'm terrified." I took out my wallet and put money on the table. "You coming?"

She pouted but stood up, gripping the back of her chair to steady herself. She let me take her arm.

We passed Carlos on our way to the door. I avoided eye contact, but Rachel gave him a look that was half leer, half sneer.

Carlos responded by standing up and blocking my way. He put his face in my face but he shouted to Rachel over the music hammering from the stage: "YOU ALL RIGHT THERE, RACHE?"

Rachel nodded. When it became obvious he hadn't seen the nod, she said, "YEAH! I'M FINE! LEAVE HIM ALONE, CARLOS!"

"SURE ABOUT THAT?"

He was a messy talker. Some of his spittle missed me, some didn't.

"YES! DON'T BE AN ASSHOLE!"

Carlos winced. Then he mouthed something I couldn't hear. He stepped out of our way, but his nail-gun stare followed us all the way to the door.

In the car, windows open, cool night air flowing in, Rachel grew moody and quiet. She didn't say anything until we reached the block where she lived, when she asked in a small voice, "I fucked up there, didn't I?"

"Not sure what you mean by that."

"Our big evening together. Rachel and Adam. What fun, huh?"

"Maybe just not my idea of a good time."

"I should have known. Taus are potheads, not drinkers. Taus are a little bit prissy, too. So they say on the Internet. I mean— oh, fuck! Now it sounds like I'm calling you names. I'm sorry!" She leaked a tear. "I just wanted us to have fun."

I helped her to the door of the low-rise building, helped her get the key into the lock. Helped her down the stairs, though she pulled away and insisted on unlocking the door of the basement apartment herself. The night had gotten chilly, but the air inside was overheated and stale. As soon as I had closed the door she leaned into me, pressed herself against my body, grabbed my hips. The smell of Bacardi and sour sweat swarmed off of her.

"Bet I know what you want," she said.

Bet you don't, I thought.

I excused myself for the purpose of using the bathroom. The parade line of brown plastic pill bottles caught my attention again. This time I was less scrupulous about inspecting them. Lithium, Depakine, Risperdol, Seroquel. Some of the prescriptions were old and expired, some were fresh.

She was slumped on the sofa when I came out. I said, "Rachel . . ."

"You're leaving, aren't you?"

"I'm sorry," I said. "But yeah, I think that's best."

"Because I fucked up."

"No. Listen—"

"Just go."

"Rachel—"

"Do I embarrass you? Well, you embarrass me! Smug candyass Tau boy. Get out! I'm tired of you anyway. You know what's better than your dick? My *finger*! My *little* finger! GO!"

Amanda was waiting in my hotel room when I got back (we shared keys). She said she wanted to see the sketches I had made. I gave them to her. She examined them approvingly. Then she asked me what happened with Rachel. And I tried to explain.

"She was showing you her world," Amanda said. "Her apartment, her daughter, the ratty bar where she spends her weekends. Even the pill bottles she leaves out where people can see them. She probably wanted to find out whether all that would offend you or whether it would turn you on."

"It didn't offend me. I was just worried the wrong people would see us . . . Why would it turn me on?"

"Tough single mom in a working-class bar where she probably screws half the clientele? Catnip for a natural bottom like you."

"What?"

"Look at you, you're so tense you're practically brittle." She reached into her purse and fished out her pipe and the tiny, ornate wooden box in which she kept her weed. "We'll share a little of this, then you can take your clothes off and I can fuck you silly."

The smoke went directly to my head. I felt an unsatisfied need to explain, but the words were elusive. "It was," I said, "I mean, I shouldn't have let her think—"

"Oh, stop. You got the sketches, right?"

"Sure, but—"

"That's what's important. The rest of it doesn't matter."

CHAPTER 9

My research team hit a snag that week. The cranial sensors used in Affinity testing were a proprietary design, and their specifications had not been among the data Meir Klein had provided. We determined that the closest equivalent was a neural scanning sensor manufactured by a company in Guangzhou called AllMedTest. These were dime-sized devices, incredibly sophisticated, and an array of six or seven would be enough to generate the kind of imaging the test required. But they were expensive, and buying them in quantity would be a major investment.

When I approached Damian about it, he said not to worry: "We have T-Bourse money to invest, and I can't think of a better use for it."

"Okay, but the sensors are fairly delicate, which we have to factor into the design. And my tech guys have to know exactly how much processing power they need to build into a portable device. They're complaining that the flow of information from the theoretical side has slowed way down."

"They're right," Damian said. "The thing is, we've come across some anomalies in Klein's data."

"Anomalies?"

"Some unsettling implications."

"Such as?"

He looked unhappy. "We'll talk about it on the weekend. You, me, Amanda, the two team leaders, plus a security detail. I rented us a place on Pender Island. We'll be out of harm's way and we'll have a couple of days to think it through. Okay?"

It sounded like trouble, and I wanted to know more. But Damian wasn't ready to talk.

The ferry from Tsawwassen to Pender Island chugged through a rainstorm that raised whitecaps on Georgia Strait and turned what should have been a postcard view into a gray obscurity. Damian was too moody to make conversation, and Amanda was using the downtime to read through a report from her team leader. I crossed the promenade deck of the ferry and found an empty seat by a rain-slicked window, took out my phone, and returned a call that had come in that morning. The call was from my brother's home, but it was Jenny Symanski who picked up.

I had talked to Jenny only sporadically since her marriage to Aaron six years ago, not because of any lingering awkwardness between us but because my brother had become the wall over which any communication had to pass. When I spoke to Jenny it was usually at Christmas or Easter, and it was Aaron who handed her the phone and Aaron who took it back when the conversation was finished. If Jenny carried a phone of her own, neither she nor Aaron had given me the number. "Jenny," I said. "Is this a bad time?"

"No," she said. "No, it's fine."

"Is Aaron around?"

"He's in DC for the day. A congressional briefing or something."

The truth was that talking to my family (my tether family) had become a duty, not a pleasure. Lately I had heard more from the house in Schuyler, since my father had entered into negotiations to sell his faltering hardware-store businesses to a national chain. "We'll be able to retire very comfortably," Mama Laura had told me, "though I dread what idleness will do to your father." (Her dread wasn't entirely hyperbolic: even a long holiday weekend could drive my father into a state of sullen, resentful boredom.)

My brother Aaron was working as an assistant to Mike Menkov, the Republican congressman from the Onenia district, and it seemed like he was making a career of it. He had learned his way around the federal labyrinth and had even drafted a couple of Menkov's speeches. I knew this because Aaron made a point of mentioning it whenever we talked, and anything he neglected to tell me would be relayed from Schuyler by way of my father. And I always congratulated Aaron when he announced his latest triumph . . . even though Menkov was a pliant tool of the corporate lobbies and would endorse any noxious idea that seemed likely to boost him up the political ladder. Lately, Aaron himself had been talking about running for office.

But Aaron wasn't home today, and Jenny had sounded a little uncomfortable telling me so. "Look," I said, "I can get back to you if this is a bad time. Tell Aaron I returned his call, okay?"

"No, wait. Geddy's here! That's why I called earlier. He wants to talk to you. Is that okay?"

"Of course it's okay. What's Geddy doing in Alexandria?"

"Well, it's a long story. You know he was playing with a band, right?"

Mama Laura had kept me posted on Geddy's music career. Some natural talent, plus a little formal instruction and Geddy's capacity for obsessive repetition, had made him a better-than-average reedman. A little over a year ago Geddy had joined a band called The Humbuckers, currently making a minor reputation for itself across the northeastern states. It was a precarious living—barely a living at all—but since the family had long ago concluded that Geddy was probably unemployable, it seemed like a good thing.

But life on the road had not agreed with Geddy. He had left The Humbuckers after a gig in Syracuse and bought a bus ticket to Alexandria. Two days ago he had shown up on Aaron's doorstep with an unhappy expression and a duffel bag full of dirty laundry. Shockingly, he had pawned his Mauriat tenor sax, an instrument he had scrimped to buy and which he had insisted on holding in every recent photograph of him I had seen. Asked why he left the band and sold his sax, Geddy would only say, "It didn't make me happy anymore."

Jenny texted me this information later; here on the Pender Island ferry, all I knew was that Geddy had expressed a completely uncharacteristic desire to talk on the phone. So I waited while Jenny gave him the handset. "Hello?" he said. It was Geddy in two syllables. Timid but somehow courageous, as if he had forced out the word on a cloud of pure bravado.

"Good to hear your voice," I said.

"Where are you? It sounds loud."

"I'm on a ferry in Georgia Strait. That's the engines you hear."

"You're on a boat?"

"Yeah, a boat."

"Do you still live in Toronto?"

"I do, but I'll be out west for a few weeks more."

"Okay." He was silent a few moments more, and I had learned to respect Geddy's silences. Eventually he said, "I wish I could visit you."

"That's not possible right now, but maybe in a few months. What are you doing at Aaron and Jenny's place?"

"They agreed to let me stay a while. I don't really have anywhere to go. I didn't want to go back to Schuyler."

He didn't want to go back to Schuyler because my father would have humiliated him for his failure. Neither of us needed to say this aloud. "Are you okay there?"

"Aaron says I can't stay forever." Now he just sounded tired. "I don't know what to do, Adam."

"The band didn't work out, huh?"

"There was a girl. I really liked her. She needed money. So I had to sell my saxophone. She took the money, but . . ."

"I understand."

"People are pretty fucking mean sometimes."

His brief career in the music business had made Geddy more casual about what he would once have called "swear words." Worse than that was the bitterness in his voice. It was entirely self-directed. Geddy would never despise the woman who had taken his money. Instead, he would despise himself for his own gullibility. And learn nothing from the experience. I suspected Geddy would go on trading luck for love for as long as it took him to give up on love. "If you need a little money to get you through, Geddy, no problem. I can send it care of Aaron and Jenny."

"No," he said quickly. "Thanks, Adam. No, I just wanted to hear your voice. It was always . . ." I imagined him blushing. "You were always pretty good to me."

Which for some reason made me feel even worse. "Okay, but listen. We'll get together, I promise. Soon as I clear up some business out here. How's that sound?"

"Sounds good."

"In the meantime, let Aaron and Jenny pamper you for a while."

"I can't really do that. I mean, they'll let me stay for a few weeks. But I don't think Aaron is really happy having me here. It's kind of . . ." He lowered his voice. "I don't like this house. It's big and it's pretty, but I would hate to live here." He added, a barely audible whisper, *"Jenny has a black eye."*

"A what? What did you say? A black eye?"

"Yes."

"What, like somebody punched her?"

A maddening pause. "I can't talk about it."

"Geddy, what do you mean?"

"Here she is. Here she is!"

"Geddy?"

Jenny came on. "We should keep this short. Aaron will be home any minute."

"Are you all right?"

"What? Yes, of course I am. Why? What did Geddy say?"

"Nothing." Or too much. "But he seems a little forlorn."

"Look . . . I'll text you about it, okay?"

"Of course."

"Great. Well. Thank you for calling back, Adam. That was nice. I know you're busy."

"Never too busy to talk to my sister-in-law."

"Great," she said. "Good-bye."

Damian had rented what the owner (a local Tau) called a "chalet" on a rural lot near the ocean on Pender Island. In reality it was a four-bedroom log-walled home with double-glazed windows and a kitchen big enough to feed and accommodate a dozen people.

We were slightly less than a dozen: me, Amanda, Damian, a tech guy from each of our two research teams, plus Gordo Mac-Donald and four of his security people. Gordo immediately scoped out the house and its surrounding territory and posted his subordinates where they could cover all approaches. "We'll be inconspicuous," he said. "We'll feed ourselves and sleep in shifts. You probably won't notice us. But if you do need us, all you have to do is holler."

Which was reassuring, though it was unlikely that anyone had followed us here. The house felt safe. Even better, with the rain falling and the daylight beginning to fade and a fire crackling in the hearth, it felt cozy.

The feeling lasted until Damian told us what he had deduced
from Meir Klein's data.

It was obvious we hadn't come here for a standard meeting, but
Damian wanted to start with a progress report, so that's what
we gave him. My team leader and I summarized the problems
we'd run into trying to design a portable Affinity-testing system. With suitable sensors, virtually any handheld digital device could record the results and run the algorithms. But another
part of the traditional Affinity screening was a DNA test. Adding a portable nanopore sequencer to the kit would triple the
cost to the end user and make the process needlessly complex,
so we were looking at workarounds: a simpler filter that would
detect only the relevant bases, or a two-part qualification process that would include a blood sample submitted to a registered
lab. Amanda's team leader said it might be possible to eliminate
the DNA test altogether, since it mainly functioned as a kind of
pre-screening, picking up a few gene sequences that were incom-
patible with any Affinity. Adding another layer of neurotesting
might achieve the same effect.

All well and good, and we chewed it over for an hour or so,
but this wasn't the main event. That began when Damian stood
up, clearing his throat and looking uncharacteristically awkward. "Okay," he said. "Thank you, and I'm really pleased with
the progress we're making. But we all know this is happening
in a larger context. The overarching goal is to cut loose the
Affinities from InterAlia, to let each Affinity govern itself according to its own interests. Meir Klein foresaw that possibility and wanted to encourage it. But he foresaw a few other
things, too, maybe not so nice. I brought along Dr. Navarro to
explain this."

Ruben Navarro was the oldest Tau on the team: he was
seventy-one and had held a chair in analytical sociology at the

University of Montreal for more than twenty years. Amanda and I had shared lunch with him a couple of times. Navarro was old enough that he had met Klein at academic conferences before Klein's work was locked up by InterAlia; they had published in the same professional journals. He sat in a chair by the window, his halo of white hair framed by the rain-silvered glass, and he spoke without getting up.

"Physicists have said that what they would ultimately like to discover is 'a theory of everything.' For the science of neurosocial teleodynamics, the equivalent goal would be 'a theory of everyone.' We're not quite there yet. Social teleodynamics is a technique for modeling human psychology and human social interactions with unprecedented accuracy. It's not a crystal ball. But like any science, it does make certain predictions. We can extrapolate from current events. We can run models based on our assumptions and see where they take us. As I like to say, the result is less reliable than a weather forecast but more reliable than divination."

It was a line that may have had them rolling in the aisles in Navarro's classes at Montreal, but we just nodded and waited for him to go on. "What is original in Klein's work," he said, "is the subtlety and complexity of the modeling. In that respect, he was far in advance of anything I have seen in the peer-reviewed literature. The method by which he derives his models is radical and contentious, but for now we can go with Klein's claim that it is reliable. So, for instance, we can ask ourselves what Klein's model predicts for interactions between the various Affinities, if InterAlia ceases to exert comprehensive control. But we have to ask that question in light of a larger one, one posed by Klein himself: How is the general culture changing, and what is the role of the Affinities in that change?" Navarro paused, and a gust of wind rattled the window. "In simple terms, Klein was asking: Is our social structure viable? Is there a future worth looking forward to? Or are we simply fucked?"

Which got a suppressed laugh from Amanda. Navarro acknowledged her reaction with a wry smile.

"Without going into detail, I can say that his research suggests that we are not entirely fucked. But it's a close thing. The problems confronting us are the obvious ones—climate change, resource competition, population stress, and all the human conflicts arising from those problems. What makes these questions especially difficult is that they cannot be dealt with comprehensively by individual action. We need to act collectively, on a global scale. But we have very limited means of doing that. We are a collaborative species, the most successful such species on the planet, but we collaborate as individuals, for mutual gain, under systems established to promote and protect such collaboration. Our global economic and social behavior is largely unconstrained. Which means that, under certain circumstances, it can run away with us. It can carry us all unwilling into the land of unforeseen consequences. Which is a very dark place indeed. May I have a glass of water, Damian?"

"Something stronger, if you like."

"No, water is fine."

Damian rustled up a glass of ice water while we fidgeted. Navarro accepted the glass, took a sip, licked his lips. "Now, all this is elementary social teleodynamics. But here again, Klein does something daring. Because he knows more about the Affinities than anyone else—and because he can model them with unprecedented accuracy—he has factored their influence into his predictions."

Amanda said, "And that makes a difference?"

"Yes! Quite a startling difference! Klein's research suggests that the Affinities could become major players in the evolution of a pan-global culture. By which I mean they will increasingly influence politics, policy, and economics. They could in fact come to serve in place of what is so conspicuously absent—a global human conscience."

"The Affinities can do that?"

"Well, no. Not every Affinity. There was a reason Klein entrusted his data to Taus."

"What," Amanda said, "we're so special?"

"Apparently," Navarro said, "we are."

We're special. It was something we may have suspected but never said aloud. It sounded arrogant and narcissistic.

But did we feel it? Of course we did.

I had felt it when I first walked through the doors of Lisa and Loretta's house in Toronto. I had felt it when I realized I was in a community of people who loved me, whom I could love freely and confidently in return, and who loved me despite my imperfections as I loved them despite theirs. I had recognized in that house the presence of what was so conspicuously absent in the house where I had grown up: the possibility of being both truly known and genuinely loved.

Which of course made us *special*. Special to ourselves; special because we were inside the charmed circle, and others were not. But Navarro was suggesting something different. He was suggesting that we might be special to the world at large . . . that something in the Tau community might help shepherd everyone into a better future.

"The bad news," Navarro said, "is that the second half of this century could be a very unpleasant time and place for the human species. In the worst case, we could be facing the collapse of infrastructure, political chaos, widespread starvation, perhaps even the beginning of a massive human die-off. But Klein is not universally pessimistic. His models suggest that there is a way through that terribly narrow passage. It's possible that we can create a better world—more just, equitable, and humane. In fact that may be the only alternative to destruction. And as Taus we are in a unique position to help." Navarro paused and looked at

Damian. "But only if the Tau Affinity is willing to assume that responsibility."

Damian stood up as Navarro sank back into his chair. "Okay, I think that gets the gist across." He surveyed the handful of us. I was aware of the rain clamoring at the window, as if God had decided to wash us all into the sea. I was aware that what we said in this shell of warm light on the edge of the cold Pacific might have consequences far beyond our own lives, if Klein's mathematics were reliable; that a word spoken or unspoken could cascade into history. "Obviously," Damian said, "this isn't something we can keep secret, either from the rest of the Tau Affinity or from the world at large. But we do have choices. That's why I wanted to have this discussion here, away from the city and away from hostile influences. So we're going to talk about this, and fair warning, we might still be talking about it when the sun comes up tomorrow morning."

"*If* it comes up," Amanda said, nodding at the window and the roaring rain.

Damian smiled. "If it does. Because there is one choice we can't share and we can't delegate. According to Klein's data, the Tau Affinity can help move the world in a better direction. But if we attempt to do that, we also make ourselves vulnerable. The world may not want to be moved, and the world can hurt us. Klein's models don't guarantee that we'll come through this unharmed. They *do* guarantee that we'll make enemies. The risk is real."

"The risk is also real," Amanda said, "for someone who runs into a burning building to rescue a child. But we do it anyway, don't we? It's the better part of being human."

"But we're not just assuming personal risks. We're putting other people at risk as well—other Taus, not to mention people outside our Affinity. If we go ahead with the project of making Affinity testing cheap and universal, it's going to force new responsibilities on us and it will inevitably put us in harm's way."

I said, "What's the alternative?"

"The alternative is not to do it at all. Lay low and let events take their course."

"And what does Klein's model say about that?"

Navarro spoke up: "It says that, if we keep our heads down, the chance of the Tau Affinity surviving as a coherent group is to some degree enhanced. But the likelihood that our current civil society will survive is proportionally decreased. In neither scenario is any particular outcome guaranteed. We're talking about probabilities here."

"So that's the question we need to answer," Damian said. "If Klein is right, a kind of war is coming. Do we enlist, and maybe do some good? Or do we sit it out and try to survive?"

Amanda said, "We could take it to T-Net."

"Sooner or later we will. I'll be talking to all the major sodality reps. But we need to have a plan to show them. There's no way to dodge the responsibility. Klein chose us for a reason."

No one spoke. For a long moment there was only the sound of the rain playing cadences on the drumhead of the house.

It rained until after midnight. Come one o'clock, Navarro pled fatigue and most of us went to bed—all of us except the security guys on the night shift. And me. I knew I wouldn't be able to sleep. I went to sit on the back deck of the house.

The cedar deck was still dripping and the patio furniture was sodden, but I didn't care. I threw a bath towel over an Adirondack chair and settled in. The sky had begun to clear. A crescent moon rode over the forest, and the air was cool and smelled of the pine woods and the sea.

I was thinking about Damian when the door creaked and he stepped out to join me.

"Sleep," he said. "Highly overrated." He looked into the distance, and the moon cast his shadow, pale as smoke, across the deck. "I keep thinking about home. You know what I mean?"

Lisa and Loretta and their big welcoming house. Yes. "We could use their advice."

Like most of us in the tranche, I had sought their advice more than once. I was thinking of the time (four years ago now) when Damian and Amanda had first gotten together. The dynamics of jealousy were different in a Tau community, but I was as capable of jealousy as any other human being. I had been avoiding both Amanda and Damian for days—I had even thought about leaving the tranche—and it was Lisa who had called me on it. She had summoned me into the kitchen to sample her tiramisu ("I used Madeira instead of Marsala"), but that was just bait. She sat me down at the kitchen table and gave me a big-eyed stare. "Adam," she said. "If I didn't know better, I'd say you were sulking."

"I don't know what you mean. The tiramisu is great."

"And you lie so very badly. But I guess it isn't easy, knowing Amanda is with another man?"

"I'm dealing with it."

"But not very well. You know she loves you, yes?"

"She says so."

"And she means it. You know she means it?"

"I guess so." That was disingenuous and childish. Of course she loved me. We were Taus. I recognized her love in the worried glances she had lately been giving me. I heard it in her voice when she tried to explain the relationship that had developed between her and Damian. And I resented her for it. It denied me the comfort of an uncomplicated anger.

"Then you need to stop behaving the way you're behaving. Your relationship to Amanda has a certain nature. You two have always conducted yourself according to that knowledge. Her need for autonomy was built into her love for you. What's the use of wanting her to be what she is not?"

"No use. I know that. I'm just . . ."

"Hurt," Lisa supplied.

Yes, painful as it was to admit it. Hurt, yes. Childishly hurt.
Hurt like a five-year-old whose ice cream cone just plopped onto
the sidewalk. Hurt by this awareness of myself as a petulant in-
fant. "I'm not sure I want to talk about it."

"Of course you don't want to talk about it." Lisa reached across
the table and put her hand on mine. Her hand was parchment-
skinned, all bones and veins. It felt wonderful. "Who would? But
here we are. You know, of course, that Damian is also concerned
about you."

That was even more difficult to accept. The thing was, I admired Damian Levay. Which hardly made me unique; everyone
admired Damian. He was passionate about the Tau community
and its welfare—not just our tranche, but the sodality, the entire Affinity. He was smart, wealthy, generous, and ten years my
senior. I could hardly blame Amanda for falling in love with him.
I was half in love with him myself.

"It is Amanda's misfortune," Lisa said, "that she's attracted to
hopelessly heterosexual men. More than once I have seen conflicts like this resolved by a jovial three-way fuck. But I think in
this case that's not an option."

Trevor had made the same suggestion more bluntly. ("So get
over yourself and go to bed with him. Are you completely blind
to his hotness?") But Lisa was right; it wouldn't have worked. I
wasn't especially proud of my heterosexuality—in our tranche
it sometimes seemed like a kind of selective sexual impotence,
for which I deserved sympathy and compassion—but I was stuck
with it. Born that way, as the old song has it.

"If you continue to cultivate your own unhappiness," Lisa
said, "you and Amanda will end up as—what? Not enemies.
We aren't that sort of people. But just friends. Do you want
that?"

"No," I said.

"Then you have to start living up to your own expectations. And—oh, do you feel that?"

"What?"

"The wind from the window!" The gingham curtains lofted as she spoke. "Rain on the way. You can smell it." She closed her eyes and inhaled deeply. "I do love that smell. Smells like thunder!" As if on cue, there was a distant rumble. "I'm nearly seventy-five years old, Adam, and I still love a summer storm. Is that wrong?"

"Of course not."

"I sense a kindred soul. You love a storm, too, don't you?"

I admitted I did.

"But we're not rivals, are we? Because there's storm enough for both of us."

"Ah. The parable of the storm."

"I'm sorry, was it too obvious?"

"Maybe just obvious enough. You are wise, oh ancient of days. Maybe Amanda's the one who should be jealous."

Lisa performed a credible blush. "I love you too, dear. Especially now that you've stopped pouting. You've finished your tiramisu, so I propose a bottle of wine and chairs in the arboretum. We can watch the lightning together. How does that sound?"

It sounded fine.

That had been four years ago. Since then, Damian and Amanda and I had arrived at a modus vivendi. Amanda would not tolerate us competing for her attention, so we didn't. And as for my feelings about Damian . . .

"Lord," he said, hands on the railing of the cedar deck, staring into the moonlit corridors of the forest, "take this cup from my lips. I'm pretty sure Lisa and Laura would make a better decision than any of us."

He was a Tau and I loved him as a Tau. But he was as imperfect as the rest of us. Left to his own devices, he would never wear anything but sweat pants and t-shirts. He believed he was a good cook; he was mistaken. He had a laugh that sounded as if someone had stepped on the tail of a small dog. He couldn't assemble Ikea furniture or operate simple appliances without a friendly intervention. Amanda had once said she loved Damian for his confidence, even when it was misplaced, and she loved me for my doubts, even when they were foolish. In a sense, we were the two sides of Amanda's own personality. Damian worked on behalf of Tau in a way that echoed the work ethic Amanda had inherited from her family: do what needs doing, and do it selflessly, efficiently, and promptly. I was the other side of that equation, impractical and occasionally impulsive, sometimes usefully creative. Amanda's personal philosophy veered between Aristotle and Epicurus. No wonder she needed two men in her life.

It was also true that these thoughts were easier to entertain now that she was sleeping in my bed again.

Mist from the drenched forest had begun to condense into a ground fog. The high moon dimmed. I was about to stand up when Damian said, "Did you see that?"

"See what?"

"In the woods. About your nine o'clock."

I tried to look where he was looking. The trees were still dripping. In the silence I could hear the creak and sway of their branches. I might have glimpsed a moving light in the deep of the woods. But it was gone before I could say a word. "Maybe it's one of the security guys."

Damian stepped away from the railing. "We need to ask Gordo," he said. "And we need to go inside. Right now."

CHAPTER 10

I went into our bedroom to wake Amanda.

She was asleep on her back, head turned to one side. She wore her hair longer than she used to, but it was still short, a dark halo against the cotton pillowcase. She sighed when I sat on the bed. I called her name.

She opened her eyes and frowned at me. "Adam? What is it?"

"Sorry, but Gordo wants us all in the main room where he can keep an eye on us. Might be some motion outside the house."

"Oh." She sat up and fished her blouse off the floor where she had dropped it. "Something moving around, you mean? Like a deer? A bear?"

"Someone carrying a flashlight."

"*Oh*. Okay. Yeah. Hand me my jeans."

In my experience the only thing better than watching Amanda put on her jeans was watching her take them off, but Gordo distracted us by knocking at the door. "Turn off the lights when you come out, okay? I don't want the whole place lit up like Times Square."

She finished buttoning up. "I thought we were here to get *away* from scary strangers."

"Probably it's nothing," I said. "False alarm."

We found everyone gathered in the main room, looking sleepy and irritable. Gordo had drawn the drapes, and he waited as Amanda and I settled onto the sofa. He had a phone in his hand and a pistol in what looked like a military holster at his hip. Usually it would have been Damian who dominated the gathering, but tonight Damian was just one more endangered Tau. He sat quietly with the rest of us.

Gordo said, "I've got three people on the perimeter and they're watching all the access points. Anybody approaches the house, they'll see him. That doesn't mean we're altogether safe. I've got Marcy Britnell on the west side, she says there was what looked like a flashlight in the woods and she's found fresh footprints tracking past the property on an oblique angle, like somebody was scouting us out. Maybe one set of footprints, maybe more, hard to tell at night on muddy ground. So we're being careful. I can't see why anyone would be out there at two in the morning after a rainstorm for *innocent* purposes, but we can't rule out a lost hiker or a drunk trying to find his way home. It may seem isolated here but there are plenty of people living closer to the docks, so let's not draw too many conclusions, okay?"

Good advice—we all nodded sagely—but easier said than done.

Amanda was still sleepy and she snuggled against me. I saw Damian's eyes linger on us a moment. He didn't seem jealous but he did look a little frustrated. Or maybe it was just the weight of the responsibilities he had recently shouldered.

It occurred to me to wonder what I might have been doing if Damian hadn't more or less adopted me a few years ago. Six months after I joined the Rosedale tranche I had been working in Walter Kohler's ad agency, putting together text and images on an Apple platform and proofreading copy on the side. The job was well paid but was only mildly interesting, and Damian told me I was wasting my time there. "Come work for me. I talked to Walter, and he's agreeable, if that's what you want."

"Work for you doing what?" Back then, Damian's main business had been his law practice. "I don't have any legal training."

He told me he was setting up a Tau-specific pension fund (which would eventually become TauBourse) and devoting some of the profits to pro-bono work on behalf of the Affinities, including petitioning InterAlia for greater transparency in their management of Affinity groups. He had already enlisted all the legal talent he needed, but what he wanted was a cadre of people who understood Tau and who were flexible enough to act in various capacities as needed, from driving cars to conducting research to writing briefs. Gophers, in effect, but we would be described as "consultants." The drawback was that none of this would exercise my artistic talent.

And I surprised myself by being okay with that. Photoshopping images of puppies for pet food ads was what I had been doing with my artistic talent lately, and the muses weren't impressed. I liked Damian's passionate attitude toward the Tau Affinity and I was excited by the idea of playing a role in its evolution. Plus—no small thing—Amanda had already agreed to join his team. The work appealed to her serious side, what Lisa had once described as her desire "to do good *ferociously.*"

Since then I had driven cars for Tau, written press releases for Tau, arranged catering for Tau, rented hotel rooms for Tau, negotiated property purchases for Tau, even mopped floors (on one memorable occasion) for Tau. Damian was my boss, but we tended not to use that word. He initiated and organized the work, but we performed it collaboratively. Even the menial work contributed something to Tau, which made it bearable, and most days I was working alongside Amanda, which was more than merely bearable. In just a few years that work and those relationships had fused into what I thought of as the heartbeat and the music of my life.

Some days it made me feel invulnerable. I was Adam Fisk of the Tau Affinity, with a host of loyal brothers and sisters—almost seven million of us, according to the most recent census. Take me on and you take on my tribe. But I wasn't invulnerable, and neither was Tau, and this weekend retreat had made that obvious.

We needed to stay together where Gordo could keep an eye on us, but that didn't mean we had to stay awake all night. Professor Navarro had the bright idea of moving sheets and blankets into the living room for makeshift beds, which we did, and he promptly curled up on one of them. Navarro wasn't one of those elderly people who have trouble sleeping: he snored like a drunken longshoreman.

Amanda stretched out on the sofa, and I was about to move to a blanket on the floor when my phone buzzed. Rachel Ragland's number. A call at this hour probably meant she was drunk, either belligerent and accusatory or wanting to make tearful amends. I considered ignoring the call. The ugly word "tether" echoed in my head. I took the phone to a vacant corner of the room. "Rachel? What is it?"

But it wasn't Rachel on the other end. It was her daughter.

"Is that Adam?"

"Suze?" I asked.

"Adam from the beach?"

"Yep, it's me. What are you doing awake at this hour?"

"I still have the picture you drew of me. I colored it."

"That's great. Suze, is your mommy around?"

"Yes but not awake."

"Maybe you should be asleep, too. Does she know you're using her phone?"

"No," she said, and for a moment I mistook the tension in her voice for guilt.

"Well, it's not a good idea to use your mom's things without her permission."

"I'm sorry." Suddenly she sounded near tears.

"Suze . . . is something wrong?"

"I *wanted* to ask her, but she *won't wake up*!"

"I don't understand. Are you at home?"

"Yes!"

"Your mom's in her bedroom?"

"*No!* She's on the *couch*! I'm looking at her *right now*!"

"What happens if you try to wake her up?"

"Nothing!"

Amanda overheard some of my end of the conversation—she sat up and gave me a concerned look. No one else was paying attention. Gordo sat by the window, his own phone in his hand, talking to one of his security people. Navarro's snoring had settled into a growling rhythm, like someone trying to start a chainsaw.

"Go to her now," I told Suze. "See if she wakes up."

"Okay . . ."

"Are you with her?"

"Yes."

"Can she see you?"

"Her eyes are closed."

"What if you touch her?"

A pause. "I don't want to."

"Why not?"

"I don't want to get the blood on me."

I closed my eyes and said, "Suze, tell me about the blood. Is Mommy hurt?"

"She cuts herself sometimes. Maybe she cut herself too much."

"Try to wake her up. Say, 'Mommy, wake up!' Real loud. Can you do that for me?"

She didn't just call it out, she screamed it. When she stopped, I said, "What happened?"

"Nothing! Maybe her eyes came open a little bit but they closed up again."

"Okay," I said, though *okay* was far from what I felt. "Okay, Suze, you need to call 911. Do you know how to do that?"

"Yeah but . . ."

"But what?"

"Mommy said never call 911 if she's passed out. Because people might come and take me away from her. She said just wait for her to wake up. But there's more blood this time. Your number was in the phone so I called it instead."

"That's good, Suze, that's smart, but you're right, this time's different. Your mommy would want you to call 911. The 911 people know how to help, and they'll tell you exactly what to do."

"I'm afraid." It sounded as if the tears were about to brim over.

"Sure you are, but that's part of being brave. Even the bravest people get scared. That's when they ask for help, right?"

"I guess."

"So I'll hang up, and then you call 911. Right away, okay? Don't wait. They'll stay on the phone with you until everything's fixed up. After that I'll call back and check on you. Okay?"

"I *guess*."

"Don't guess, Suze. Just do it."

"Okay."

"I'll hang up now, but I need you to promise to make that call. Do you promise?"

"Yeah."

"Say it for me."

"I promise."

"Good girl."

I ended the call and looked at the phone in my hand. The phone was shaking. Because my hand was shaking.

Amanda came over and touched my shoulder, and I told her what Suze had said.

She frowned and nodded. "God, that's awful. It sounds like Rachel's a cutter."

"A what?"

"Self-injury. It's a personality disorder. People cut themselves, burn themselves, things like that. Enough to hurt, but not enough to do real damage. So it probably wasn't a suicide attempt. You said she had psychiatric drugs in her bathroom?"

Her stash of pharmaceuticals, the kind prescribed for ADHD, OCD, depression, anxiety, even a couple of antipsychotics. Most of them had been prescribed to Rachel, though I had seen a different name on a couple of the labels—Carlos something-or-other, her barroom buddy.

Amanda's Tau telepathy was acute enough for her to guess what was going through my mind. "You didn't take advantage of her, Adam. You didn't know she was crazy until—"

"Until after I took advantage of her."

"No. You didn't do anything wrong. *Rash*, maybe, but not wrong. That's the thing about outsiders. They're unpredictable. Not always bad, but dangerous in all kinds of ways, to themselves and others."

I opened my phone again and tried Rachel's number. I was gratified that the line was busy. I hoped it meant Suze was doing what I had told her to do.

Amanda said, "Rachel's damaged in ways you couldn't have known about. I just don't want you to be collateral damage."

"I'm thinking about Suze. Does she count as collateral damage?" I looked at the others in the room, my tribe, all of us leaning on each other in one way or another. Suze didn't have a tribe. She barely had a mother.

Amanda took a step back and said, "What I mean is—"

I could guess what she was about to say. My welfare was more important to her than Rachel's. She didn't want me to get hurt. Outside Tau, people were unpredictable and relationships could go wrong in countless ways. Misunderstandings were inevitable. And so on.

But she didn't finish the sentence.

At the time—when the window glass shattered, when the drapes billowed as if an invisible finger had tugged them, when Amanda looked startled and then fell down—we didn't understand what was happening. Later, we reconstructed it this way:

Gordo MacDonald had put his security detail on alert. Marcy Britnell, a Tau from Cleveland and formerly a second lieutenant in the US Marine Corps, was working the tree line at the western edge of the property, armed with a pistol and equipped with a pair of IR goggles, when she spotted a figure in the forest. The figure appeared to be carrying a long gun, and Marcy quietly called the news in to Gordo while keeping the stranger in view.

Gordo didn't want Marcy tackling the intruder by herself, so he told her to hold her position while he sent out a couple more of his people. And that's what Marcy did, until she saw the figure raise his weapon and aim it toward the house. At which point she leveled her pistol and shouted to the gunman to lower his weapon and stand down.

The gunman didn't lower his weapon. Instead, he began to swing it toward the sound of Marcy's voice. Marcy wasn't sure how visible she was in the moonlight, but she was taking no chances. She squeezed off a shot.

The gunman twisted to the left, obviously hurt, and reflexively fired a round of his own.

The rifle he carried was a Remington 783, and the bullet he fired went nowhere near Marcy Britnell. Instead it flew toward the house, clipped a pine bough, penetrated the glass of the sliding doors that adjoined the deck, pierced the coarse fabric of the curtains, passed within inches of the phone Gordo was holding to his ear, and struck Amanda just under her left shoulder and inches from the curve of her spine.

I looked away from her at the sound of the bullet cracking

the window. I saw the curtain billow and settle back as if a wind had lifted it, and I saw Gordo pause in mid-conversation, mouth open but motionless as he tried to sort out what was happening. When I turned back to Amanda she looked perplexed. Then she fell toward me, eyes open, and I caught her.

In those days we liked to talk about "Tau telepathy." It wasn't really telepathy, of course, but we understood each other so deeply, so intuitively, that it often felt that way. What we discovered that night on Pender Island was something even deeper than Tau telepathy. Call it Tau rage.

Amanda tumbled into my arms, struggling to say something that emerged as a choked whisper, and time began to stagger forward in a series of static moments, snapshots taken in a glaring light. Probably everyone else in the room could say the same thing. But we worked in concert despite our confusion. I went to my knees, Amanda's weight carrying me down. I helped her to lie on her right side. I could see the wound now, a flower of blood on the back of the wrinkled white blouse she was wearing. The wound was bleeding freely but not gushing. Her eyelids fluttered and the pupils of her eyes rolled upward.

I said, "Amanda?"

Hands pulled me away from her, and Gordo MacDonald knelt down in my place. "I'm qualified in emergency first aid," he said, "and Marcy's on her way in—Marcy did time in Afghanistan as a field nurse. Let us look after her."

Before I could answer he had taken a knife from his belt and cut away her blouse. Amanda gasped, a sound like water bubbling over rocks.

The exterior door flew open almost immediately. It was Marcy, breathless, with a plastic case the size of an overnight bag in her hand. A med kit, which she had stashed in the trunk of one of the cars that had come over on the ferry. She looked frazzled and breathless, but she moved straight to where Gordo was tending Amanda. She inspected the wound, checked Amanda's pulse, called her name and got a weak response. "Hang in there," Marcy said. She turned to Gordo and added in a low voice, "We need professional help."

"The shooter?" Gordo asked.

"Nelson's bringing him in."

Damian was on the phone to a Tau contact back in Vancouver. He put down the handset and began a brief, intense conversation with Gordo. I couldn't hear what they said. All my attention was still focused on Amanda.

She was alert enough to murmur something about the pain. Marcy took a syringe from her kit and with practiced efficiency gave her a shot of morphine. Almost immediately, Amanda's eyes drifted to half-mast. "She'll be okay, Adam," Marcy told me over her shoulder. "I mean that."

"She needs a hospital."

"Setting it up right now," Damian said from across the room.

There were a couple of local physicians on Pender and a small regional hospital not far away on Salt Spring Island, but we needed a better and faster option. Late as it was, it took Damian only three calls to find a Tau who ran a helicopter-commute service out of Tsawwassen. A Sikorsky S76 was in the air twenty minutes later, by which time Damian had located a Tau physician near Ladner with access to a fully equipped clinic. The doctor agreed to assess and treat Amanda without reporting a gunshot wound, as long as she didn't require complex surgery—which Marcy had said she would not.

As that was being arranged one of Gordo's security guys, the one called Nelson, came up the stairs to the rain-sodden deck with the wounded shooter clinging to him. Damian stopped him at the door: "Not in here—we can't have his blood all over everything." The shooter slid down to the hardwood planks.

When we talked about it later, that was what we called him: *the shooter.* Because we had heard the word on TV and in the movies. But that wasn't how I thought of him at the time. Not when Amanda was still losing blood. I thought of him instead as the son of a bitch who had tried to destroy everything that made my life worth living.

Marcy and Gordo headed for the deck, and I followed them. The shooter was a skinny dude with one of those long faces you sometimes see on very tall people, as if his features had been stretched vertically. His hair was wet and dangled over his forehead in two black wings. His eyes were anxious but unfocused. Marcy's bullet had taken him mid-body, below the ribs and to the left. Blood had clotted on his cotton shirt and discolored his jeans from the waist to the left knee. Marcy looked at him and said in a small voice, "Oh, Christ. Gordo—"

"I know," Gordo said.

The man was dying, and there was nothing Marcy or anyone else could do to save him. That was what I surmised from their silences.

It made me glad.

Hatred is a purifying emotion. Before that night I would have said I hated a few people. But dislike and disdain aren't hatred. They're pallid, hollow emotions. Real hatred is a bulldozer. It wants to demolish and destroy. It brooks no opposition.

I looked down at this piece of shit in the form of a human being, and he looked back at me through a haze of pain. Furious or frightened tears leaked from his eyes. I knelt down and put my face close to his face. His pig eyes narrowed. His breath stank of cloves and halitosis, mingled with the coppery smell of all the blood he was spilling. I ordered him to tell me his name.

Gordo, behind me, tried to get my attention. "Adam—"

The shooter wasn't saying anything, though I had his complete attention. So I put my hands on his throat. I felt the stubble where he had shaved that morning. I felt his Adam's apple frantically bobbing against my fingers. His lips struggled to form words. I let him take a breath.

"Fuck you," he whispered.

Gordo pulled me away before I could do any damage. "Adam, *we know who he is*. We've got his wallet. His driver's license. His credit card. His phone." He looked at the dying man and I realized that the same hatred I felt was running through Gordo, Damian, Marcy, everyone else in the house. It was one big river. Maybe what they felt was a little less white-hot than what I felt, but it was real, visceral hatred.

"This time tomorrow," Gordo said, "we'll know everything about him. Where he lives, who his friends are, who he's working for. We already know he's an amateur. Carrying his personal shit on him like that."

The shooter moved his mouth again, seemed to be trying to say something that wouldn't come out.

Marcy fetched her medical kit. After a brief, hushed conference with Gordo and Damian, she produced a syringe and filled it from a small brown bottle.

"Hold him steady," she said. "I don't want him knocking this out of my hand."

Gordo leaned across the shooter, pinning his legs and his left arm. I tugged his right arm straight out as Gordo used a pocket knife to slice his shirt sleeve from cuff to shoulder. When Marcy jabbed the needle into the shooter's bicep, he arched his back in a feeble spasm of resistance. I asked Marcy what she was giving him.

"Painkiller," she said curtly.

"What, to make him feel better?"

"Enough for that," she said. "Enough for that and more."

The shooter thrashed and struggled when he heard her. But not for long.

CHAPTER 11

Maybe understandably—or maybe not—a couple of days passed before it occurred to me to call Rachel Ragland.

She didn't answer her phone, and I left an apologetic message and asked her to get in touch. Another day passed. Nothing. I drove to Rachel's building, parked, and buzzed her apartment from the lobby. Silence. So I called the local hospitals and found her at Vancouver General. She was in "for observation," and unless I was family, visiting hours were two to six, at Rachel's discretion.

By my watch that left a window of three hours, and the hospital was only twenty minutes away. It hadn't rained since the weekend. The weather had slipped into an autumn lull, all soft blue skies and crisp breezes, and it was an easy drive. But I felt as if some transparent part of me had become opaque: I looked at the world through a lens of clouded glass.

It turned out that Rachel was in a ward in the hospital's psychiatric wing. A locked ward, though that wasn't as bad as it sounded; all it meant was that patients and visitors needed authorization to pass through the glass-and-mesh doors next to the nurses' station. I waited twenty minutes for someone to find Rachel, give her my name, and find out if she was willing to see me. At last a nurse (a young guy in powder-blue scrubs) waved me in. I followed him to Rachel's bed.

She was dressed in slacks and a plaid flannel shirt. There were slippers on her feet, and she was sitting up, an ancient paperback novel in her hand. She gave me a long, searching look. She was clean and reasonably alert but I could tell by a certain slackness around her eyes that she was back on her meds. Before I could speak she said, "They think I'm suicidal. That's why I'm stuck here. But I was only cutting." She held out her left arm to show me her bandages, a swatch of cotton and tape that ran from wrist to elbow. "You know about that? People who cut themselves sometimes?"

"I've heard of it," I said.

"Well, I'm one of them."

"I'm surprised. I never saw—"

"What—scars? This was the first time I did my arm. I used to just cut my legs. Up high, so I could wear shorts and not show anything. But not a bathing suit. Which was okay because I don't swim. And I was pretty healed up when you saw me without my clothes on. I'd been good. On the mend. But you could have found scars if you'd looked for them." She put a bookmark in her paperback novel and set it aside. "So why are you here?"

"Suze called me," I said. "That night."

"Yeah, I know. I heard all about it. You told her to phone 911."

"Yeah."

"Even though she wasn't supposed to do that."

"She said so, but—"

"Because I trained her that way. You know why? Fucking *social workers*, that's why! There were a couple of incidents back before I got my prescriptions and now I'm on their watch list or whatever. I'm on, like, bad mother probation."

An orderly passing by with a box of gauze in his hand slowed and cocked his head. Rachel moderated her voice until he was out of sight. "They're like the NSA in here, always watching. This is where they put people who can't be trusted."

"You were unconscious when Suze called. She couldn't wake you up."

"I'd been cutting, yeah, and maybe a little too deep, and I was ashamed of myself, so I took a double dose of meds and washed 'em down with orange juice and vodka. Because I really, really wanted to sleep. And hey, it worked. Out like a light, right there on the sofa. Still bleeding a little. I leaked before I clotted. So I guess Suze got scared, which I'm really *really* sorry about. A miscalculation on my part. But would you take away my kid for that?"

"No . . ."

"No, but you did. That's *exactly* what you did when you told Suze to call 911. Now they're putting her in temporary foster care. Pending an assessment. They won't even let me talk to her. They say we can schedule a visit, but not until the doctors decide I'm up to it." Her eyes brimmed with tears that were perhaps equal parts loss and anger. "They took away my baby!"

"I'm sorry," I said.

"I would *absolutely fucking love it* if this were totally your fault. That would make me feel a little better. But, taking Suze's call? Being worried about me? I can't really blame you for that."

"Thank you, Rachel."

"What I *do* blame you for is—" She hesitated and bit her lip as if debating how to proceed.

"Go ahead. Say it."

"I don't know exactly *how* to say it, but . . . I'm here, and Suze is in foster care, and I can't help thinking, none of this would have happened if I was a Tau. If I was a Tau, you wouldn't have called 911, would you? You would have called some other Tau. Or a bunch of other Taus. Some nice little Tau couple would be looking after Suze, and after I got attention from a Tau clinic, and with a whole tranche to make sure I kept on my meds, I'd have her back right away quick. What do you think, Adam? Is that about right?"

I didn't have to answer. It was absolutely true.

I stayed a few minutes more. A nurse came by with three pills and a paper cup, and Rachel dutifully swallowed the pills and chased them with a gulp of water. She opened her mouth to show the nurse she'd swallowed the meds. I think Rachel wanted me to see this small humiliation. The fate to which I had delivered her.

As I turned to leave she said, "Are you okay? No offense, Adam, but you look like shit."

"I haven't slept much."

"Yeah, well." Her gaze went a little quavery. "Welcome to the club. Oh, I remembered something. Something I meant to tell you. About the guys who came to visit me? The ones you drew a picture of at the beach?"

It seemed like a long time ago. "What about them?"

"The guy who did most of the talking—you asked about his face, and that's what I was trying to remember. But he had another, uh, distinguishing feature. Not his face. His hand. There was a mark on it."

"A mark?"

"A tattoo. A little one. Actually not his hand but just above the wrist? I saw it when his shirt cuff rode up."

"What did it look like?"

The medication was beginning to kick in. She smiled dreamily. "A window."

"I'm sorry—a window?"

"A box. A rectangle. A tall box. With a line across it. Like an old-fashioned window, the kind where you lift the lower pane. Know what I mean? Like a letter H, but with three cross lines, top bottom and middle. Does that mean anything?"

"Yes," I said. "It does."

We rolled up our Vancouver operation in November of that year. Which was good, because by then I was desperately homesick. I missed Lisa and Loretta. I missed their big, warm house in Toronto. I wanted to be there when they put up the Christmas tree—usually a huge spruce, decked out with Victorian ball ornaments and spun-glass angels and silver menorahs and any other ecumenical or secular decoration any tranche member felt like attaching to it. I wanted to be home for Christmas, Hannukah, Kwanzaa, Dognzhi, Pancha Ganapati, Shabe Yaldā, Saturnalia, and what-have-you. That was what I wanted.

Damian needed to be back in Toronto for another reason. Toronto was where his law offices were, and the war between Tau and InterAlia was being fought with writs and court appointments. That wasn't necessarily a bad thing: InterAlia was in a severely weakened condition, which gave us some leverage. The company's stock had declined to record lows and there were rumors of an impending bankruptcy.

Damian and I went out for an early dinner on our last day in the city. A couple of blocks down Robson there was a restaurant that served good and reasonably affordable schnitzel. The staff had come to recognize us as regulars, and I assumed they also recognized the two Tau security guys who habitually followed us in and kept watch over us from a table of their own. The evening crowd hadn't arrived yet, and we had enough space and privacy to speak freely.

For years Damian and his law firm had been conducting pitched battles with InterAlia over the autonomy of Tau. The corporation was jealous of its intellectual property, and the last thing they wanted was any kind of legal judgment that might recognize the Affinities as quasi-ethnicities, even invented ones. But what had lately crippled InterAlia were the legal challenges from unaffiliated sources: class action suits, discrimination cases. Most of the Affinities—Tau on the vanguard—had created institutions that served their members exclusively. We had established, for example, a network of Tau rehab clinics, staffed by Taus and catering to Taus with substance-abuse problems. The success rate of our clinics was spectacular, with a recidivism rate half that of standard treatment. But we routinely turned away non-Taus. Did that mean our clinics (or our financial services, another area Damian had pioneered) were discriminatory? InterAlia didn't officially sanction these Affinity-specific businesses, which meant Tau had been forced to fend off similar legal attacks; in all of these cases our lawyers had attempted to subpoena InterAlia's sorting protocols; and in every case InterAlia had resisted, which meant costly out-of-court settlements or lengthy legal challenges, several of which were currently wending their way toward Supreme Court decisions.

But that was old news. As of yesterday, Damian told me, InterAlia had folded its cards and pushed away from the table. "Partly because they found out Klein had arranged for their proprietary algorithms to be posted all over the Internet. Between that and the ongoing litigation, the writing was already on the wall."

"I guess I understand. But then, why go to the trouble of murdering Klein?"

"Simple. They didn't."

I blinked. That had been our theory from the day we first heard about Klein's death: InterAlia was behind it. Who else could it be?

Damian sat a moment, watching customers come and go through the revolving glass door. Our waiter poured fresh rounds of coffee but knew better than to hover. "Remember what Rachel Ragland told you about the tattoo on that guy's hand?"

The Phoenician letter Het. The guy who interrogated her had belonged to the Het Affinity. Which was disturbing in itself. There was nothing about the Affinities that precluded criminal behavior. All the Affinities were, in effect, low-crime districts, but that was because our collaborative potential made crime less inviting. Within the Affinities jealousy was blunted, greed was marginalized, and basic human needs were usually met. Statistically, Tau was the most law-abiding of all the Affinities, if only by a hair. We liked to think of ourselves as good people, and that was statistically true. But we were free moral agents like everybody else, perfectly capable of committing crimes under the right circumstances. So were the Hets.

"I saw the same kind of tattoo the night Amanda was shot," Damian said. "On the guy who fired the rifle."

"What do you mean—it was the same guy?" In which case my career as a forensic sketch artist was over before it had begun. The Pender Island shooter had looked nothing like either of my drawings.

Damian shook his head. "Not the same guy, a similar tattoo. The shooter had it on the back of his neck, just under the collar of his shirt. So we've had our experts take a deeper look at Klein's models of Affinity interactions and how that might play out when the Affinities are autonomous and self-governing. The results are surprising. Some of the smaller Affinities, like Mem and Rosh, eventually wither up and vanish. Some get bigger. Some get big enough and rich enough to exert real political and economic influence."

"Which is why Klein gave us the information, right? He saw Tau as a potentially powerful influence. A good one."

"Others might be powerful but maybe not so good. And that raises a huge red flag, especially concerning Het."

"Does it? I mean, why would the Hets want to kill Klein in the first place? Why would they be stalking our people?"

"It's not clear that the guy on Pender actually intended to shoot anyone. He was probably there for reconnaissance, carrying the weapon in case he needed to defend himself. He had his wallet in his pocket, and Gordo says that marks him as an amateur. We have his name, we know where he lived, we've identified his tranche. We should have better answers soon. But our best guess is that the Hets also acquired Klein's data, and they read the same auspices in it as we did. Potential conflict, Het versus Tau. It's possible the Hets wanted to get in the first blow by keeping Klein's data out of our hands, and when that didn't work, by interfering with our analysis of it."

I thought again about the man who shot Amanda. He hadn't been aiming at her, but he must have been willing to kill any or all of us—that was why he had come armed. Gordo had disposed of the rifle and taken charge of the shooter's effects. But I hadn't talked directly to Gordo since the night I had ridden with Amanda on the helicopter to the mainland. I knew the shooter was dead because I had seen Marcy deliver the lethal injection. Damian had been reluctant to say anything more about the incident until our investigation was complete, and for weeks he had discouraged questions. But since the subject had come up, I asked him what happened to the remaining evidence from that night—the shooter's car, if he had one. The body.

"The shooter left his car parked at Tsawwassen ferry docks, but it'll be found—if it's ever found—on a logging road down by the US border."

"Gordo's people moved it?"

"Gordo and his people were extremely helpful, everything from finding spent cartridges to sluicing down the back deck. That's something we're going to need, by the way—a permanent Tau security force. Taus who have the appropriate skills and can be called on when we need them. Once we stop paying dues to InterAlia we'll have to allocate revenue to set that up."

"And the body?"

"Our helicopter pilot came back to pick up the body."

"And?"

"And . . ." Damian looked at me, then looked away. "There's a lot of water in Georgia Strait. It's easy to lose things in it."

We booked a flight to Toronto as soon as Amanda's doctor cleared her to travel.

The plane arrived at Pearson International, and we caught a cab at the beginning of an early snowfall. Bright, small flakes of snow, the kind that dart up at the merest breeze and snake in narrow lines across the roads. "Just a taste of winter," the cabbie told us. "Just a little taste."

Damian smiled thinly but didn't answer. Amanda wasn't talking much, either. Her left arm was in a sling, to protect the healing musculature of her shoulder. She was somber, as she had been ever since she had woken up in an outpatient clinic in the suburbs of Vancouver. Chastened by what had happened to her, as anyone would be. But not frightened, not traumatized: I felt that, and I loved and admired her for it. No fear, but a new and tangible anger. It was as if, along with the bullet, something sharp and coldly luminous had lodged inside her.

Lisa was waiting on the porch when we arrived at the tranche house. Damian paid the cabbie, then we mounted the wooden risers to the porch and took turns hugging her (though Amanda had to do it cautiously, favoring her injury). Lisa was two years shy of her eightieth birthday, and hugging her was like wrapping my arms around a porcelain figurine. Her white hair smelled of this morning's shampoo and this afternoon's loaf of cinnamon bread. "Welcome home," she said. "Come in, all of you. Loretta's not too mobile today but she's waiting in the front room. And I expect you're cold. Not to mention hungry and thirsty."

This was home, I thought. This was worth fighting for. Worth dying for, if it came to that.

By the first of December our tech guys had assembled a functioning prototype of a portable Affinity tester, and we put it to work on the tranche as a test of its effectiveness.

The social-theory guys were still trying to work out the long-term implications of the availability of such a device. At the tranche Christmas party Amanda and I tried to explain all this to Trevor Holst, who had flown home after the annual convention and had been out of the loop during the Vancouver crisis. There had been things we couldn't say to him over the phone, which was awkward because he was close to Amanda, too. But we could talk freely now.

Trev's hair had a hint of gray that hadn't been there when I first met him seven years ago, but he was as physically imposing as he had ever been. He had been living alone for six months, since his last lover moved to Phoenix and married a roofing contractor he'd met at a Tau mixer. No hard feelings, "but it's not easy to get used to. The bed still feels empty when I'm the only one in it."

He wasn't asking for sympathy, just catching us up on his situation. His eyes had gone wide as dinner plates when he first saw Amanda's sling. "It doesn't hurt," she reassured him. "At least not anymore."

The shooter's bullet had spent much of its momentum by the time it penetrated the windowpane and the drapes of the house on Pender Island. It had struck her high in the back, chipped her shoulder, cracked a rib, and done a fair amount of soft tissue damage. If the wound had been even slightly worse she would have required serious surgical intervention, in a hospital where awkward questions would have been asked. As it was, she would carry the mark for the rest of her life.

And maybe some less visible scars as well. Tonight should have been a happy occasion. Lisa had been in the kitchen all day, and the buffet was overflowing. Loretta's arthritis had reduced her mobility but she hobbled gamely through the crowd, as quietly amiable as ever. The whole tranche had turned out, plus some old members who had moved out of our catchment area, plus a bunch of friendly Taus from nearby tranches. This was the span of my social universe, people I loved and who loved me, many of whom had passed briefly and pleasantly through my bed and might do so again if the stars were suitably aligned. It *was* a happy occasion. But Amanda had something serious on her mind, and Trevor and I both sensed it. So, after dinner, as the house filled with the murmur of gentle and happy talk, we headed upstairs.

Had it been summer we might have climbed out on the roof and watched the moon rise over the city. It was too cold for that now, so we went to the attic instead—not really an attic but a dormer room on the third floor, too small to fix up for a tenant and too hot in summer, where Lisa and Loretta had stored a few sticks of old furniture, and where a single-paned window overlooked the backyard and the ravine full of leafless oaks and maples. There were three ancient easy chairs in the room, lined up to face the window. The glass was opaque with frost, and we sat in the eerie luminescence of moonlight through ice as Amanda fetched a pipe from her bag and filled it with finely ground cannabis. When she passed me the pipe I tasted her lipstick on it. I looked at her and smiled, and she smiled, but there was a sadness behind her eyes, and I thought: *Just say it. Whatever you need to say, say it.*

The Tau Affinity had reached a tipping point, a point of accelerated change, a point beyond which nothing would ever be quite the same. The evidence was everywhere. The retesting we had done, for instance. Our tech guys had presented us with their prototype of a portable Affinity tester: a plastic box with a couple of data ports and with eight cranial sensors dangling from it like the arms of an octopus. It was clunkier than the product we would eventually manufacture, but in full working order. Everyone in our tranche had been retested, and Lisa had announced the results this morning: we were all Taus, tried and true.

"Except one of us," Trevor confided, taking a long hit from the pipe.

Amanda and I stared at him. The moonlit dormer room was quiet enough that I could hear a train sound its whistle all the way from the Canadian Pacific tracks a mile north. "Who?" Amanda asked.

"A guy who was assigned to the tranche just a couple of weeks ago. He replaced Jody Carmody, who's moving to Lunenburg, something to do with her job. Tonight would have been his first official meet-up. I ran the test on him myself. He seemed a little nervous at the time, but I didn't give it much thought. But Lisa told me last night he came up as a ringer. Near enough to pass in the social sense, but definitely outside what they call Tau phase space." The cluster of characteristics that defined Tauness.

"So how'd he get assigned to a tranche?"

"InterAlia tested him, right? So it's possible they might have slipped in a ringer. Somebody who could report back to them about Tau politics."

"You think that's what this was?"

"I went to see the guy this morning, give him the bad news. He was already gone. His apartment had been cleared out overnight. So yeah, he knew. It wasn't anybody's innocent mistake. Somebody sent him to infiltrate us."

"InterAlia?"

"Possibly. In which case it would have to have been set up before InterAlia went bankrupt. So of course the guy buggered off—he was already redundant."

Amanda looked thoughtful, the icy light glinting in her eyes. "So if he wasn't actually a Tau . . . did Lisa say whether he qualified as anything else?"

"He was pushing several categories. Almost a none-of-the-above result. But he would have qualified as a Het, if only just."

I thought about all the half-true stereotypes, fodder for countless stand-up comics and video sitcoms. Wealthy, pot-smoking Taus. Indolent, cheerful Zens. Sex-crazed, bisexual Delts. And stern, efficient Hets, with their complex pecking orders and finely graded hierarchies. Their creased trousers and their businesslike expressions.

All of which was bullshit, but bullshit with a kernel of statistical truth. Most of the stereotypes had emerged from journalistic overstatement of the earliest sociological studies of the Affinities. As a Tau I was in fact a few percentage points more likely to be a regular cannabis user than someone from the general population, and our comparative business acumen was a matter of public record. And it was probably also true that Hets were quantifiably more likely to be overcontrolling, know-it-all dicks.

Which, in the world as we had known it, hardly mattered. All the Affinities shared the same goal: to bring together people selected for their mutual compatibility. Hets weren't all hopeless assholes, or they wouldn't have been able to leverage their own not-inconsiderable worldly success. (Tau and Het were the top-earning Affinities.) And Het wasn't a problem for Tau, as long as the Affinities weren't competing against one another. But that was in the old days, when InterAlia called the shots and made the rules. New rules now.

"It's the Wild West," Amanda said. "We need to be a lot more careful. Watch our backs."

She had talked about this at length with Damian. The general scenario was pretty simple, she said. With the availability of cheap, portable testing, the population of the Affinities was about to explode. And not just in North America and Europe, but in places that had been legally closed to Affinity testing, like Russia and China. And without InterAlia to enforce the rules, non-aligned people were likely to sense their disadvantage and agitate for greater oversight. Whether the Affinities survived would depend on whether we could influence the inevitable legislation. "Because if we don't," she said, "we'll be driven underground, like terrorist cells or something. And given the huge number of people involved? We could be looking at something like civil war."

"Bullshit," Trevor said. "Civil war?"

"Of one kind or another. I mean, look at what Tau does for us. TauBourse is like Social Security, and we have a Tau medical network that takes care of us whether we're insured or not. Now Damian says we need a permanent security force and a fair way of making Affinity rules, so no tranche or sodality feels cheated or left out. That's an army and a parliament, basically. Those are government functions. And governments tend to be jealous of their power."

"Sure," Trevor said, "but even if they pass laws against us, I can't see Taus taking up arms."

"Maybe not Tau. Other Affinities might, and that could make life difficult for all of us."

She didn't say which other Affinities she had in mind. But the Hets, or some faction among them, had already taken up arms. One Het soldier was dead, his body entrusted to the tidal currents of Georgia Strait, and we had discovered what may have been a Het spy in our midst. If there was a war coming, the first shots had already been fired.

———

But there was more than that on Amanda's mind. She needed to tell us something, and it was something we didn't want to hear, and both Trevor and I had figured that out. Her attention kept drifting to the ice-covered window, as if she saw something unsettling there.

"It's all going to change," she said. "That's what I've been talking about with Damian."

Back when he was young my stepbrother Geddy used to get what he called "the Sunday night feeling." Neither of us had much liked school. Friday afternoon was great, the whole inchoate weekend in front of you, and Saturday was also fine, twenty-four hours of distilled freedom. Even Sunday morning was okay, as long as Mama Laura didn't insist on church, and Sunday afternoon flowed as sweetly as an autumn creek. But by sunset you could feel the ominous weight of the week ahead. The homework you hadn't finished, the book report you hadn't written.

I had spent seven years in the Tau Affinity, and it had been the longest, happiest weekend of my life. But suddenly I had the Sunday night feeling.

"We're like the Lost Boys," she said. "You know? *Peter Pan*. But it's time to grow up."

Even worse.

"We have to take responsibility for ourselves. Lay down a foundation and build some walls. Damian's already doing that. And he's not the only one. He's been conspicuously successful, but there's somebody like Damian in almost every tranche. Dozens of them in the Canadian sodality and hundreds in the US, just waiting to be organized. Damian's calling a meet-up in February, in California, to start discussions. He expects to devote the next few years to creating a Tau political structure."

"Great," Trevor said, not quite ironically. "What about us?"

"He still needs us," Amanda said. "Maybe more than ever." She turned to face Trevor. "We're going to need people to organize and run a Tau police force. Damian wants you to be one of them."

Trev didn't say anything. He was startled, clearly. Flattered, but also freaked out by the idea. Amanda didn't wait for an answer. She turned to me.

"You have different skills. Good memory, you can follow instructions, you can improvise if you have to, and you know how to interface with people who aren't Tau."

That seemed dubious. I thought of Rachel Ragland. My interface with Rachel had not been a raging success. "Which makes me what?"

"A diplomat," Amanda said.

"You must be joking."

"Actually I'm not. But you need to talk to Damian. He can explain it better than I can."

I said, "And how about you? Does he have plans for you yet?"

She looked at the window again. "I'm going to California with him."

Which was how I found myself, long after the end of the party, sitting at the kitchen table telling my troubles to Lisa.

The rest of the tranche had gone home. Those who lived in the house had retired to their rooms. Loretta was upstairs, asleep. But Lisa had always been a night owl. I think she liked the quiet of the hours before dawn, the house restored to order, the dishes washed. She looked tired but content. I told her about what Amanda had said, and about the choice Amanda had made, and Lisa nodded. "Things change," she said. "I know, that's terribly trite. A static existence is impossible, and who would want such a thing? But change comes at a price, doesn't it? And we all pay in full, sooner or later."

She was probably thinking of Loretta, whose health had been

fragile lately. I had come to Lisa for sympathy, but that began
to seem like a dickish move on my part. I said, "I'm sorry if I—"

"Oh, stop. Don't apologize. There's no reason we can't com-
miserate together." She sat back in her chair and gazed around
the cooling kitchen. "Winter nights like these, I think of what's
changed over the years. Even in our tranche. I think about the
people who've moved on."

Plenty of us had, even in the seven short years since I had
joined. People took new jobs, went to live in different cities,
joined different Tau tranches. And they were always replaced
by new faces, new friends. Tau was a river. I said, "That includes
some of the people I met the first time I showed up here. Remember Renata Goldstein?"

"Of course. Yes. And her girl, the one with Down syndrome."

"Tonya."

"Yes, Tonya. She used to hide out in the basement and watch
cartoons."

"*SpongeBob SquarePants.* With the sound turned off."

"That's right. And you used to sit with her. Until Renata left
the tranche, what, four years ago now? Five?"

"Moved out west, didn't she?"

"Mmm . . . that's what she told people. Actually she's still in
town. I ran into her on the subway last February."

I was surprised. "Really?"

"She quit the tranche and never joined another one."

"What—did she drift?"

"Drift" was a problem buried in the fine print of Affinity test.
The human brain and the human mind were malleable. Affinity scores tended to be robust, but they could change over time;
it was possible for someone who was only barely a Tau to drift
out of the range of qualification altogether, and InterAlia had
always mandated five-year retests. The phenomenon was thank-
fully rare—in my years with Tau I had heard of only one case of
terminal drift in the city, a suburban car wash owner who failed

to re-up and was forced to leave his tranche, tears all around—
but it was a terrifying concept.

"Perhaps she drifted," Lisa said. "More likely it was just family conflict. *Tethers.*" Lisa pronounced the word with audible
scorn. "Usually it's a spouse. In Renata's case the tether was that
girl. The girl was Renata's tether."

"Not her *tether*, Lisa. Her *daughter*."

Lisa gave me hard look. "Yes, of course. The tether was her
daughter."

She pushed her chair away from the table and stood up slowly,
wincing. "I'm going to bed. You should do the same, Adam. You'll
feel better when you've closed your eyes for a while."

We didn't know it yet, but it was the beginning of the hard years.
The harrowing of the Affinities.

PART THREE

Tranche Warfare

Have we reached a new stage in the peculiar history of the Affinities?

It's been just a quarter of a century since the science of social teleodynamics discovered new ways to model the boundary between consciousness and culture. And it was only a few years after the field's founding that one of its most prominent figures, Meir Klein, traded the classrooms of Tel Aviv University for the corporate corridors of a then-obscure data-mining firm called InterAlia.

It must have seemed like a smart move, back in the day. InterAlia used Klein's theories to launch the Affinities in North American markets, and both Meir Klein and the people he worked for grew very rich indeed. For a while. Until Klein was strangled in his sleep and InterAlia collapsed under the weight of the class-action suits brought against it.

Anybody remember how seductively fashionable the Affinities once seemed? Klein named the twenty-two Affinity groups after the letters of the Phoenician alphabet, for no better reason than that he was friendly with a colleague who taught ancient Near Eastern literature, and suddenly everyone was reciting those syllables as earnestly as Proto-Canaanite schoolchildren: Eyn, Pey, Qof, Rosh. And of course the biggies, Tau and Het. Some of us were bold or curious enough to take the test. Some of us qualified to join a local tranche. And some of us didn't, and some of us envied those who did, as if they had been admitted to an exclusive fraternity, the one all the cool kids belonged to.

Yes, it was like that. Really.

A few years more and it became obvious that the pitch about how people "cooperate more successfully" inside the Affinities wasn't just a come-on. Some of the Affinities were cooperating themselves into big money by way of entrepreneurship or investment. Outsiders weren't invited to that party, either. And we did begin to feel very much like outsiders, those of us who failed to pass the test or who refused to be tested. We all knew someone who had vanished into the black hole of an Affinity group and no longer had the time or patience to show up for the cousin's wedding or the niece's bat mitzvah. Some of us were angry enough to join advocacy groups like NOTA (None of the Above) or, less formally, to get up in the faces of strangers who declared their allegiances a little too smugly. Amazing how a few well-publicized swarmings and knife fights brought the long sleeves down over those old Het or Wau tattoos. Big profits for the laser-tattoo-removal industry—and for tattoo artists who know how to hide a Phoenician letter under even more elaborate skin art. (Have you ever wondered how many thirty-somethings are walking the streets with a delt hidden in their dragon or a tau concealed in their pot leaf?)

Cheap, quick, universal Affinity testing—and the publication of Klein's teleodynamic source code—saved the Affinities from the financial collapse of InterAlia. But it also created the Affinities as we know them today: circled wagons in a hostile desert, sometimes locked in fierce intergroup conflict. Tranche warfare, so to speak. Het is to Tau as Hatfield is to McCoy, insiders say, and rumor has it that actual bullets have been exchanged, though both groups deny it.

Social-tech regulatory bills currently before Congress will either defang the Affinities or delete them altogether, depending on which version of the legislation passes. It remains to be seen whether the remnants of Klein's Affinities can survive the rigors of government oversight and increasingly stringent tort law.

But an even more serious challenge to the Affinities may be lurking on the horizon. People have been playing with the teleodynamic data by which Klein invented the original Affinity *groups. There are other ways of interpreting those numbers, these people say. Other ways of sorting the human socionome. Radical new teleodynamic algorithms have been proposed and are currently being tested.*

We've learned too much about ourselves to go back to the old ways. But how do we connect with one another, post-Affinities? That remains an open question. And, potentially, a very scary one.

—Editorial, "Groupthinking," NewYorkNewsSite.org

Meir Klein identified cooperation as the keynote human skill, and he sorted humanity's best cooperators into twenty-two hypercollaborative groups, the Affinities. It was his hope that these networked hypercollaborators would act together to further human progress.

But having your hand on a lever means nothing unless you know which way to throw it. The capacity to do work is only as important as the work we do.

New Socionome has designed powerful new outcome-directed social algorithms, open-sourced and freely available. Telos is the Greek word for "purpose" or "goal." You might say we're putting the telos back in teleodynamics. Inventing a better world, one hookup at a time.

—*New Socionome Manifesto* (Cambridge/Shahjalal draft)

CHAPTER 12

One January night when I was sixteen years old my stepbrother Geddy came into my room, terrified for no apparent reason.

When the sound of his anxious breathing woke me, my first thought was that something was wrong in the house: a fire, a break-in, somebody was sick. A glance at the window showed winter darkness and a lacework of ice and a few snowflakes drifting past the fogged glass, as the clock on my nightstand ticked from 4:10 to 4:11. "Geddy?" I said. "What the fuck?"

"You shouldn't swear," he said.

Geddy was a month shy of ten and still very much under the influence of Mama Laura, for whom even "hell" and "damn" were forbidden words. I told him that if he wanted to wake me up in the middle of the night he should brace himself for the possibility of a curse or two. Then I said, "So what's wrong? Bad dream?"

It was a reasonable guess. Geddy suffered from chronic bad dreams. He was also an occasional bed-wetter, though the flap of his PJs looked dry tonight. He was pretty amorphous in his pajamas: a heavy kid, clumsily proportioned, strands of hair pasted to his forehead with sweat. Mama Laura kept the house swelteringly hot in winter. The furnace was roaring like a chained dragon down in the basement.

"Can I ask you a question?" His voice was plaintive.

"Can't you ask Mama Laura?"

He hung his head. "No."

"Why not?"

"I'd wake up Daddy Fisk."

Fair enough. My father was pretty touchy. Geddy was still getting used to his hair-trigger temper. Dad had not yet uttered an unkind word to or about his new wife in the six months they had been married, but his attitude toward Laura's son Geddy was increasingly impatient. If Geddy was reluctant to wake the old man with a question, I couldn't blame him.

Nor could he have gone to my brother Aaron. Aaron resented the way the family had changed since Dad's second marriage. He was polite to Mama Laura—Aaron was too fond of being the old man's firstborn and favorite son to put that status at risk. But he was only barely cordial to Geddy, and only when he thought he was being watched. When he figured the rest of us were out of earshot he could reduce Geddy to tears with a few choice words.

"Okay," I said, "ask."

"Can I sit on the bed?"

"Is that the question?"

He was impervious to irony. "No."

"Okay, sit. If you're dry."

He blushed. "I'm dry."

"Okay then."

He perched at the foot of the bed. I felt the mattress compress under his weight. "Adam," he said, "is the world *old* or is it *young?*"

He stared at me intently, waiting for an answer.

"Jesus, Geddy, is *that* what's bugging you?"

"Please don't swear!"

"What's the question even *mean*?"

He frowned even harder and groped for an explanation. "It's like, is everything all used up? Is history almost over? Or is it just getting started?"

Crazy little guy. I had no real idea what he was talking about it, but he wanted an answer so badly I felt obliged to give him one. "Jesus, Geddy—sorry—but how should I know? I guess it's kind of in the middle."

"In the middle?"

"Not so old it's finished. Not so young it's new."

"Really?"

"Sure. I guess. I mean, that's how it seems to me."

He thought it over, and finally he smiled. I didn't think I'd solved the problem for him—whatever his problem was—but I seemed to have made it easier for him to bear. "Thank you, Adam."

"You're incredibly weird, Geddy."

I had said those words often but I always said them affectionately, and Geddy's smile widened. "You too," he said. As always.

"Go to bed now, 'kay?"

"Okay," he said.

Neither of us would mention the conversation in the morning. Nor would we report to anyone in the family. Geddy probably figured I would forget about it altogether.

But I didn't, and neither did he.

Four years had passed since I had sat with Amanda Mehta and Trevor Holst in an attic room in our tranche house in Toronto, confronting a future we could barely comprehend. Many things had changed since then.

For one, I was wearing an absurdly expensive suit. For another, I was in New York City. For a third, I was doing something I was good at.

But I was not, at the moment, doing it very successfully.

I sat in a midtown restaurant opposite a woman I had met more than once, for professional reasons, since that night in Toronto. The woman's name was Thalia Novak. She was in her forties, skinny, with a narrow face and a halo of tautly curled hair. She wore a green blouse and a necklace of strung glass beads the size of playground marbles. Thalia was a sodality rep for the Eyn Affinity, and I had a feeling she was about to deliver some bad news.

But we shared dinner first, like civilized people. I supposed it was even possible she might change her mind as we talked, if the decision in question had not already been taken at some higher level of the Eyn hierarchy. I was acting as a Tau negotiator, fully empowered to make a deal on behalf of the North American sodalities, and Thalia was my opposite number.

The restaurant was fairly new. By the look of it and the faint smell of sawdust and plaster, it had opened or been remodeled within the last few weeks. The prices were high and the customer count was low—we very nearly had the place to ourselves. I guessed most folks were home, checking screens to find out whether Pakistan and India had graduated from conventional warfare to the thermonuclear variety. The food was good, maybe because the chef wasn't juggling a lot of orders. Thalia had ordered salmon and I had ordered paella, both on Tau's tab. The Eyns were a small Affinity with no financial superstructure and very little collective wealth, and it didn't hurt to remind her of that.

I let her talk through dinner. The stereotype was that Eyns loved to talk and that they were a little goofy. I liked Thalia— we had negotiated complex inter-sodality covenants on a couple of other occasions, most notably when Eyn and Tau organized opposition to an insurance-reform act that threatened Affinity-based pension funds—but she wouldn't have overturned anyone's preconceptions about her Affinity. She told me she had just started a course in "tantric flexing," an exercise routine with some kind of spiritual component. She said it made her feel more centered. I wondered if it made her feel better about backing out of her Affinity's commitment to Tau.

I raised the question over dessert, in the bluntest possible way. "If you sign this agreement with Het, you know you'll be out of the Bourse."

She raised her napkin to her mouth and then folded it over the remains of her raspberry zabaglione. "I do understand that. Obviously, it's an important concern for us."

Four years ago Damian Levay had opened up TauBourse to investors representing other Affinities. To date, we had created rock-solid pension funds for twelve of the extant Affinities. The Eyns could certainly pull out their money and invest it elsewhere. But TauBourse had outperformed benchmark Wall Street funds for all our members, and by a wide margin, in part because we invested preferentially in Tau-operated enterprises. Leaving Tau-Bourse would have an immediate financial downside for Thalia's Eyns.

But she was still talking. "We see potential legal issues with the Bourse, though, Adam. We're not sure it's a stable, sustainable business model."

"It's perfectly stable, unless the Griggs-Haskell bill passes."

"Which looks increasingly likely, however."

"More than just likely, if you throw the support of Eyn behind it."

"We're not a political Affinity. You know that."

"But Het is. And if you back them up—"

"If we back them up, and if Griggs-Haskell passes, and if the president signs the bill, we'll be better off if our money *isn't* tied up in TauBourse. That's the bottom line."

"Did Garrison tell you that?"

"I can't talk about what I discussed with Vince Garrison."

Vince, not *Vincent*. She was already on familiar terms with the Het negotiator. That was when I realized she was trying to let me down easy. Which meant Eyn had already secured an accord with Het.

"I'm sorry, Adam," she said. "I like you personally. You've been more than fair to me and to the Affinity I represent. I do appreciate that. But you have to understand, it's an existential issue for us. Even if the Griggs-Haskell bill doesn't make it out of the Senate, some kind of legislation is inevitable. Sure, I'd prefer the kind of legislation Tau would write. And I know the Hets are jockeying for king-Affinity status. But it was only three weeks ago that the Russians blamed Tau for its role in the attempted coup—"

"It was a revolution, not a coup. And Tau's role has been exaggerated. We don't really have a huge footprint in the Russian Federation."

"No, and it won't be getting any bigger, will it?"

"United Russia is running an authoritarian regime. Are we supposed to collaborate with it?"

"Het did."

"Het kissed Valenkov's ass. Repeatedly. Until he gave them everything they wanted."

"What Het did was eminently practical. Call it realpolitik if you like—it carved out a space for the Affinities in a closed society."

"Except for Tau."

"Well, yes."

"What does that tell you?"

"It tells me the writing is on the wall. Do you know the story from the Old Testament? It's where the saying comes from. King Belshazzar stole the sacred vessels from Solomon's Temple and used them to praise false gods. A disembodied hand wrote on the wall: *Mene, mene, tekel, upharsin*. It meant Belshazzar's days were numbered. He was killed by Persian soldiers the same night. Moral of the story, there's nothing to be gained from signing up with the wrong god, even for a short-term benefit. Gods are jealous, and gods remember. And right now, Tau is the wrong god."

She stood up. I stood up. She gave me her hand. "The world's moving on, Adam. Tau can't stand still. Compromise or be left behind. That would be my advice to you."

"I guess Eyn's famous concern for social justice only goes so far."

"Don't make this worse. You're alone in a world of trouble, and you know it." She turned away, then turned back. "Thank you for dinner. It was very good."

I called Trevor from the sidewalk outside the restaurant. This early on a Thursday evening midtown should have been crowded, but the street was mostly empty. "How was dinner?" he asked.

"The restaurant was lucky to have us. The city feels like a ghost town."

"Otherwise?"

"No joy," I said. "So it looks like Plan B."

Which meant we were heading for Schuyler, New York. My old hometown. To do something that would tear my family apart.

CHAPTER 13

We got on the road in the morning. Trev took first turn at the wheel. It was a warm day in late May, pretty enough to make our troubles seem distant. Once we left the city the road wound through farmland and fallow fields where faded exit signs announced the names of equally faded small towns, and Trev cracked his window and let in a breeze that smelled of alfalfa and manure, and sunlight swayed across the dashboard as the road curved west and north.

Somewhere behind us was a second vehicle, a van, with six of Trev's security guys in it. They were keeping a protective eye on us. So were various Taus along the route, locals alerted to watch out for suspicious or unusual vehicles. We didn't really expect trouble. But we took precautions: there had been trouble in the past. In February a delegation of English Taus from a Manchester tranche had been run off the road and killed as their bus passed through the Lake District—no charges were laid, but we had reason to suspect the work of a Het undercover team. A month later one of our sodality leaders had been found dead in his hotel room in Chicago. Again, no actionable evidence, but the victim had been about to finalize an agreement that would have allied us with the Res Affinity and disadvantaged Het. And we had known for years that Het was capable of extreme action. The scar Amanda Mehta still carried was evidence of that.

It was possible but not likely that a Het team might follow us to Schuyler. I had good personal reasons to visit the town. Sure, there would be a sitting congressman in Schuyler at the same time. Yes, that congressman would soon be casting a potentially decisive vote on the Griggs-Haskell bill. And yes, I would be meeting that congressman face-to-face.

But none of that was surprising, given that the congressman was my brother.

On the road to Schuyler I took one call and made another.

The call I took was from Damian Levay, from the Laguna Beach property he shared with Amanda. I docked the phone to the dashboard port and tilted it toward me. Damian frowned out of the tiny screen, and beyond him I could just make out the suggestion of a balcony railing and the blue sweep of the Pacific in early-morning sunlight. I told him we were on our way to Schuyler. He said, "I just want to make sure you're okay with this."

"If Jenny's okay with it, I'm okay with it."

"That's good. But things are never really simple, though, are they? When it comes to family."

He said the word *family* with a faintly disparaging emphasis. Non-Tau family, he meant. Biological family. Family as tether.

"It's not a one-way deal. She helps us, we help her."

"If we succeed, you probably won't be going back to Schuyler for any more family reunions."

Meaning I would probably never speak to my brother or my father again, after this weekend. But it wasn't as if we spoke much now. It wasn't as if I stood to lose much in the way of happy familial intimacy. Tranche or family: I wasn't the first Tau to face the choice.

And Damian knew that. There was something else on his mind. It wasn't about my family, it was about me. Damian was a sodality leader now, and he had assigned me diplomatic duties because he believed I had a knack for dealing with non-Taus, a little extra dollop of empathy or something: supposedly, the trait showed up in my Affinity-test numbers. But that could cut two ways. A little sympathy for those outside the tribe was a useful thing, as long as it didn't generate dangerous mixed loyalties.

But I understood what I was getting into, and I reassured him of that. Going back to Schuyler wasn't "going home." I had just one real home, the home I retreated to whenever possible, a house in Toronto (Lisa's house, since Loretta's death last year), where there was a room set aside for me, folks who genuinely loved me, no simmering rivalries, no hidden sexual violence . . . "I just hope what we do this weekend makes a difference."

"It will," Damian said. Then he looked away from the screen and looked back. "Somebody wants to say hi."

Amanda.

The last few years hadn't much changed her. The same hair, shiny as the wings of a perfect black bird; same flawless skin, the color of coffee with cream; same sharp, observant gaze. Time had left subtle marks, ghosts of expressions that had lingered long enough to set, a hardness of purpose where there had been a playful openness, resolve where there had been uncertainty. But the smile she gave me was eternal. "Hi, Adam," she said.

We hadn't talked much since her marriage to Damian. Not out of any awkwardness, just lack of opportunity. She had moved to California with Damian; I had stayed in Toronto. She was a sodality leader, I was just a functionary. She had made it clear, as had Damian, that although the marriage solemnized a real commitment, it didn't mean she and I were finished. But we saw each other far less often than we once had. And to be honest, I was a little uncomfortable about sleeping with a married woman.

Not because the relationship was immoral but because it was brutally asymmetrical.

So we said pleasant and inconsequential things to each other for a couple of minutes and finished the conversation with smiles that were genuine but seemed weirdly distanced from the present crisis. Then Damian got back on the line.

"One more thing. And this is for Trevor as much as it is for you. We've got information that there's a Het security detail en route to Schuyler."

I relayed this news to Trev, who gave me a look signifying something like: "Whoa—really? *Why?*"

"I can't tell you anything more than that. It might be they want to keep an eye on Congressman Fisk prior to the vote. Or it could be more sinister. So keep your guard up, right?"

Right.

Getting closer to Schuyler, as farmland gave way to scrubby forest and outcrops of glacial debris, I called my father's house.

A voice call, not a video call. Neither Mama Laura nor my father believed in paying good money for a little extra bandwidth. The last time I'd been there, the phone had been a landline with a clunky handset. My father carried a contemporary phone for business purposes, but he had never given me the number.

"Adam!" Mama Laura exclaimed. "So good to hear your voice! Where are you?"

"Just a few miles out of town, actually."

"Wonderful! Your old room is all ready for you. You're not the first to arrive—Aaron and Jenny aren't here yet, but can you guess who is?"

"Geddy?" I hoped it was Geddy. I hadn't seen Geddy for years, but he still called from time to time.

"Yes, Geddy! And he brought a friend!"

"Oh?"

"A girl friend." I could hear the pause she put between the two words: she wasn't sure whether the girl friend was in fact a girlfriend. "Her name is Rebecca. Rebecca Drabinsky. She's from New York City, one of those places in New York you read about, I don't know, Brooklyn? Queens? I forget."

This was Mama Laura's way of telling me two things. One, Geddy's new friend was Jewish; and two, Mama Laura was okay with that. Which suggested to me that my father *wasn't* okay with it, and that Mama Laura wanted to get her own opinion on record before any controversy erupted.

"I look forward to meeting her."

"She's quite a character! But I like her. Can you still find your way to the house or do you need directions?"

"I could find it in my sleep."

"That's good. I can't wait to see you! And I can tell you Geddy's very excited, too."

And still not a word about my father. "What time do you want people arriving for dinner?"

"You're welcome anytime. Say five o'clock if you want to freshen up first?"

"Five it is."

I ended the call and Trevor drove a few more miles. We passed what I recognized as the quarry road, winding into a patch of wild scrubland where you could break your leg tripping over glacial till or stumbling into some ancient kettle hole buried in the duff. "Family," Trevor said philosophically. "Remember what Robert Frost called it? The place where, when you have to go there, they have to take you in."

"Doesn't always work that way," I said.

We approached the outskirts of Schuyler. There was the usual strip of highway-exit businesses—gas stations and fast-food franchises—and then a couple of motels, sparsely populated. We could have stopped there, but Trev wanted accommodations closer to town. That left two obvious choices, a Motel 6 just off the main drag or a Holiday Inn a little farther north. Trev started to pull into the Motel 6 but paused before making the turn. We could see most of the parking lot in front of us, cars fronting a two-story row of rooms with doors painted Pepto-Bismol pink. "Huh," he said, and pulled back into traffic.

"What?"

"You see that? In the lot? Four black Chevy SUVs, identical models."

"So?"

"Those are Het cars, bet you any money. And I'd rather not share accommodations with Het enforcers if I can help it."

So he registered at the Holiday Inn. He talked to the concierge about arranging a rental car, and I took the vehicle we had come in. Alone on the drive to Mama Laura's, I turned on the radio and tuned in a news site. The announcer was using solemn words like "international crisis" and "ultimatum," but nobody had actually nuked anybody. Yet.

CHAPTER 14

Polite commentators liked to call the state of affairs between Tau and Het a "rivalry." In reality it was a fight—a fight for the future of the Affinities. Tau wanted to preserve and defend what Meir Klein and InterAlia had created. Het wanted to take absolute control of it.

Het was winning.

Het had about as many members as Tau, according to a recent census, and we were the most populous of the twenty-two Affinities. So we brought roughly equivalent numbers to the field, but Het had an immediate advantage: in sociodynamic terms, Het was *monohierarchical*. Which meant it possessed a *single hierarchy*: just one rigorously denominated chain of command, one leader, stacked ranks of followers. It was a classic form of human collaboration: horizontal equality among members of any rank, but top-down decision-making. Usually that takes a certain amount of policing and coercion, but the genius of Het is that its members tended to fall into place as neatly as Tetris pieces. The result was a kind of instinctive monarchy. They didn't call him that, but the Hets had a king: I had seen him in passing, during sodality negotiations. His name was Garrison, and when Garrison said jump, Het jumped.

Tau, on the other hand, was *polyhierarchical*. When we did the leader-follower thing, we did it to address some specific task or local problem. You want to put out a fire, you let the fire chief call the shots. You want to build a house, you defer to an architect and a carpenter. We had hierarchies, but we were constantly constructing and dismantling them, hierarchies like temporary circuits in a vast neural network.

It made us versatile, adaptable. It also made us loose and complex and slow, where Het was blunt and simple and fast.

And Het had brought blunt, simple weapons to the battlefield. Weapons like bribery and expensive lobbyists, backroom threats and hired lawyers. Not to mention, should you step out of the light and into the shadows, actual guns and muscle. Whereas Tau had come to the fight like earnest Quakers, armed with little more than a love of justice and the power of persuasion. In brief, our asses had been kicked.

At least at first. Slowly, slowly, we were bringing our own weight to bear. We didn't punch with much strength but we knew how to swarm. How to find a vulnerable point and work it from many angles. How to crowdsource a counterattack.

One thing you look for is the unexpected connection: say, between a Tau member and a congressman who might be about to cast a critical vote.

Say, between me and my brother Aaron.

Then you look for an exploitable weakness. A troubled marriage, maybe, in which one partner has a great many secrets to keep.

Like Aaron's marriage to Jenny.

You find the weak point. Then you press until something breaks.

It was Mama Laura who had engineered this family reunion, and it was Mama Laura who answered the door when I knocked.

Late afternoon, and the sun was behind me. Sunlight came through the branches of the budding willow, and Mama Laura shaded her eyes as the door swung open. She gave me what she sometimes called her "big old welcome-home smile," but with a hint of uneasiness in it. "Adam," she said. Then, almost as an afterthought, she opened her arms and I hugged her. "Come on in," she said.

She had grown a little grayer and a little portlier in the years since I had left Schuyler, but time had been relatively kind. The same was true of the house itself, from what I could see from the entrance hall. Same carpet, same faded furniture, same heavy drapes, but all of it freshly scrubbed and dusted. The air smelled of wood polish and savory overtones from a slow roast sweating in the oven. "Geddy absolutely cannot wait to see you! He's up in his old room. And your father is upstairs, too . . . Can I get you something to wash away the road dust? We have lemonade, Coke . . ."

"I'm fine," I began to say, but I was interrupted by the pounding of footsteps on the stairs.

I doubt Geddy could have reached me any faster if he'd slid down the banister. He had never been good at concealing his feelings, and now he wasn't even trying. He had a grin as wide as his mouth could make it. He was practically laughing with pleasure. "Adam!" he said, and took me in an embrace that nearly bowled both of us over. "I heard the doorbell!"

"Hey, Geddy," I said.

He stood back. "You look great! You dress better than you used to."

Mama Laura and I both laughed. I wasn't wearing my thousand-dollar suit—it would have gotten me expelled from the house for the crime of pretension, I suspected—but I guessed a tailored shirt and wool pants looked upscale to Geddy. Geddy wore blue jeans with a checked cotton shirt tucked in at the waist, a style Mama Laura called "Walmart formal." He was thin enough to be called skinny these days: this was what had emerged from the chubby cocoon of his adolescence.

"Still playing the changes?" It was the question I asked whenever I talked to Geddy on the phone. Originally a reference to his music career, now a general-purpose what's-up.

"Still working at the warehouse," he said. "Mostly indoors now. I sit in with a band on weekends. Some guys I know. Trad jazz, but we're pretty tight. Rebecca says—but you have to meet Rebecca! She's in the basement, going through some old boxes—"

Mama Laura took my arm in a firm grip. "I think Adam should say hello to his father first."

It was why this reunion had been arranged, after all. It was why Geddy had come from Boston, it was why Aaron and Jenny had traveled from DC, and it was at least one reason why I was here.

My father had received his diagnosis last winter, but he had forbidden Mama Laura to share it with us until a month ago. Even then she had been reluctant to talk about the details, as if his disease were an intimacy she dared not discuss except in the most basic outline. Cancer. Inoperable. Stage IV. Originally in the lungs, now throughout the body.

He had refused chemo out of some combination of terrified denial and stoic acceptance. He said he felt fine, which meant his pain was mostly under control. His main symptoms, Mama Laura said, were debilitating fatigue and loss of appetite. Plus heightened irritability and moments of confusion.

I went upstairs to see him. He was in the bedroom he shared with Mama Laura, but he wasn't in bed; he was dressed and sitting stiffly upright in the upholstered chair by the window. The little video monitor on the dresser was babbling quietly away, but he had turned his face to the sunlight. Maybe he was appreciating the spring of a year that would likely not include, for him, an autumn or a winter.

"Adam," he said, swiveling to face me, putting his features in shadow. "Nice you could make it."

"Good to be here."

"Laura was real happy about you coming. She sets great store by family."

"You can tell by her cooking. The roast smells great."

"It's lost on me. I can't smell a damn thing anymore. Food tastes like sawdust and library paste."

"I'm sorry," I said.

"It's not your fault. It's not anybody's fault but God. You look like you're doing all right."

"More or less."

"Still working for your club?"

"It's not a club."

"Yeah, I know, it's been in the news. The Affinities. They got in everywhere, didn't they? Like Communists. Or Freemasons. You don't know who is one, unless they tell you. But you've obviously had some success at it. Good for you, I guess. It's just that we can't boast about it, the way we can boast about Aaron."

"Well, at least you can boast about one of your sons."

It occurred to me that I didn't know what to call him. When we were kids Aaron and I had been trained to call him "sir." But I hadn't addressed him as "sir" since the day he insulted Amanda. It was decades too late to start calling him "Dad." And if I had called him by his first name he would have considered it a shooting offense.

He gestured at the TV, a little Samsung panel at least twenty years old, and said, "All this shit going on."

"Anything new?"

"Is there ever? Bullshit threats from one side, bullshit threats from the other. Now and then a bomb goes off. Only difference this time is, the bombs are getting bigger. I guess I won't live to see who's left standing. I can't bring myself to feel much regret about that." He raised his hand—it shook a little—and smoothed the wing of graying hair that was supposed to disguise his baldness. The expression in his eyes grew vague. "I want to tell you something. While I'm thinking of it, before I forget. That's a problem these days, forgetting things."

"Okay. What is it?"

"You know I sold the business. Couldn't stand up to those chain-store bastards forever. So there's money. Enough to pay for my dying, enough to support Laura. And plenty left over. I had my lawyer draft a final will. Most of the money's going to Aaron. I'm sorry if you feel insulted by that. The thing is, Aaron has been around when you weren't. He doesn't need the cash, but he'll be a good custodian. I set up a trust fund for Geddy, and Aaron agreed to manage it. If it ever happens you fall on hard times, talk to Aaron—I told him to let you have whatever you need, if you really need it."

"Okay."

"Like I said, it's not an insult. I'm thinking of you. It's just that . . ." His words faded; maybe he lost track of the thought.

But I wasn't insulted, and I understood perfectly. The family was a hierarchy. My father had always been the indisputable boss. Aaron had never openly challenged that presumption, though I suspected he honored it only when he was within spitting distance of the old man. He performed the part of the dutiful son impeccably, whereas I had left Schuyler at the first opportunity and found myself a more congenial sort of family. That was the sin my father could never forgive.

"Okay," I said again.

"What?"

"It's fine. Whatever you want to do about your will, I'm okay with it."

"You just don't give a shit, huh?"

"I didn't say that."

"But it's what you meant."

"No." I took a step closer. Close enough to smell the illness on him. His body was starting to burn fatty acids as his illness advanced. The chemical products of the process included acetone, exhaled through the lungs. His breath smelled like nail polish remover. "What I meant was that you don't need to worry about me, and you aren't obliged to take care of me, and I don't expect anything from you."

"You haven't expected anything from me since you left this town."

Which was about absolutely true but not worth acknowledging. "I think I'll head on downstairs now. Will you be joining us for dinner?"

"I'll sit with you," he said. "I don't promise to eat."

As I approached the kitchen I heard Geddy talking with Mama Laura, a flow of happy conversation I was reluctant to interrupt. So I turned the opposite way and opened the door to the basement, where Geddy had said his friend Rebecca was sorting through boxes.

She looked up as I came down the steps. She was sitting on a pea-green folding chair, one of the set Mama Laura had retired from the backyard a decade ago, and she had her hands in a cardboard carton on which GEDDY'S THINGS was scrawled in enthusiastic black letters—Geddy's own printing, years old. The basement was as gloomy as it had ever been, raw drywall and exposed cinderblock, an elderly washer/dryer vented to the exterior world through a dusty aluminum port. Rebecca Drabinsky looked tiny, perched among the boxes in what we called "the storage corner." She stood up when she saw me. I said, "I'm Adam."

"Hi, yes!" Small body, small face, a pair of oval glasses that magnified her eyes, dark wirebrush hair that reminded me of a fox terrier one of my tranchemates owned. Off-brand sneakers, jeans, a black t-shirt under an unbuttoned flannel shirt. She would have looked at home in the cafeteria of any American university, sitting at a table with a book or tablet propped in front of her. "I didn't hear you at the door."

"I was just upstairs saying hello to my father. Geddy was going to introduce us, but he's busy in the kitchen. You're going through his old stuff?"

She nodded, a decisive bob of her head. "Geddy asked me to. To set aside anything I think is important and maybe organize it a little bit. He wants to take the best stuff back home. He'll go through it himself, of course. I just think he wanted me to see what he left here. Like, pieces of his life before he knew me."

I saw what she had selected and set aside on a yellow blanket thrown over the dusty concrete floor. Paperback books, including some I had given Geddy. Staff paper and practice sheets from when he was first learning to play the saxophone, plus some unused Vandoren reeds in their original boxes. A stack of Grammy Fisk's old LPs. What Rebecca was going through at the moment was a box of childhood drawings. I remembered Geddy's drawings: mainly fire trucks, tall buildings, and airplanes, meticulous as blueprints.

But she had a particular drawing in her hand, and she held it out to me. "You must have done this one."

I took it from her. It was a pencil sketch of Geddy when he was about ten years old, executed on yellowing printer paper. It was mine, but I barely remembered it. I must have drawn it out at the quarry, by the suggestion of trees and water in the background. Amateur as hell, but it caught a little of Geddy's wide-eyed gaze and big toothy grin.

"You must have said something funny, to get that smile out of him."

"It's a good smile. I used to tell him jokes, just to see him laugh."

"I know what you mean. When he's happy, it's just so— *wholehearted*."

I liked her for using the word. "How did you guys meet?"

"Well, that's kind of a story. I tell people I first saw Geddy when he was busking in the MBTA. Which is true, in a way. I must have passed him dozens of times on my way through Davis Station. But that's not really how I *met* him. You're a Tau, right?"

It wasn't exactly a polite question in the current social climate. But of course Geddy would have told her about me. "Yeah," I said warily. "Why?"

"No offense. I like Taus. I think they're the best Affinity. You know Geddy took the test, back when InterAlia was running it? He was really disappointed when he didn't qualify. Deep down, I think he wanted to be a Tau like you."

"It's not a question of failing, Rebecca. It's not that kind of test. I mean, it's too bad Geddy doesn't have an Affinity, but—"

"No, I know all about that; that's not my point. He envied what you found in Tau. He wanted what you had, and he never stopped looking for his own version of it. He bought a test kit when they came out, one of the old clunky ones with the scalp sensors. Just to make sure. He recorded his own teleodynamic profile. And that's how we met."

"I don't understand."

"New Socionome."

"Ah."

"An algorithm hooked us up." She watched my face. "You don't approve?"

"No, I just—I don't know a whole lot about it."

Which wasn't entirely true. I understood the general concept. Hackers and activist math geeks were trying to find new, non-Affinity ways of linking people together. Maybe that was useful for people like Geddy, who couldn't be sorted into a proper Affinity. But it had no relevance for me and I had pretty much ignored the phenomenon.

"Anyway, that's how we met. Geddy submitted his teleo profile to New Socionome. I was already registered. His name popped up on my linklist and we got in touch. He invited me to one of his weekend gigs. So that's how we *really* met—I was at a table in South End bar and Geddy was up on stage with a singer and a drummer and bass player and a rhythm guitarist. Under the lights he looked . . ." She laughed, a high happy sound. "Earnest and goofy and, I guess you know how he gets, kind of *outside of himself*. He came over after the set and we started to talk."

"So what do people talk about, when they've been introduced by an algorithm?"

"Making a better world," she said.

Upstairs, the afternoon was wearing on. Sunlight from the dining room window tracked over the big table as I helped Mama Laura set it. My father remained upstairs, and we were all conscious of the fact that he was mortally ill, but that didn't stop the talk or the laughter—it was therapeutic, not insensitive, and Mama Laura said at one point it might be doing him good, the sound of us all together down here, like the old days.

Around five o'clock the phone rang. Mama Laura had never replaced the slate-black landline phone my parents had owned when I was a teenager; picking up the handset, she looked like a character from a historical drama. It was easy to guess by her grin who was on the other end. "Aaron," she announced when the call ended. "He and Jenny just landed." At the Onenia County regional airport west of Schuyler, that would have been, probably on a chartered flight from DC. "They'll be here in forty-five minutes or so."

Geddy and Rebecca exchanged uneasy glances, by which I guessed Geddy had shared some of the family's less savory secrets with her. I excused myself, went into the bathroom, and took out my own phone. I called Trevor Holst at the Holiday Inn. "They're coming," I said.

"Okay. Keep me posted."

Five hours before the lights went out.

CHAPTER 15

Much later, I looked at some of the posts Rebecca Drabinsky had left on her own website and others. Some of what she had written struck me as prescient, and this is one of the passages I bookmarked:

> We are falling.
>
> Everything made of matter is falling. We call it entropy. Matter decays. Stars eventually stop shining; planets grow cold, or are scorched to embers which themselves grow cold. Matter falls, and sooner or later it hits bottom.
>
> Life is part of that process. Life is entropic. We dissipate the energy of the sun. Life is a falling-in-progress.
>
> What makes living things unique is that they are teleodynamic. By dissipating the sunlight stored in food we sustain ourselves at a level above our natural rest state, which is death. Our falling is an act of self-creation. We FALL FORWARD, as individuals and as a species.
>
> For most of the history of our species, the goals we fell toward were simple. Food to eat, food for our families,

food for our tribe. Shelter for ourselves, our families, our tribes. The imperatives of love and reproduction.

But in the contemporary world, for a significant proportion of the world's human beings, those basic needs have been met, if only partially and inadequately and unjustly. Under such circumstances, what does it mean to fall forward?

The Affinities were an attempt to harness and enhance the human genius for collaboration. And they succeeded . . . for those who qualified for membership. But the Affinities are a tribal model. Twenty-two pocket utopias, each with an entrance fee. Twenty-two Edens, and every Eden with a wall around it and with a crowd of hostile, envious outsiders peering in.

Because it's not enough just to favor collaboration. Collaboration is a means, not an end. Tribes devise goals that benefit the tribe, and tribes come into conflict. Endless Affinity warfare—or the capture of political power by any single Affinity—is not an outcome we should endorse or permit.

New Socionome works differently. The social nuclei we create are open and polyvalent. We make social molecules that hook up complexly and create the possibility of new emergent behavior. Our algorithms of connection favor non-zero-sum transactions, as the Affinities do, but they also facilitate long-term panhuman goals: prosperity, peace, fairness, sustainability. The arc of human history is long but our algorithms bend toward justice. We aren't just falling. We're FALLING FORWARD.

I was struck by what she had written because it explained much of what happened that weekend in Schuyler. And my role in it, and hers.

Aaron and Jenny arrived an hour before dinner, carried from the regional airport in one of the ancient black Lincoln MKTs the local taxi company passed off as limousines. Aaron rang the bell, he and Jenny were duly hugged and handshaken, and Mama Laura sent Geddy out to fetch their luggage: two identical hard-shell travel cases of a high-end German brand.

My elder brother had learned to carry himself with the kind of assumed authority people call "statesmanlike." Shoulders square, chin up. His hair was styled and streaked with gray at the temples. The gray didn't look natural, and I pictured him in front of a bathroom mirror, painting it on. Maybe a good move for an inexperienced junior congressman. His handshake was a quick, decisive squeeze. This, too, felt rehearsed. "Hey, little brother," he said.

"Hey back at you, Aaron."

Jenny gave me a hug. She lingered a moment before we broke apart, but I tried not to read anything into it. The obvious question was on my mind: was she still willing to do what she had offered to do?

But there seemed to be no uncertainty or indecision about her. The old tentative, soft-spoken Jenny—the it's-okay-with-me-if-it's-okay-with-you Jenny, the Jenny I had known and half-heartedly courted as a teenager—was gone. In her place was someone not just older but vastly more cynical. Her eyes were wary, her smile more mechanical than genuine.

Mama Laura called us to dinner as soon as Aaron and Jenny had dropped their bags and washed up: "You got here just in time!"

We took our places. The head of the table was empty until my father came shambling downstairs. He wore dress pants and a crisply starched white shirt, tragically loose on him now. We waited in silence until he had eased his body into the chair. He nodded at Jenny and gave Aaron what was probably intended as a cheery wink. "All right then," he said. "Let's eat."

"Not before the blessing," Mama Laura said. She asked Aaron to say some words, and he bowed his head and reminded the Lord that we were all thankful for what we were about to receive.

Four hours before the lights went out.

I harbored a faint hope that my father's illness had mellowed him, but there wasn't much evidence of that. True, there were no lengthy tirades, and for most of the meal it seemed as if he had abandoned his lifelong habit of correcting the opinions of others. He put a serving of Mama Laura's glazed ham and a mound of Mama Laura's candied sweet potatoes on his plate but did little more than poke at them with his fork. He looked at each of us in turn, rotating his gaze around the table, pausing at each face as if he needed to commit it to memory. Our talk was amiable but subdued and he listened to it with an unreadable expression.

Then, as the serving dishes made a second round, Rebecca asked him whether there was any news from India.

She knew he had been upstairs watching television news, and I guessed she meant to include him in the conversation. Full credit for good intentions, but I held my breath like everyone else at the table.

My father focused his eyes on her and pursed his lips in an expression of distaste. After a long moment in which the only sound was the screech of Geddy chasing peas across his plate with a fork, he said, "There are drones."

"Drones?"

"Yeah, drones, you know, pilotless aircraft?"

"I know what a drone is, but—"

"Probably Chinese. From their ships in the Arabian Sea."

"Surveillance drones?" The Indian government had been complaining about Chinese surveillance drones for weeks now; they had shot down a couple and put the wreckage on display.

"No. They're blowing things up. Big news."

That caught the attention of Aaron, who had recently been appointed to a House subcommittee on military affairs. He said, "Blowing *what* up?"

"Military installations. Whole cities, maybe. The TV people don't know anything. Communications are down all across the subcontinent."

"Jesus!" Aaron said. Mama Laura shot him an injured look. "I apologize for the language," he said, "but if things get really hot I might be called back to DC."

He started to reach for his phone. *"Aaron,"* Mama Laura said before his hand made it past his lapel.

"I should check my messages, at least."

"Did the people you work for have our home number?"

"Sure, but—"

"In that case, in the event of an emergency, the phone on the side table will ring. Until then, please enjoy your meal with the rest of us, no matter what's happening halfway across the planet."

It was not a negotiable demand. "Of course," Aaron said, though for the next few minutes he cast reflexive glances at the video screen in the next room, blank and silent in its corner. I couldn't help exchanging a look with Jenny. If Aaron's visit was cut short, we might have to change our plan. Or abandon it altogether.

But Rebecca's question seemed to have piqued my father's interest in her. "You're Geddy's girlfriend," he said, though they had already been introduced.

"That's one thing I am."

"I guess that means you're a *lot* of things."

"Aren't we all?"

"They tell me you belong to one of those Affinity groups?"

"Actually, no—"

"Adam here works for one. I forget which."

"He's a Tau," Rebecca said. "But I'm not a member of an Affinity, Mr. Fisk. I'm enlisted with New Socionome."

"Enlisted with *what* now?"

"New Socionome. It's kind of a global collective for designing new ways to connect people, outside of the framework of the Affinities."

"You're probably wise not to call it an Affinity, given that Aaron wants to pass a law against them."

"He means the Griggs-Haskell bill," Aaron said. "You've heard of it?"

"Of course," Rebecca said.

"It's just a way of regulating a troublesome and problematic business. I'm no fan of government regulation, but in this case it's necessary. I guess you approve of that, given that you've chosen not to join an Affinity?"

"Actually no," Rebecca said. "I don't approve of it. I think it's worse than unnecessary. As it's written, the bill would grant oversight powers to the largest Affinity, which is Het, which would just give an authoritarian Affinity even more political clout than it already has. It's a clusterfuck." She blinked into the silence that descended on the table. "Uh, sorry, Mrs. Fisk."

My father was less offended by her language than by her refusal to defer to Aaron. "How's *your* club work?"

"New Socionome's not a club. It puts together small circles of people in ways that enhance cooperation toward loosely defined long-term goals. Each circle has open valence, which means they can expand any way they want and include anyone they feel like including. It's like creating the grain of dust that nucleates a snowflake."

"My word," Mama Laura said, awed and bewildered in equal parts. "I've never heard it put that way."

My father said, "I guess it's not a particularly *exclusive* club. For years, the golf club here in town? You couldn't get in if you were a Jew. But they relaxed that rule."

Geddy flushed but said nothing. Rebecca seemed, not *startled*, exactly, but at a loss for words.

It was Mama Laura who finally spoke up.

"Charles," she said, in the tone she usually reserved for misbehaving children. She waited until she had my father's complete attention—a hostile, skeletal stare. "Charles, we all know you're ill. Believe me, *I* know it. The doctors told me exactly what to expect. I know what my duty is. I will feed you if necessary, clean you, see to your needs. Speaking plainly? I'll empty your bedpan when the time comes, and I don't expect to be thanked for it. But Geddy has come home with a new friend he wants us to meet. And I think she is a lovely person. And I am very happy for both of them. And it matters a great deal to me that my son is happy. So even though you're sick, and even though the fact of your sickness has tied the tongue of everyone else at the table, I won't let you ruin this meal as you have ruined so many others. Speak civilly or keep your mouth closed, because I mean to have a pleasant dinner this evening, with or without your help."

My father gaped at her, eyes like cueballs in pockets of crepepaper skin.

"There's peach streusel for dessert," she said. "Or ice cream, for those who don't like streusel. And I can start a pot of coffee as soon as everyone's ready."

The conversation veered into less nervous territory. Mama Laura asked Jenny about her mother. Jenny's father Ed Symanski had died a year and a half ago, of liver cancer. Her mom continued to live alone and in a condition of alcoholic dementia in the family house, which was falling into disrepair. Jenny had recently

been granted power of attorney and was in the process of relo-
cating her mother to an extended-care facility. There was a facility near Utica that was well regarded and prepared to deal with
Mrs. Symanski's alcoholism as well as her chronic confusion, but
the chances that Jenny's mom would move there without a fight
were slim to none.

That was all true, but it was also a convenient excuse for Jenny
to stay in Schuyler past the weekend, after Aaron would have
flown back to Washington. And once Aaron was out of the way,
Jenny could do what she had agreed to do for Tau. And for herself, of course. Mainly for herself. Incidentally for Tau.

My father had made no response to Mama Laura's rebuke.
He was silent during dessert but seemed more sleepy than sullen. After coffee he excused himself and allowed Mama Laura
to escort him upstairs. Aaron took a bathroom break, but his
hand was reaching for his phone even as he left the table. Soon
we could hear his voice from behind the door off the hallway,
terse unintelligible questions blurred by the echo of an enclosed
space.

"I think it would probably be okay to turn on the TV in the
living room," Jenny said, meaning it would be better to get some
news we could all share rather than insult Mama Laura by trawl-
ing our phones for information. Geddy located the remote and
pushed the button. The old panel lit up weakly, already tuned
to a news channel, a pixilated image of night over water with
lights in the sky. The newscaster's voice was offering carefully
hedged speculation: *according to the best available reports* . . . .
the fog of war . . . we cannot confirm . . .

Mama Laura came back downstairs, gave the TV a dubious
glance, and asked whether anyone might be willing to help with
the dishes. I volunteered. Dishwashing was traditionally a fe-
male task in my father's household, but he wasn't here to complain and Mama Laura accepted my offer with a smile. We were
drying the china when she asked me about Amanda: "That

girl from India you brought here years ago, do you still see her at all?"

"She's from Canada, not India. And she lives in California now, so I don't see her very often."

"Too bad. I liked her. I know you did, too. Is there anyone special at the moment?"

"I know a lot of special people."

"Yes, in your Affinity. But I meant someone, I guess you could say, *intimately* special. A girlfriend."

"Lots."

She toweled a chipped Noritake serving dish and set it in the drying rack. "That sounds kind of sad to me. Don't you ever wish you could just be with someone you love, as simple as that?"

"Is it ever as simple as that?"

A rueful smile. "Maybe not. And, Adam, let me say I never did believe what your father said about Tau, that it's all homosexuals and dope smokers."

"Well, not *all*," I said. "But we're well supplied with both."

"I'm not sure that's funny."

"I didn't mean it to be."

Three hours before the lights went out.

Aaron called us into the living room. He had been on his phone again, but he tucked it back into his pocket as we settled into chairs. Geddy left the TV on but turned down the volume so we could hear my brother's news.

"Okay," he said. "Mama Laura, I'm sorry, but we have to go back to Washington tonight. They're prepping a plane at the local airport, and the very next thing I have to do is call a cab."

"Is it as bad as that," Mama Laura asked, "what's happening in India?"

"No one's sure. There's absolutely no electronic communication of any kind coming out of the country right now. We think that's because Chinese malware took down all the telecom infrastructure—Internet nodes, telephone exchanges, satellites, and relay stations."

The Chinese were allied with Pakistan, and a small fleet of Chinese naval vessels had been parked in the Arabian Sea for weeks, but this was the first direct intervention by China, if that was in fact what had happened. "Most likely it's just a smokescreen," Aaron went on. "It's not that the Chinese are attacking India, more like they're drawing a curtain so Pakistan can stage an attack the rest of the world can't see. Maybe also limiting India's capacity to respond. We'll know more in a few hours, if our own communications aren't affected."

Rebecca said, "Why would they be?"

"Part of the smokescreen. Our own military has the finest surveillance satellites in the world, but about half of them have stopped talking to us. We've also got unexplained power grid problems in New York City, Los Angeles, Seattle. Some kind of highly engineered, cleverly targeted software virus, possibly bleeding over from the attacks on Indian infrastructure. And it might get worse before it gets better. That's why they need me in Washington. Congress is being recalled to convene an emergency session tomorrow morning."

Mama Laura said, "Are we in danger?"

"Nobody's bombing *us*, if that's what you mean. But an infrastructure attack is technically an act of war. Of course, the Chinese are denying responsibility. Nobody really knows where it goes from here. The situation will get better eventually, but it might get worse before it improves. Jenny, you need to pack the bags. I'll call a taxi."

"I'm not going," Jenny said.

We all stared at her.

"Not an option," Aaron said. "Travel's going to be disrupted. That's inevitable. If you don't fly back with me, you might be here a lot longer than you expect."

"All the more reason. I can't leave my mom where she is. Sooner or later she'll hurt herself. And . . . dealing with her won't be easy, but I'm psyched up for it now. Postponing it would be hard on both of us."

This was the moment, I thought. If Aaron suspected anything, Jenny's reluctance to leave would confirm his suspicions.

But he didn't so much as glance at me, and the look he gave Jenny was merely contemptuous. "Look, if that's what you want . . . ."

"It's what I want."

"Well . . . I'll miss you, of course." This was for the benefit of the family. I gave Jenny credit for not rolling her eyes. "The rest of you, please try not to worry. This is very bad news for the folks in Mumbai, but the most it'll mean for Americans is a few days' inconvenience. I'll be in touch when I can."

"Go on up and say good-bye to your father," Mama Laura suggested.

"Right, of course," my brother said.

Another limousine pulled up out front and carried my brother away.

It was a clear night, moonless, cool but not cold. An hour later we could have stood in the backyard and watched his chartered plane cross the sky from the regional airport on its trajectory to DC, navigation lights strobing green and red in the darkness. Two hours later we could have stood in the same place and seen the Milky Way wheeling overhead like a scatter of diamond dust, free from any obscuring urban glare. Because that was when the lights went out.

CHAPTER 16

Growing up, I had never considered my brother Aaron to be a bad person.

A pain in the ass, sure. Often. And with an undeniable streak of cruelty. The first time I noticed that streak—the first time his meanness struck me as something characteristic about my brother, distinct from the usual schoolyard cruelties—was when I was nine years old and Aaron was a week shy of his twelfth birthday. We had been in the park adjacent to the school on a slow Saturday morning, me pitching softballs (pitching was my only athletic skill) and Aaron taking practice swings. Neither of us was likely to make the MLB draft, but I was drawing my own measure of smug satisfaction from Aaron's inability to hit my slider.

Also enjoying Aaron's swing-throughs was Billy-Ann Blake, ten years old, who lived three streets east of us and who was amusing herself by heckling from the otherwise empty bleachers. Billy-Ann was a tall, gawky girl whose parents let her run around in pink denim overalls. That morning, the summer sun hammering down from a silvery-blue sky, she repeated what must have been every scatological epithet she had ever overheard at the town's Little League tournaments, which was quite a catalog. Aaron was frustrated and embarrassed, and with every taunt from Billy-Ann his complexion turned a deeper shade of red. Finally he threw down the bat (*"Sore loser!"* Billy-Ann shrieked) and walked off the field, tossing a terse *see you later* in my direction.

I gathered up glove, bat, and ball and made my own way home. Aaron showed up around lunchtime, sweaty and sullen and uncommunicative.

Not long after lunch, Billy-Ann Blake's mom knocked at the front door. Mama Laura took her into the living room, and after a brief talk Aaron and I were called to join them. It seemed that Billy-Ann, after taunting Aaron, had been walking through one of the park's paved trails when she was pushed from behind, fell face-first into the asphalt, and suffered a spectacularly bloody broken nose. She was at the hospital with her father now, and although she hadn't seen who pushed her, she was certain it was Aaron Fisk.

Mama Laura asked Aaron whether this was true. Aaron gave her a somber, troubled look. "No," he said flatly. "I mean, Billy-Ann was watching us play ball, but we came right home from the park. Somebody else must have pushed her."

Mama Laura had spent the morning in the kitchen assembling her contribution to tomorrow's church bake sale and she had not paid attention to our whereabouts. She returned Aaron's stare without reaction. Then she turned to me. "Adam, is that so?"

I didn't hesitate. I knew what was expected of me. "Yeah," I said. "We came right back."

Billy-Ann's mom went away unsatisfied, and Mama Laura may have had her suspicions, but no more was said on the subject in the Fisk household. Because Aaron was gold. Firstborn son, pride of the family, star of the debating team . . . shitty on the baseball diamond, maybe, but a first pick for soccer and a rising star of the school's swim team. Sure, Aaron had been angry, and yeah, he had probably shoved Billy-Ann hard enough to break her nose.

But stuff like that happened. It didn't make him a bad person, did it?

And lying to protect him: that was just family loyalty. Even if Mama Laura started looking at Aaron a little differently from then on. Even if she spared some of those same glances for me.

Jenny Symanski spent plenty of time at our house in those days, but she never seemed to buy into our idolization of Aaron. Which was good. As far as I was concerned, the best thing about Jenny was that she liked me more than she liked my brother. Which is why, years later, even after I joined Tau, even after Jenny and I broke up, I was astonished when she married him. It was flattering to think she had settled for Aaron because she couldn't have me, but it was also possible that some kind of mutual attraction had smoldered away unacknowledged until they were in a position to act on it. And, well, why not? By that time Aaron was a college graduate, involved in the family business, and already catching the eye of the local Republican party elders; I was the standoffish art-boy geek who had traded his family for some kind of pretentious, dope-smoking social club.

Geddy stayed in touch with Aaron and Jenny more consistently than I did, and it was Geddy who had flagged the first signs of Aaron's abuse. He had hinted at it back when I was in Vancouver, but it wasn't until months later that he raised the subject in another phone call.

"He slaps her," Geddy had said. "Punches her sometimes. Maybe worse things."

"Really? You've seen this?"

"When I was staying with them. I mean, I didn't see it *happen*. But some nights I could hear the yelling. And in the morning she might have a bruise. Or she might be walking a little carefully, like something hurt. So I knew. And she knew I knew. She tried to talk about it sometimes."

Jenny had never been a complainer, but neither had she suf-

fered fools gladly. I asked Geddy why she didn't go to the police.

"She's worried Aaron could pull strings and get a complaint
shut down. And then it would be even worse for her. But she's
thinking about it."

One thing I had learned from watching my tranchemates
disentangle themselves from their tethers was that these things
don't get better all by themselves. "There are shelters," I said.
"There are people who can help her with legal problems.
Geddy, if she wants to talk to me, I'm sure I can set up a secure
line. Aaron wouldn't have to know about it."

"Okay," Geddy said. "I'll tell her that."

But I didn't hear from her. And a year later, Geddy said the
trouble had been resolved.

"Resolved how? They're still married, aren't they?"

"That was part of the deal. Jenny decided she needed evidence,
right? So she set up her tablet in the bedroom with the camera
recording video. Night after night, until she had all the evidence
she needed. Yelling, slapping, grabbing, hair-pulling—Aaron's
a hair-puller, did you know that? Including threats. What he'd
do to her if she tried to tell anyone and how he'd bankrupt her
if she left him. Because he's afraid of a public scandal."

And here was another aspect of Jenny's personality I had failed
to discern: this calculated stoicism, the ability to endure something terrible until she had devised a tool to end it. Twenty-five
minutes of video recording, Geddy said, which she had wisely
copied and stored in multiple locations. I pictured a thumb drive
in a safety-deposit box in some DC bank, an insurance policy
by any other name.

But still, she hadn't divorced him.

"That's part of the deal. She keeps the video to herself and
goes on pretending they're happily married. In return they lead
totally separate lives, separate bedrooms, separate vacations, he

pays her a monthly stipend and guarantees payments on her car, things like that. She hardly has to see him, except at public events."

"Not as good as a clean separation."

"It's what she wants, Adam. She feels like it gives her some power over him. She's saving all the money he gives her, in case he tries something. But he sees other women. What he calls discreet short-term relationships. Which Jenny says means high-priced hookers and bar pickups, basically."

And that was how things had stood until a couple of months ago, when Jenny herself had called me. She used Geddy's phone (he was in DC with his band), which meant she distrusted her own phone, which meant the situation with Aaron must have heated up again.

At first I didn't recognize her voice. Jenny had been a social smoker almost as long as I had known her, but her years with Aaron had ramped it up into a full-blown pack-a-day habit, and her voice was a charcoal drawing of the voice I remembered. It had lost its tentativeness, too. "A while back you told Geddy you'd be willing to help me. Is that right?"

I felt blindsided. "Of course. But I'm not sure—I mean—"

"I know Geddy told you about Aaron and me. So I don't have to rehash all that business, do I?"

I told her what I knew. "So you had an arrangement with Aaron—I guess something changed?"

"I want to go public," she said. "I want the video to go viral. But I can't just post it online. I need legal advice. And I need protection. I thought of you because I know Aaron has been cozy with the Het sodality, and I know Tau isn't okay with that."

This was when the Griggs-Haskell bill was being vetted in committee. Damian and other sodality leaders had been looking at how various congressmen were likely to cast votes. Aaron was one of the congressional reps who were firmly in the pocket of the Het lobby. He had benefited considerably from PAC funds we had traced to wealthy Het contributors. So yeah, Tau had an interest in seeing Aaron discredited, if it would affect his vote on Griggs-Haskell. Though I had a fleeting wish Jenny hadn't pitched it quite so bluntly. Clearly, she wasn't pinning her hopes on my own refined sense of moral duty.

"I can have a word with some people if you like. Can I ask what changed your mind?"

She paused, then said flatly, "Aaron's in what I guess you would call a long-term extramarital relationship."

"And you're not okay with that?"

"I don't give a rat's asshole about Aaron's affairs. Except . . . I've *met* this woman. She's someone perfectly trivial, but she shows up now and then on the cocktail circuit. She's reasonably good-looking but mousy and timid, which is how Aaron likes 'em. And lately I've noticed how she dresses. Long sleeves in summer. How she walks sometimes. I ran into her in a bathroom at the Blue Duck Tavern, putting makeup over what looked like a serious bruise. Doesn't take Sherlock Holmes to add it up."

"That's what changed your mind?"

"Well, yeah. Because I thought I had solved a problem. But I had only solved *my* problem. The real problem is Aaron. He's still out there, doing what he does. The only difference is that some other woman is feeling the pain."

"And you want to stop him."

"I want to paint the word *abuser* on his fucking forehead. Or as close as I can get."

Okay: I promised to speak to someone, see whether Tau could help. Then I said, "How are things otherwise? Jesus, Jenny. I haven't talked to you in a dozen years."

"Thanks, Adam." The intensity drained from her voice. "I'm pretty busy, actually. No time to chat. But you can reach me through Geddy when you need to."

CHAPTER 17

The lights went out all over North America and across much of the rest of the world that evening, but from Schuyler it looked, at least at first, like any other power blackout.

So we did what everyone else does when the lights wink off. Geddy peeked outside and reported that the whole neighborhood was dark, so we knew it was more than a blown fuse. Mama Laura handed me a flashlight from a drawer in the kitchen and sent me to the basement to fetch the emergency candles she kept there. (A years-old box of yahrzeit candles, no doubt from the tiny kosher aisle in the local supermarket. I was sure Mama Laura didn't know the use for which they were intended, though Rebecca winced when she started lighting them.) Jenny tried to call her mother but reported that her phone was also dead. Mama Laura went upstairs to see if my father was still awake (he was not) and to fetch the battery-operated radio they kept by the bedside.

We gathered in the living room. Geddy put the radio on the coffee table and cranked up the volume. The radio was an old analog model, and the only station we could tune in was a local one. The evening news-and-sports guy was struggling to keep up with the situation: he said the blackout appeared to be continent-wide and that wireless and internet service was disrupted and intermittent. There had been no official statement from the federal government, "that I know of." He said people should shelter in their homes. He repeated something Aaron had suggested, and which the wire services must have announced shortly before the blackout became complete: telecom and utility problems were probably due to viral malware that had been released in India but had spread uncontrollably. There was still no reliable news from that part of the world, but the last social-media posts from the city of Surat showed "a bright cloud and column of smoke" from the direction of Mumbai more than a hundred miles distant. "But of course that doesn't prove anything," the newscaster added.

"Isn't this awful," Mama Laura said.

Mumbai. Amanda had relatives there. There were Tau communities there, too, not to mention countless people who would have qualified as Taus had they ever taken the test. Relatives of a different kind.

I took a candle and navigated my way to the bathroom, where I tried to call Trev. But my phone was as dead as Jenny's. Which meant I was out of touch with my team. Which created a whole new set of problems, and I needed to talk to Jenny about that.

Fortunately for our chances of having a private conversation, Jenny was a smoker. Mama Laura wouldn't allow a cigarette to be lit in the house, so Jenny excused herself to step outside. Geddy and I followed her onto the back porch, but Geddy hurried back inside as soon as she took out her pack of Marlboros—he hated the smell of burning tobacco. I waited for the screen door to swing shut behind him.

Jenny gave me a careful look. The night was cool but windless, and her face was softened by the light of the rising moon. She could almost have been her younger self, Jenny Symanski and Adam Fisk, just hanging out. She said, "Okay, so what now?"

The plan had been admirably simple. What Jenny wanted from Tau was protection. Not just from Aaron but from the media shitstorm that would follow her release of the video. One official press conference, one official statement, a signed affidavit, then she wanted to disappear. Because, as she had said when we first discussed this, "It's not just a career-killer for Aaron. It's an embarrassment to *me*. I look at myself in those videos and all I see is someone—what's the word? *Cowed*. Cringing. Like a whipped dog! It's fucking humiliating. Not exactly what I want to show the world."

"But you *weren't* cowed," I told her. "That's why the video exists, because you *weren't* cringing, you *aren't* letting him get away with it."

At the end of the weekend I was supposed to take Jenny to a Tau enclave in Buffalo, with Trev and his security detail for escort, and after a prearranged press conference we would drive her over the border into Canada. She wanted a clean break with her past life, and that was what we promised her: our own version of the Witness Protection Program. A new name with all ancillary credentials, a new home in a pleasant university town out west. A job, if she wanted one. The sodality had ways of quietly and invisibly ensuring the employment of fellow Taus—and fellow travelers, in this case. Once the video was public she might be recognized, but I doubted it; Jenny had the kind of pleasant but commonplace looks that could be rendered utterly anonymous by a bottle of L'Oréal and a change of clothes.

"We should proceed as if nothing's changed," I said, though much *had* changed. For one thing, the international crisis might cause the vote on Griggs-Haskell to be postponed. For another, we wouldn't be releasing any videos or staging any press conferences until power was restored. "We leave here Monday morning and head for Buffalo. By then we might have a better idea what's going on in the rest of the world. In the meantime I'm going to have to find a way to contact my friend Trevor out at the Holiday Inn." I didn't mention the contingent of Het enforcers Trev had spotted earlier. No need for Jenny to worry about that. "And we need our own copy of the video."

"Okay," she said softly. "Now?"

"As good a time as any."

She looked into my eyes as if she were hunting for some kind of reassurance there. Then she rummaged in her purse until she came up with a cheap thumb drive, which she pressed into my hand.

She smoked her cigarette and we listened to the night. In neighboring houses, candles moved like restless ghosts behind darkened windows. The backyard opened onto a stretch of marshy, unimproved land where bullfrogs croaked out what Mama Laura used to call "that *jug o' rum* noise." Jenny and I had caught a huge bullfrog there, a year or so before puberty began to complicate our relationship. The frog was six inches snout to tail—I had held it still while she applied a tape measure from her mom's sewing box. The frog had croaked all night in a box in Jenny's garage, and in the morning her parents had made her turn it loose.

"Must be strange for you," she said, "being back here."

I shrugged.

"It is for me," she said. "So many memories kind of overlapping, you know, like a multiple exposure. Things we did back in the day. I look at Geddy and I still see the chubby, awkward kid he used to be. All the crazy enthusiasm he couldn't keep inside himself. You ever think about that stuff?"

"Sometimes."

"About your family?"

"Sure. Sometimes."

"Because I think it must be strange, coming back here, your

father on his deathbed or close to it, and you and me about to hand Aaron a nasty ticket to obscurity."

I almost wished I could tell her I had spent sleepless nights worrying about it.

"I have a different family now," I said. "I hope it doesn't sound callous, but whatever love I got in this house, I got mainly from Grammy Fisk, and she's been gone a long time. I'm sorry for my father. I really am. But I was never much more to him than an afterthought and a distraction. He fed me and he tolerated me and he allowed me a place in his house. And I guess that's worth thanking him for. But it's nothing like love, and I can't say I ever really loved him."

Jenny looked at me as if from a great distance. "Actually," she said, "yeah, that *does* sound a little callous."

"The first people who took me into their home with genuine love were two old women with a big house in Toronto. I expect my father would call them a pair of rich old dykes. I still live in that house when I'm not on the road. I love everyone who lives in it with me. One of those women—Loretta—died a couple of years ago. Cancer, not very different from my dad's. I cried when she passed, and I feel her absence every day, even now. I know what grief is, Jenny. I know where it comes from, and I know how people earn it."

She sighed a plume of smoke to the starry sky. "Okay," she said. "The funny thing is, that's how I used to feel about *this* house, back when my folks were drunk or arguing or both. I came here because Grammy Fisk was nice to me, and Mama Laura never yelled, and I liked being with you, and Geddy was pretty entertaining. And if Aaron ignored me, that's just because he was older and so good at everything. Some nights the only way I could get to sleep was by pretending this *was* my family, and that the only reason I had to go home was because I'd been born at the wrong address."

It was a memorable phrase. *Born at the wrong address.*

"So maybe I think about those days more than you do," Jenny finished.

"Maybe so."

"But I doubt it, because some things you just don't walk away from."

"I walked away from here a long time ago."

She smiled, a humorless compression of her lips. "Well, one thing hasn't changed. You're still a lousy liar."

"I hope that's not entirely true. The work I do these days, I'm a kind of diplomat. I help Tau negotiate deals with other Affinities. I need to lie from time to time. I'm one of the best liars we've got."

She stubbed out her cigarette on the rim of one of Mama Laura's big ceramic planters. "Then God help Tau, and God help us."

I tried twice more to call Trevor Holst, without success. I needed to talk to him, but it looked like I wouldn't be doing that before morning. It was late now. Mama Laura was tidying up the kitchen for the night, and the rest of us huddled around the radio, learning nothing. Geddy began to yawn.

Then there was a terse knock at the front door. "I'll get it," Mama Laura called from the kitchen. Twice tonight we had had visitors come to the door: neighbors who were running portable generators, offering to let us join them if we needed anything. Probably more of the same, I thought, until I heard Mama Laura's stifled screech of alarm.

We all leaped up, but I was first to grab a flashlight and reach the door. Mama Laura stood in the door frame with her hand to her mouth. I aimed the light outside and saw what had scared her: a huge dark-skinned man with elaborate facial tattoos and blood oozing from a gash above his right eye.

"Trevor, Jesus," I managed.

"Sorry," he said meekly. "I would have called first, but . . ."

"Adam," Mama Laura said, "do you *know* this man?"

"Yes. He's a friend. Mama Laura, this is Trevor Holst."

She relaxed visibly and exhaled a pent-up breath. "*Oh.* Then come on in, Mr. Holst. You seem to be hurt—I'll get the iodine and some washcloths."

Trevor clearly needed to talk to me privately, but we were obliged to do introductions and explanations. I took him to the living room. The candlelight made him seem even more intimidating than usual: his *kirituhi* tats looked inky black, and drops of blood had trickled down the bridge of his nose and dried on his cheeks like tears. He wedged himself into a chair and put on his biggest hey-I'm-harmless smile, but even that seemed somehow vulpine.

I introduced him as a Tau friend who had been traveling with me and who had taken a room at the Holiday Inn for the weekend. Trev blamed the cut on his head on the blackout: "Streetlights went dark and I walked into a lamppost. Back at the hotel there was a bunch of folks trying to get rooms—a bus broke down at the town line and the driver couldn't contact anybody for help. So I gave up my room for an older couple from Tennessee. Figured I'd transfer to the Days Inn, but they're full too. Which is why I came by here to tell you I've got no place to stay and maybe get a recommendation—one of those motels up the highway closer to the county line, I'm thinking."

By this time Mama Laura had come downstairs with a bowl of warm water and towels. She put the bowl on the coffee table and bent down to swab Trevor's forehead. "Any other night," she said, "I would recommend you get the folks at the Creekside Clinic to put in a couple of stitches in this cut. You gashed yourself pretty good. It might heal to a scar. But a cotton bandage will keep body and soul together for now. As for those motels on the highway, they're chock full of bedbugs. You can stay here tonight, Mr. Holst."

"That's very generous, Mrs. Fisk—"

"You'll have to sleep in the bed in the attic, I'm afraid, even though you're too long for it by half. Is that all right?"

"Very much all right. Thank you. Please call me Trevor."

"Everyone calls me Mama Laura."

"Thank you, Mama Laura."

She smiled. "You're very welcome. You say you're traveling with Adam?"

"From New York back to Toronto by way of Schuyler."

"Then shame on Adam for leaving you at the Holiday Inn. His friends are always welcome here."

Trev shot me an amused look. *Yeah, shame on you.* "It was my choice. I didn't want to intrude on a family gathering."

"Thoughtful of you, but I think it stopped being just a family gathering when the lights went out."

Making up the bed in the attic, Mama Laura came across an ancient portable radio to supplement the one in the living room. Geddy installed fresh batteries and took it upstairs when he and Rachel retired.

Which left me and Trev and Jenny free to talk. Trev told Jenny he'd be driving when we left Schuyler and that he would make sure she was safe. Jenny gave the bandage on his head a careful look. Clearly, the plan had already gone awry. But she nodded her agreement and went upstairs without further questions.

Which made it possible for me to say: "Trevor, what the fuck?"

He kept his voice to a low rumble. "We lost the security detail. Both cars. I was riding in the lead vehicle, we were doing a drive-around to get the lay of the town. This was maybe an hour before the lights went out. The fucking Het guys ambushed us, forced both our vehicles off the road. My car went into a ditch, the other vehicle hit a concrete planter. Tracy Guitierrez was driving—she's in the local hospital with most of the rest of my guys, not critical but definitely out of business for the time being. Lost a lot of skin on the right side of her face. Those of us who could walk quit the scene as soon as we called for help. I didn't want to have to waste time telling stories to the cops while the Hets do whatever they feel like. And then the black-out. I had to walk here."

I processed this. It was the news about Tracy that really made me angry. She was a fairly new Tau, still full of that oh-my-God-I'm-home-at-last giddiness. I wanted to hurt somebody on her behalf. And it didn't take Tau telepathy to feel a similar sentiment radiating from Trev like heat from a woodstove.

But we had to be smart about this, too.

"Raises the question," I said, "of why they would do that."

"I've been thinking about that on the walk here. Obviously they know something is up. Probably they know it involves Jenny. My guess is, the Hets got wind of our plan. And they mean to do something about it."

"Like what?"

"I wish I knew. Have you been able to get in touch with Damian or Amanda?"

"No."

"Me neither. Which means we're on our own right now. On the other hand, so are the Hets. And Hets are lousy at acting without orders, so maybe that buys us some time."

"What do you suggest we do?"

"Tonight, post a watch. The two of us, I guess. One of us should be awake and vigilant at all times. And in the morning, we take your car and get Jenny Fisk out of town ASAP. How's that sound?"

"Reasonable, I guess."

"So who gets the first watch of the night?"

"I'll take it. You look like you could use some rest."

He didn't object. "Show me the way to the attic room," he said. He checked his watch. "And wake me at three. Sooner, if you see anything suspicious."

He was at least a foot longer than the fold-out Mama Laura had set up for him, but he made himself comfortable. Back downstairs, I blew out the candles and put a chair by the big front window where I could watch the street. Then I poured myself a cup of cold coffee from the pot that was left after dinner and stared into the darkness.

CHAPTER 18

I had been on watch for about an hour, half dozing by the window, when there was a scream from the second-floor hallway, followed by violent shouting.

I grabbed a flashlight and ran upstairs. But when I made it to the landing all I saw was my father lying on the floor in a pair of white pajama bottoms, and Mama Laura bending over him, and Trevor at the far end of the hallway looking startled and contrite.

Apparently my father had gotten out of bed and headed for the bathroom, carrying one of Mama Laura's yahrzeit candles on a saucer. He found the bathroom door locked. He knocked and rattled the knob, and when the door opened he dropped the candle and screamed. He screamed because he had been asleep when Trev arrived, and Mama Laura had neglected to warn him that if he needed to take a leak during the night he might encounter a muscular two-hundred-and-forty-pound stranger with extensive facial tattoos. He dropped his candle (it rolled to the verge of the stairs, flame extinguished) and managed to back away three steps before he tripped over a knitted rug and fell to the floor. Mama Laura, running from the bedroom, found Trev standing over her husband and repeating the words, "Dude, are you all right?"

It was possibly the first time in his life my father had been called "dude." He wasn't taking it well. Now that he was no longer frightened, his belligerence came roaring onto center stage. "Who the fuck invited *you*?"

"I did," I said. I scooped up the fallen candle. "This is Trevor. He's a friend of mine."

"You have some pretty fucking peculiar friends!"

"He needed a place to stay for the night."

"Well, welcome to the Fisk Hotel!"

"Don't be ungracious," Mama Laura said, helping him to his feet. Because he was dressed in pajamas it was easy to see how much weight he had lost. His knees poked at the white cotton fabric like knotted cords. He had no belly, just a declivity under the barrel of his ribs. "And don't swear, if you can help it. Come back to bed, Charles."

"I still need to take a piss, goddammit!"

Even by candlelight I could see Mama Laura blush. "Go on, then."

He grunted and headed for the bathroom, skirting around Trev as if he were radioactive. Then he paused and looked back at me.

"Figures this is one of yours," he said.

Mama Laura apologized for the excitement. I went downstairs with Trev behind me.

"Other than that," he said, "anything happening?"

I smiled. "All quiet on the western front."

"Okay. You want me to take my shift now? I mean, I'm fully awake."

"So am I. You should get another couple of hours if you can."

Alone again, I settled back into my chair. Outside, the street was empty and stayed empty. Silence inside and out, until I heard more footsteps on the stairway. This time it was Geddy's friend Rebecca, barefoot in a cotton nightie. Her skinny frame and halo of dark hair gave her the look of a Q-tip dipped in black paint. "Couldn't sleep," she explained when she saw me. "What with the noise and all."

I asked without thinking, "And Geddy slept through it?"

"I guess so. We're in separate rooms, remember?"

Of course they were: Mama Laura's Protestantism wouldn't countenance an unmarried couple cohabiting under her roof. Rebecca headed for the kitchen, and I heard the refrigerator door open and close. She came back into the living room with a glass of milk in her hand. "I put the rest of the carton in the freezer, where it's still a little cold. But if this blackout goes on much longer you'll have to start throwing away perishables. Mind if I sit?"

I did mind, because as long as she was in the room my attention would be divided between her and the street. But I couldn't say that. I shrugged, and she sank into the big easy chair that used to be reserved for my father. "I guess you couldn't sleep either."

"I'm a light sleeper at the best of times."

"Uh-huh." She sipped her milk.

Outside, a car drove past. It didn't stop. I watched until its taillights vanished around the nearest corner. "I apologize about the candles."

"I'm not religious, and I'm not sentimental about yahrzeit candles. Though I still light one on Yom HaShoah, like everyone else in my family."

"Big family?"

"It seems like it, when we get together for the holidays."

"Have you introduced Geddy to them?"

She sipped her milk and wiped her lip with her wrist. "My

Gentile boyfriend? Of course I have. They love him. There's no problem, except with a couple of Orthodox cousins whose opinions no one takes seriously. An awkward moment now and then, no big deal."

"As awkward as all this?"

"Well, maybe not *quite*. But Geddy told me what to expect, especially concerning his dad. So no shocks there. And I know how it is with families."

I nodded and looked back at the window.

"Conventional families, I mean," she said. "Your friend Trevor is cute, by the way. I like the way you are with him. There's obviously some real love there."

Her gaydar had surely blipped when Trevor came within range, and I wondered if she was making an unwarranted assumption about my relationship with him. But if so, so what. "Real love" was a fair call.

"Being in an Affinity must be like that. That's what I think. I mean all these wonderful, complex relationships just spilling out of the air practically—a million possibilities, a million flavors of potential happiness. You were an early adopter, right? It must have been great back then."

"It's great now. Anyway, I thought you disapproved."

"No, I totally get it! I mean I *do* disapprove, in a way, but I don't disapprove of what an Affinity gives you."

"So what do you disapprove of?"

"The fact that it's *in an Affinity*. The fact that there's a wall around it. All due credit to Meir Klein—he knew utopia isn't one-size-fits-all. You could put a hundred people together and they could live better, fuller, freer, happier, more collaborative lives—but only the *right* hundred people, not a hundred random people off the street. So once you know what to measure and how to crunch the numbers, *voilà*: the twenty-two Affinities. Twenty-two gardens, with twenty-two walls around them. No disputing it's nice inside, for anyone who can *get* inside. But think about what that means for all the people not included. Suddenly you've segregated them from the best cooperators. Which puts outsiders in a walled garden too, but it's not really a *garden*, 'cause all the competent gardeners buggered off and the trees don't bear much fruit. And a walled garden that *isn't* a garden looks like something different. It looks like a prison."

"Colorful metaphor, but—"

"And that's not the only problem. You've created twenty-two groups—twenty-*three*, if you count those of us left out—with competing interests. The Affinities are all about cooperation *within* the group, not *between* groups. So, hey, look, a new world order, twenty-three brand new para-ethnicities and meta-nations, and what prevents them from going to war with each other? Nothing. Apparently."

"We've done good in the world, Rebecca. TauBourse, for instance. It benefited a lot of people who weren't Taus, directly and indirectly. As for war, we had people in high places in India and even a few in Pakistan, trying to prevent all the trouble."

"And how's that going?"

I shrugged and looked back at the window. A pair of headlights appeared at the end of the street, approaching. The vehicle behind them was big, but it was too dark to make out more than a boxy shape. It drove past without slowing or stopping. Then the street was empty again.

"I don't think you're down here because you can't sleep," Rebecca said. "I think you're down here standing guard."

"What makes you say that?"

"In addition to the way you can't keep your eyes off an empty street?"

"What would I be standing guard against?"

"Het, I'm guessing."

"And why would you think that?"

"Because your sister-in-law talks to Geddy, and Geddy talks

to me. I know what Jenny's situation is. I know how Aaron treated her, and I know what she means to do about it. I also know you're helping her—Tau is helping her—and I know why. You think her video will discredit Aaron and maybe force him to step down before the vote on Griggs-Haskell. Win-win, right? Except for Het."

I looked at her with fresh respect and a degree of wariness. Maybe Geddy had trusted her enough to confide in her. But I wasn't Geddy, and I wasn't sure I trusted Geddy's judgment.

"Assuming any of this is true," I said, "what's *your* interest?"

"Personally, you mean? Or from the point of view of New Socionome?"

"Either."

"New Socionome isn't an Affinity. There's no *us* and *them*. No single point of view. No consensus. It has no interests to advance, except to facilitate non-zero-sum collaboration. So the only opinion I can offer is my own. I think the Affinities are doomed whether Griggs-Haskell passes or not. Because they have a toxic dynamic. The sooner they fail, the better. I think Jenny needs to get away from Aaron, and I think she's brave to want to out him as an abuser. Short-term, I approve of what you're doing to help her. Even though it's messy. I assume you've thought about what it's going to do to this family?"

At length. I told her so. "But I believe it's worth it."

"For Jenny, you mean. And to do the right thing."

"For Tau," I said. "And to do the right thing."

Rebecca asked me one more question before she carried a yahrzeit candle back upstairs with her: "Do you really think there might be Het people out there who want to hurt us?"

I wondered whether it was wise to answer her question. I didn't want to confirm her suspicions or reveal more than she already knew. "Look at it from Het's point of view," I said.

"They've kept a close eye on Aaron and they probably know at least a little about his troubled marriage. If they don't know about the video, they may at least suspect Jenny of being a loose cannon. They also know the most direct connection between Jenny and Tau is through me. So any occasion that brings me into contact with Jenny is going to interest them."

"Interest isn't the same as a threat."

"Suppose they figured out what Jenny intends to do. How do they respond? They can't take control of the video—it's already been copied to remote servers, and they would have to assume Tau already has access to it. The only real leverage they can exercise is over Jenny herself, by making the price of releasing the video too high to bear."

"How would they do that?"

"The usual tools are threats and intimidation."

"What kind of threats and intimidation?"

"No way to predict. Plus there's the communication shutdown. Hcts are strongly hierarchical, which means the people they sent to Schuyler might be unwilling to act without authorization. Or maybe they have contingency orders—there's no way of knowing."

"You have any evidence they actually have hostile intentions?"

Solid evidence: a bunch of Tau security guys in the local hospital. But that was news Rebecca didn't need to hear. "Better to assume the worst."

"So your plan is to sit by the window and worry?"

"Until we can get Jenny out of town."

"I see. Okay."

"I'm glad you approve."

She gave me another of her conflicted smiles, one part sincere, one part cynical. "I'm not sure I do. But I guess I understand."

Trevor came down to relieve me in the chill hours of the morning, looming out of the darkness like a candlelit Goliath. "Hey, Trev," I said. "Quiet so far."

"Hope it stays that way," he said, small-voiced and careful not to wake anyone, settling into the chair I had just left.

So I went to bed and got a useful few hours of sleep. When I opened my eyes it was morning, the house beginning to warm up in a bath of late-May sunlight. Downstairs, Mama Laura fixed breakfast for those of us who were awake (Rebecca was still sleeping). The electric stove wasn't working, but she had fired up the gas grill in the backyard and used it to scramble eggs in an iron pan, standing in the dewy grass in her bedroom slippers with a goosedown jacket over her nightdress. She delivered the eggs to the table with a satisfied flourish: triumph over adversity. Plus coffee, boiled in a pan over the grill.

Trev ate heartily even as my father sat in sulky silence, glaring at the gigantic Maori who had somehow invaded his home. Geddy had been keeping an ear on the radio in the living room, and he brought us up to date on the latest news: phone and data services had been partially restored to parts of the west coast but were operating sporadically and unreliably. New York City and Washington, DC, also had intermittent telecom coverage, but the rest of the country, and most of Europe, and all of the Indian subcontinent, were still down. A few unconfirmed reports hinted that Mumbai was burning. All this information was being relayed through private broadcasters running on self-generated power, whispers passed from one ear to the next.

As soon as possible, I took Trevor and Jenny aside—once again, Jenny's tobacco habit gave us an excuse to segregate ourselves in the backyard. I said we should leave for Buffalo as soon as possible. Trev was clearly uneasy about undertaking the trip without an escort, but he didn't want to alarm Jenny by raising the possibility of a Het attack. Jenny herself was fine with leaving this afternoon. "I'll pack," she said, "and we can leave as soon as Geddy gets back."

I said, "Geddy left?" Trev, simultaneously: "Back from where?"

"My mom's. I need to know how she's doing. She really does need to move out of that house and into a care facility, sooner rather than later. I can arrange that through Tau, though, right? Even when I'm in Canada living under an assumed name?"

I managed to nod.

"So Geddy offered to go check on her. She's always been nice to Geddy, even at her worst."

"When did he leave?"

"Just now. Said he'd be about an hour."

But an hour passed. Then two. And Geddy didn't come back.

CHAPTER 19

I borrowed the keys to Mama Laura's Hyundai while Trev stood guard at the house. My plan was to check in at the Symanski house and see whether Geddy had been there. I was also prepared to check the local hospital and police station, and Trevor had supplied me with the names and addresses of some local Taus in case I needed help.

The car was well maintained but very old: it had always been hard to convince Mama Laura to trade in a vehicle that was "still perfectly good," and she had never felt comfortable at the wheel of my father's Cadillac. Which was actually helpful, because the car's radio was an analog relic, which meant it brought in the local station, itself an analog relic. The announcer's voice periodically gnarled into incomprehensibility, but the gist of the news came through. Such as it was.

And it seemed almost preternaturally strange, these rumors of apocalypse whispered against the morning calm of Schuyler, lawns just days shy of needing their first mowing of the season, a few cars on the road, a few pedestrians on the sidewalks, nobody hurrying, as if the blackout had created not panic but a sort of unpremeditated vacation. The most sinister thing I saw on the way to the Symanski house was a Great Dane lifting its leg over a maniacally grinning garden gnome.

It was clear that something dreadful had happened in Mumbai and elsewhere on the Indian subcontinent, though it wasn't at all clear who was benefiting by it. Our own continent-wide blackout was an echo of that conflict, a reminder that we weren't exempt from it. Before I left the house we had had a brief visit from our neighbor on the left, Toby Sanderval, who owned the Olive Garden franchise off the highway; he advised us to keep the doors and windows shut "so the fallout don't get in." Which terrified Mama Laura, until Rebecca and I assured her that any fallout from a nuclear exchange in India—had there been one—would have to travel across the equator and through nearly a dozen time zones before it presented any danger to the good citizens of Schuyler, New York.

But it was not all bad news that crackled through the car speakers. Municipal power had been restored to parts of Washington, DC. A presidential statement calling for calm and patience had been released to all extant media. There was even a report of intermittent cell phone service in New York State, though not locally—I tried.

As I drove, I kept my eyes open. I had biked and driven from my house to Jenny's house so often that the route was familiar, even all these years later. I looked for Geddy's car, an eye-poppingly yellow Nissan Elysium; I saws no sign of it, and it wasn't in the driveway of the Symanski house when I pulled up.

The house where Jenny's mother lived had not been well maintained. From the curling shingles to the faded siding, it announced neglect. Jenny's dad had left enough money for upkeep, Jenny said, but her mom was too far in the bottle to hire a contractor or even a handyman. I parked and went up the three wooden stairs of her front porch and knocked at the door, wondering if she would recognize me.

A couple of minutes passed before she answered. As the door opened, the house exhaled a sour effluvium of tobacco smoke and body odor. Mrs. Symanski stood in that invisible wind, oblivious to it, wearing a stained gray nightdress, a nasty caricature of Jenny's mom as I had once known her. She gazed at me and said, "Have you come to fix the electricity?"

"No. Mrs. Symanski? It's me, Adam. Adam Fisk."

She squinted. "Aaron?"

"No, *Adam*. Aaron's brother."

"Fuck me, I believe it is. Well, well. What brings you here?"

"Actually, I'm looking for Geddy. Has he been here today?"

"What—Geddy?"

"Yes. My stepbrother. Geddy."

"What would Geddy Fisk be doing here?"

"Well, that's the thing. When he went out this morning he said he was going to call on you. But that was quite a while ago, and he hasn't come back. I was wondering if he made it here at all."

"Why would he come here?"

"He's in town and wanted to say hello."

"Well, he didn't. Say hello, I mean. Is he lost? How do you get lost in a one-horse town like Schuyler?"

"So you haven't seen him at all?"

"Not since Jenny was a girl." She gave me a longer look, as if trying to locate me in the crumbling firmament of her memory. "Adam Fisk. Looking for Geddy? Can't you just, uh, phone him?"

"Unfortunately no. The phones aren't working."

"Or the lights. *Or* my fucking stove. *Or* the refrigerator. Food spoiling. Nothing works right anymore."

I guessed on olfactory evidence that her food had been spoiling long before the blackout. Or else she didn't bother taking out the trash. "Mrs. Symanski, I wish I could stay—"

"You should have married her."

"Excuse me?"

"If you'd married Jenny she wouldn't have to live with your brother. I guess it won't shock you to learn Aaron's an asshole. But I knew that about him. I always knew that about him, always, always. The way he looks at people. You were different. You didn't have that, um, assholiness in your eyes. Yeah, but you *didn't* marry her, did you? You gave her to Aaron like she was some bicycle you got too big for."

"You haven't seen Geddy, then?"

"No, I haven't seen Geddy Fisk, for better or worse."

"Then I need to keep looking. Thank you for your time, Mrs. Symanski."

"Don't you want to come in?"

It was an invitation to enter the kingdom of futility and despair she had made of her life. The world the Affinities were meant to redeem. "I can't right now."

"Should have married her," she said, closing the door in my face.

I thought obsessively about Geddy as I drove to Schuyler's small police station. And the memory that came to mind was of the night he had burst into my bedroom, tearfully demanding to know whether the world was *old* or *young*.

So typically Geddy, that attack of philosophical anxiety. So impossibly difficult to anticipate or answer. Moments like this were what had made Geddy an outsider, friendless at school, mocked behind his back and often enough to his face. I loved Geddy dearly, loved him maybe more than I loved my biological brother Aaron, but his strangeness was a constant admonition: *There but for the grace of God go I.* I had been a solitary kid with a sketchbook and a penchant for keeping my own company, and Geddy was just a few steps farther down the same road—and that much closer to the annihilating loneliness at the end of it.

The police station was on Schuyler's main street. Downtown traffic was almost nonexistent today, and most businesses were closed for the obvious reason, but I noticed the Sunnyside Diner and a couple of coffee-and-muffin places running on generator power, doors open and decent crowds inside. It was Sunday, and the parking lots at both the Catholic and Methodist churches were full. I pulled into the first vacant space in front of the Town of Schuyler Police Department. Inside, I told the uniformed officer at the front desk that I was looking for someone who hadn't come home and I wanted to make sure he hadn't been in an accident.

The officer told me 911 was down or intermittent, so there could have been any number of situations not reported, and in any case his people were "working their asses off" responding to the calls or notifications they *had* received, so he couldn't really help me—except to say that most of the problems they had encountered so far seemed relatively minor and he hadn't heard about anything involving serious injuries. But I could check with the county hospital if I liked.

Onenia County Regional Hospital was on the other side of town, usually a ten-minute drive but I made it in eight, ignoring the speed limit and thinking about Het. It was likely that the Het enforcers who had run Trevor's vehicles into a ditch were also responsible for Geddy's disappearance. For that reason, Trev had not wanted me riding around town by myself—but his first duty now was to protect Jenny, and he had relented. The question was, if the Het guys had taken Geddy, what did they want with him?

Het was a secretive Affinity, but we had learned a few things about it since the time Amanda took a stray bullet from a Het rifle some years ago. Being a Het meant, among other things, knowing who was entitled to give orders and who was obliged to follow them—and being okay with that. Hets were happy to take orders from other Hets as long as the pecking order felt rational and clearly defined. Individual members deferred to their tranche leaders, tranches were organized by region, the regions elected representatives to national sodalities, the sodalities sent delegates to an annual pan-Het convention. They were cagey about publicly naming leaders, but there was rumored to be a ruling council of ten overseen by their head man, Garrison. Other Affinities tended to be less rigidly organized, Tau being an obvious example, and the laborious process of consensus-building meant we couldn't carry off the kind of turn-on-a-dime political maneuvers for which Het had become famous.

Back when InterAlia was still fighting for control of the Affinities, the corporation had seen Het as a useful ally. InterAlia had offered them a deal: help us manipulate our opponents and we'll make you a silent partner, a sort of King Affinity. And when Meir Klein defected from InterAlia, it was most likely Het assassins they had sent to deal with the problem.

Not that Het was an Affinity composed of cold-blooded murderers—far from it. Most Hets never learned about the occasionally lethal skirmishes their sodalities undertook, and no such case had ever been prosecuted in the courts. But individual Hets were fiercely loyal to their Affinity; only rarely would an individual Het question orders from above or pry into the sodality's motives; and they were not above threatening or harming an innocent person to achieve their ends. They had made that abundantly clear. But still, if they had taken Geddy—why *Geddy*?

The waiting room in the emergency department of the regional hospital was mostly empty and the woman at the admissions desk seemed almost pleased to see me. I gave her Geddy's name and description and asked whether he had been admitted this morning. She didn't even have to check the records: Nope. She had been on duty all day, and the only admission had been a seventy-eight-year-old man who suffered a myocardial infarction while visiting his daughter in the maternity ward.

I thanked her and left.

I had a couple more places to visit. Trevor had given me the names and addresses of some Taus from the local tranche. But as it turned out, I only needed to see the first of them.

Her name was Shannon Handy.

Shannon was fifty-seven years old, a Tau for more than a decade, and she lived alone in a bungalow east of downtown and south of the highway. I knocked at the door, identified myself as a visiting Tau with sodality connections, and told her I needed to speak to her about an urgent matter. She invited me in.

Her home was clean and smelled faintly of maple smoke from a modern wood-burning stove in the kitchen. "Pollutes the atmosphere—it's a carbon sin, I guess—but it comes in handy when the power goes off. Warms the house and I can make a pot of tea to pass the time. Would you care for a cup?"

We sat at her kitchen table while she waited for the water to boil. Because she was a Tau, we didn't need to dance around the proprieties. She knew without asking that I was worried and I knew without asking that she was willing to help. She listened attentively as I explained the situation, twice asked me to clarify some detail or other, and when I finished she poured tea for both of us and doled out sugar and milk and sipped from her cup for a few silent moments.

"Big happenings for Schuyler," she said eventually. "Huh! Aaron Fisk, local hero, junior congressman, friend to the beleaguered middle class—and raging asshole, apparently. So we need to find your brother Geddy, and we need to do it as soon as possible, assuming these Het folks haven't already spirited him out of town."

"I think the blackout might work in our favor," I said. "Typically, Het enforcers won't act without instructions from their superiors, and unless they have magic telephones, they aren't getting any."

"They might be working from some prearranged plan, no need for instructions."

"They might. But as I said, Geddy's not directly involved in any of this—he's not even a Tau. Kidnapping him, if that's what they've done, seems kind of, I don't know, improvisational."

"And even if the blackout does help us, it could end at any time. So whatever we do, we should do it as soon as possible. Which means we don't really have time to appreciate a nice cup of Earl Grey." She stood up. "Let's go."

"Go where?"

"I manage a store in Schuyler. It's called Gizmos—you must have passed it on your way to the police station. We sell personal electronics, cell phones, coffeemakers, shit like that."

"Sure, but—"

"See, there are twelve Tau households in Schuyler. More in the neighboring counties, especially Duchesne and Flaxborough—our tranches all party together—but twelve inside the city limits. We're well connected in the community and we're mostly long-time residents. We know the town and the people who live in it."

"That's great, but—"

"Hush and let me finish. I did the annual inventory at Gizmos just last week, so I know we've got at *least* sixteen pairs of two-way radios in stock—what you call walkie-talkies. Little Motorolas with a range of fifteen miles or so. You get one, your friend Trevor gets one, every ambulatory Tau in Schuyler gets one. Once we're hooked up we can get coordinated, make a plan, do what we do best. How's that sound?"

Strength in numbers. I felt a little surge of optimism, the possibility that this awful day might have a non-tragic ending. Shannon gave me a sympathetic smile. "We'll take my car," she said.

CHAPTER 20

Driving back from Gizmos with a trunkful of two-way radios, I shared a few more details about Jenny and Aaron and their relation to Geddy.

Shannon listened thoughtfully. "Well," she said, "maybe these I Iet goons just screwed up. Maybe they wanted Jenny Fisk, but Geddy was the one they could get, so Geddy's the one they took. My opinion, for what it's worth? They'll probably try to cut a deal. Give you Geddy in exchange for, I guess, not releasing the abuse video."

"Either way, it's an impasse until the blackout ends."

"Because they can't even negotiate Geddy's release until they can talk to you. In the meantime, they keep Geddy somewhere we can't find him."

Geddy had never much liked traveling. He hated sleeping in strange rooms, rooms in which strangers had slept. That had been the worst of part of touring with a band, he once told me. *All those ugly little beds in all those ugly little rooms.*

"Well, hang in," Shannon said. "This isn't a big town. Unless he's already gone, we'll find him."

We pulled up at her house. She offered to cook me dinner; I told her I needed to get back to Rebecca and Jenny and Mama

Laura. She wanted to talk to Trev, who could describe the Het vehicles and maybe some faces. "He can contact me by radio," she said. "And in the meantime—"

She didn't finish the sentence. She was interrupted by a trilling that emanated from the left hip pocket of her faded jeans. Wide-eyed, she pulled out her phone. But the ringtone stopped before she could answer it. "False alarm," she said. "Huh."

But it was more than a false alarm. It was a promise and a warning. The engineers and IT geeks of the world were working the problem. Communications would be restored soon, maybe any minute now. For better or for worse.

It was dusk by the time I got back to my father's house. Trevor came down the front porch as I parked and met me when I stepped out of the car. I told him where I'd been and what I'd learned, and he nodded approvingly when I showed him the two-way radios.

"Gives us a fighting chance, anyway. I'll talk to this woman—Shannon?"

"Shannon Handy."

"Living up to her name, seems like. You go on inside."

"I need to explain all this to Mama Laura."

"Jenny already had a talk with her. About Aaron. And the video."

"I should have been here."

"They don't know about the Het troops, but they both figure Geddy's been kidnapped for the purpose of keeping the video quiet. This is hard on both of them, especially Mama Laura. We need to be solving the problem, not explaining it."

"I still need to talk to her," I said.

———

But Mama Laura was in no mood to talk.

I found her sitting on the bed in Geddy's old room, her hands folded in her lap, surrounded by the relics of Geddy's early life: his old desk, his record collection, the faint rectangles on the wall where his posters had once sheltered the paint from sunlight. She seemed to be studying these things, as if she wanted to commit them to memory. She barely glanced at me as I came through the door, and the glance was contemptuous.

"You came here under false pretenses," she said.

"Mama Laura, I'm sorry. What happened is—"

"Stop! Just *stop*." She clenched and unclenched her small hands. "Jenny told me everything I need to know. All about Aaron. And what he did to her. And what your interest in the matter is."

"We should have told you sooner."

"Perhaps you should. Or perhaps I should have guessed. You know, when I married your father, I was a single woman with a young child and poor prospects. Joining this family—I can't quite say we were *welcomed* into it—it seemed like Geddy and I had been delivered from a world of trouble. But that was wrong, wasn't it? On the contrary. We were delivered into a den of vipers."

"I'm sorry," I said again, uselessly.

"You were smart to leave this town. I wish you had stayed away. Because, I don't know who or what you are when you're with your friends, but here? You're just another Fisk, no better than your brother or your father. Maybe you pretended to be nice to my boy, but—"

"I never pretended."

She shook her head. "Don't try to excuse yourself. There is only one thing I need to hear from you right now. Do you know what that one thing is?"

"We'll bring him home, Mama Laura."

"See that you do," she said.

———

"The trouble with these walkie-talkies," Trevor said, "is that any-body who cares to can listen in on them. Anybody with a scan-ner or a similar unit, anyway. And we have to assume anybody who owns one of these things maybe took it out of the closet during the blackout. So I don't want us discussing anything crit-ical over the air. I had a little chat with Shannon, and she says we can use her house as a base. Get the local Taus together and make plans where we won't be overheard. Are you cool with that?"

"If we're at Shannon's house, who stands guard back here?"

"Jenny and Rebecca want to come with us—they pretty much insisted on it—and I don't think Het is much interested in your father or Mama Laura. Also . . . Shannon couldn't say much over the air, but it sounds like she might already have an idea about what happened to Geddy."

So we ended up taking two cars. Rebecca drove with Trevor, and I went with Jenny. Jenny sat in the backseat, mostly silent, staring out the window as the headlights swept the darkened streets of suburban Schuyler. Twice she checked her phone, but there was no signal.

As we turned a corner onto Shannon's street she said, "They took Geddy because of *me*, right?"

"If Het took Geddy, it was for the purpose of protecting Aaron."

"To keep me from talking about him."

"Almost certainly. But there hasn't been any actual threat."

"Because of the blackout."

"Maybe."

"Well, if they mean it as a threat, it's working. I'm not saying anything about Aaron until Geddy's safe. And even then . . . this is like an object lesson, that I'm vulnerable. That I'll always be vulnerable. I can go to Canada, I can go into hiding, but they can always get to Geddy or my mother, say, or Mama Laura—somebody who matters to me. They can hurt me no matter where I am, and they *will*."

"Once Aaron's exposed, they have nothing to gain by threatening you."

"Unless they want to punish me for crossing them. Can you tell me they wouldn't do a thing like that?"

"It's not likely."

"But it's possible."

I had no answer for that.

"Look," she said, "I don't want Aaron to get away with what he did to me and what he's doing to other women. But not at the price of someone's life."

"No one's been killed."

"But Geddy's already been kidnapped. And it's Geddy—it's *Geddy*, Adam! Geddy wilts if someone looks hard at him. Being taken captive? Physically coerced, maybe beat up, kicked around?"

"We don't know that anything like that has happened."

"But it might have."

I didn't say anything. Because she was right, of course. It might have.

Trevor made some kind of instant emotional connection with Shannon Handy. It was a Tau thing, but more: Trev had dedicated himself to protecting Taus, and Shannon had honed her own protective instincts (and other skills) during a tour of duty in Afghanistan many years ago. They looked like the ultimate mismatch—a middle-aged white woman who owned a consumer-electronics franchise next to a dark-skinned guy with Maori-style facial tattoos and the body of a bar bouncer—but they fell into earnest, focused conversation as soon as they were introduced.

They turned Shannon's kitchen into a command-and-control center. I waited in the living room with Rebecca and Jenny and a couple of local Taus who had already been briefed on the situation: a young IT guy named Clarence, who nodded a cautious hello, and a forklift driver, Jolinda Smith, who lived outside of town and who had brought with her some crucial information.

"Soon as Shannon came to my door and asked me whether I'd seen anything unusual," Jolinda said, "I knew what she was talking about." Jolinda was a big woman, muscular, and she leaned forward in her chair, eyes intent. "Because not much traffic comes out my way. I live on Spindevil Road, up past the gravel pit, you know that area? Nothing much past my house but some old hobby farms, most of 'em run down or abandoned. I was on my porch this morning, smoking a little kush and waiting for the power to come back on—not that it did. So I was surprised to see a, like, convoy coming up Spindevil away from the highway. Because that's not something you ordinarily see up there. Four black SUVs and a late-model sedan of some kind, all together, all moving at a serious clip."

"Any idea where they were headed?"

"Nope. But Clarence here has an idea."

Clarence was a twenty-something stringbean in chinos who sat up straight and cleared his throat before he spoke. "We've been keeping an eye on the local Het tranche since the troubles started. No troubles *here*, but be prepared, right? So we know who all the Hets in Schuyler are."

"And who are they?"

"Harmless people for the most part. Very tranche-loyal, but they work in local businesses like everybody else, so you run into them now and then. None of them has criminal records, or at least nothing beyond an occasional DUI or traffic ticket . . ."

"You checked?"

He smiled. "We have contacts with the DMV, local and state

police, the municipal registrar. I've been in some databases, yeah. And like I said, nothing criminal or suspicious."

"But?"

"But one of the local Hets is a guy named Carson Dix. He's a foreman at Schneider's Dairy. He also buys distressed properties, fixes them up and flips them. A couple of months ago he bought a two-story farmhouse on its last legs, real isolated, more like a vacation property than anything you could actually farm, with a view of Killdeer Pond which I guess Dix thought would be a selling point. He hasn't started the renovation yet. Point is, that property is Het-owned, it's remote, and the only way to reach it is to drive straight past Jolinda's house."

"So we need to check it out."

"That work has already commenced," Clarence said. "We thought it would be too obvious to be doing drive-bys, so we have a guy on the far side of the pond with a pair of binoculars and one of Shannon's walkie-talkies. He says the house is definitely occupied. Smoke from the chimney and lights in the windows. The vehicles Jolinda saw are parked in back, bunched up so they're not visible from the road. One of them is a sedan that meets the description of the car your guy was driving. We can't confirm that your guy is present, but that's the obvious inference."

Your guy. It was strange to hear him use those words to describe Geddy.

"So if that's where he is, how do we get him out?"

Jolinda said, "I believe that's what Shannon and your friend Trevor are trying to figure out right this minute."

Their voices droned out from the kitchen, the words indistinguishable, an ebb and flow of urgent talk that went on for more than an hour. Then the scrape of kitchen chairs on linoleum. Shannon led the way when they came into the living room, looking tired but flushed with excitement. "Let us run our idea past you. But if we decide to do this, we need to act real soon. All right?"

She outlined the plan, with explanatory asides from Trevor, and she ticked off a list of things we would need: a disposable vehicle, gasoline, people in place both here in Schuyler and at the farmhouse on Spindevil. What she described sounded plausibly effective but unavoidably dangerous. "So the question we have to ask is, are we sure it's better to do this than to let the situation just kind of evolve?"

"If it evolves," I said, "it's likely to evolve right out of our control. If we don't get Geddy back they'll take him somewhere better defended, someplace we can't find."

"So we act now?" Shannon asked. "Can we get a consensus on this? Because it'll take time to put everything in place."

"Act now," I said. "That's my vote."

Jolinda turned to Shannon. "You think this has a decent chance of working?"

"I make no promises, but yeah, I do think it might work."

Jolinda nodded once. "All right. I say yes."

And: "Yes," Clarence said.

Trevor nodded. "Yes."

No one asked Jenny or Rebecca to weigh in: they weren't Taus. But they made no objection. "We go, then," Shannon said.

She got on her walkie-talkie, summoning local Taus to the house for a briefing. The only thing that might hinder us now was an end of the blackout, which would put the Het detail back in contact with their leaders and probably back in motion—which was why Trevor let out an anguished "Oh, *shit*!" when the lights flickered on.

Followed by the pinging and chiming of multiple phones. I took mine out of my pocket. Signal strength was at two bars, and the incoming call was from Amanda Mehta in California.

CHAPTER 21

People grabbed their phones and walked in different directions. I took mine into Shannon Handy's kitchen.

The link was dicey. I plugged in an earbud for privacy and so I could pay attention to the screen, since Amanda was using her standard video service. Her voice came through reasonably well, but the video was a cascade of Picasso distortions and checkerboard monstrosities. "We have to talk fast," she said. "Coverage east of the Mississippi is still sporadic and we could lose it at any time."

Then, momentarily, an image froze on the screen: Amanda with a wisp of hair spanning the bridge of her nose, black eyeshadow framing each eye in a paisley shape she called a *boteh*. I was helplessly reminded of the way she had looked the night we first met, the night she took me up to the roof of the tranche house in Toronto to smoke weed and listen to the sounds of the city. On that night I had fallen in love with her, and she with me, but with this difference: I was not her first Tau lover, but she was mine. She had known that, and she had gently and sweetly walked (and fucked) me through the process of learning to distinguish my love for her from my burgeoning love for my Affinity. The years since then had forged a connection between us, fragile but still more substantial than this image of her, which shattered into noise even as I was gazing at it.

I began by laying out the situation here in Schuyler. I told her Jenny was with us but that a group of Hets had kidnapped Geddy for the purpose of threatening her into silence. I explained that Jenny was now unwilling to cooperate with our release of the incriminating video, but she would likely change her mind if we got Geddy back, and I said Trev and some local Taus had cooked up a plan to recover him.

"You can't do that," she said.

Another image of her froze in place (her lips in a querulous frown, as if she had caught sight of something troubling on the periphery of her vision), provoking another memory: the way she looked when she talked about what she called my "unfortunate tendency" to form relationships outside my Affinity. There was never any real disappointment or disapproval in that look, just an acknowledgment of a problem that couldn't be ignored or dismissed. As if to say, *We're Tau, but none of us is perfect; each of us carries some burden of veniality or naiveté; this is Adam's.* As if to say, *Adam hasn't quite learned how to love us exclusively.*

"Things are more complicated than you can imagine," she said. "We're starting to get reports from every country with a Tau sodality—physical attacks on tranches all over the world. Some of it is probably random. There are plenty of people out there with grudges against the Affinities. But some of it looks targeted. We think Het's taking advantage of the opportunity to do us some strategic damage. But it would be very hard to prove that, and any kind of clumsy retaliation will just make us look like the bad guys, reckless and violent. Which plays into their hands. Which is maybe the whole point. So, *no*—Damian and I have been in touch with every sodality rep who can take a call, and the consensus is, we have to stand pat until we can organize a coordinated response. This is critically important. You absolutely *cannot* go vigilante with an armed tranche right now."

I thought of Geddy, locked in a room in some moldering farm-house. He would be terrified. But he would also believe we were working to get him back. He would trust us to do that, without question. "We're talking about my brother here."

"Your stepbrother. Not even a blood relative."

I wondered if it was possible that the bad connection had fucked up our Tau telepathy. "I grew up with him, Amanda."

"I know. But, Adam, we all grew up with *somebody*."

The camera captured an image of her bare right arm as she turned in her chair. A Chinese dragon lived between the dimple of her elbow and the ball of her shoulder, green-scaled and with black ophidian eyes, coiled around what could have been a letter X but was in fact a Phoenician tau. A declaration of fealty, carved in the clay of her body.

The kitchen ceiling light flickered. "We can do this," I said. "We can do it cleanly. And with Jenny's cooperation we can still release the video."

"No—Jenny's cooperation doesn't matter anymore."

"How do you figure that?"

"You copied the video to us before the blackout. We can release it as soon as we have reliable access to media, with or without her consent."

"But it won't work if Jenny doesn't back it up. People will say it's CGI. Nobody trusts raw video without corroboration."

"Jenny's not the only one Aaron pissed off. We've been in contact with his most recent ex-girlfriend, and she gave us a signed affidavit about his treatment of her. It's all the corroboration we need. We can take it public anytime."

But no one had told me that. The screen offered one more frozen image, Amanda with her head half turned, the *bodeh* curving from her left eye like a crow's wing, and I thought of the night we had come back from Vancouver, her arm in a sling and her bullet wound still fretting her, how she had sat with me and Trevor in the attic room of the tranche house and confessed that she was going to California with Damian, how at the end of that confession she had turned to kiss Trevor and then leaned the other way to kiss me, long kisses fraught with meaning, three breaths conjoined.

Her voice began to break up. "Adam, are we clear on this? You absolutely *cannot* go after Geddy. We have complete consensus at the sodality level. Do you need Damian to confirm that? He's in the next room talking to Europe, but I can fetch him if I have to."

"No." What would be the point?

"So it's agreed?"

I said, "Agreed."

Long pause. No image now, just a confetti of random pixels and a background noise that sounded like ghosts conversing in a language of sparks and echoes.

"Are you sure?"

Rrr you sssure?

"Of course I am."

"Because it sounds like—"

Bekkkuz it sssouns lie-kkkkk—

Then the audio died, the signal bars on the display drained to zero, and the kitchen light went dark again.

I went back to the living room, where everyone was staring at dead phones. Trevor looked at me expectantly. I bought a moment by asking him who he had been talking to.

"Brecker," he said, "at the hospital." One of the Tau security guys who had been run off the road shortly before the blackout. "Everybody's stitched and bandaged, but I don't think they'll be of much use to us in the short term."

"Okay."

"So—you were talking to Damian?"

"Amanda," I said.

"And?"

"I made her aware of the situation regarding Geddy. I told her we're working on a plan to get him back."

"And?"

For the last eight months I had worked for Tau as a diplomatic liaison, and I had learned how to deploy a strategic lie. But lying to a tranchemate was different. Trev was giving me a puzzled look, which I met and held, because eye contact mattered: avoiding eye contact was a liar's tell. But I felt like I was staring, and I had to remind myself to blink.

I said, "She wants us to go ahead and get Geddy back."

He cocked his head as if he had heard a distant but ominous sound. Then he shrugged and smiled. "All right. Let's get it done."

CHAPTER 22

Shannon's house was suddenly crowded with local Taus, and over the course of the next couple of hours we finalized the details of the plan to retrieve Geddy. It had a reasonable chance of succeeding, I thought, but we needed time to assemble resources, and it was already well past midnight. Best to come at them at dawn, Shannon suggested. Which gave us three or four hours to place people and supplies and make the necessary preparations.

Assuming the telecom system didn't reboot during that time. A word from Damian or Amanda to Trevor was all it would take to stop the project in its tracks.

Shannon added more wood to the stove as the night progressed. A drizzling rain set in, fogging windows and slicking the dark streets. Rain would make everything more difficult. But we were committed now, and we told ourselves it didn't matter. Trevor moved around Shannon's living room briefing Taus, rehearsing them in their roles, making sure everyone knew his or her task and was suited for it. It was a kind of collaborative choreography, the genius of the Affinities manifesting itself in this apparently random collation of ordinary people: I felt it, and Trevor felt it, too. He sat with me for a few minutes as we waited for one of Shannon's tranchemates to come back with a car. A gust of wind threw rain against the window like a handful of pebbles, and he said, "You know what this reminds me of? That time way back, not long after you joined the tranche, when Mouse was having trouble with her crazy ex."

Mouse, right. Mouse had moved west a few years ago. She lived in Calgary now, working as an accountant for a mostly-Tau construction firm. But she kept in touch, called the tranche house every Christmas and always made a point of speaking with Trev and me. "We were amateurs," I said. "It was lucky we didn't get hurt. Worse."

"We were learning what it means to be a Tau, taking risks we wouldn't take for a stranger. But yeah, we're better at it now. Still the same impulse, though, right? The way you feel when someone tries to hurt the people you love."

"Right."

"Except this time it's not a jealous ex with a baseball bat, it's a bunch of Hets who want to take down our entire Affinity. We're not protecting one guy, we're protecting Tau as a way of life."

I nodded.

"So it's not about Geddy, and it's not about Jenny. It's about all of us. We need to keep that in mind."

He was looking hard at me again.

"Right," I said.

"Okay. So you're up for this?"

"I'm up for it."

"Good." He grinned. "Because I think that's our ride pulling up at the curb."

The car, supplied by one of Shannon's tranchemates, was a Toyota sedan that had seen twelve winters; its paint was blistered and the interior smelled like tobacco smoke and stale Doritos.

But its motor was fully functional, and it was a good choice, given what we had in mind for it. I volunteered to drive.

My passengers were three local Taus, and they were mostly quiet. We drove through the north end of Schuyler toward the highway, and the town was eerie in the misting rain, streets deserted, dawn just beginning to reveal a sky of tumbling clouds. The car's radio picked up the analog radio station that had been our only source of news since the blackout, and the news this morning was mixed and mostly speculative. Something terrible had happened in Mumbai, and there were rumors of pitched battles in Karachi and Islamabad. Unnamed experts claimed that a cyberattack aimed at Indian military systems had spread catastrophically and globally, which had triggered retaliatory responses from major players: the unleashing of dozens of varieties of military malware targeting infrastructure nodes in virtually every industrialized nation on the surface of the earth. But electrical power had lately been restored to the west coast of the United States and to some urban areas in the east, and telecom providers were slowly and erratically coming back on line. Which was good news for the world, but maybe not for me—or Geddy.

I told myself Geddy would be okay. He could be spectacularly earnest and naïve, but there was a strength in him, too, a stoicism he had learned the hard way. I had seen the change in him when he was just thirteen years old. Before that, my father could reduce him to sobs with an unkind word. After that, when my father said something vicious, Geddy's face would cloud but he would clench his jaws and stare furiously. Not suppressing the hurt—I didn't think he was capable of that—but refusing to give my father the satisfaction of tears.

I imagined Geddy in captivity, showing his captors the same silent defiance. Unless someone even less forgiving than my father had managed to beat it out of him.

The sky was light by the time we reached the highway and headed east. The rain had tapered a little but it was still coming down, soft shifting sheets of it. The Toyota's wipers creaked over the windshield. After a few minutes of this we reached the unmarked exit for Spindevil Road.

Spindevil was two lanes of potholed blacktop, long neglected by county repair crews. It curved past the abandoned quarry where, many summers ago, I had gone on swimming expeditions with Aaron and Geddy and Jenny Symanski, and pushed on through scrub forest and rocky wild meadows, past isolated properties bounded by split-rail fences and weathered NO TRES-PASSING signs. The only other cars I saw were Tau cars, part of our loose convoy, one ahead of me and three behind. We all stopped when we reached Jolinda Smith's little house, which would serve as our outpost. The farmhouse where the Hets were holding Geddy was three miles farther north, and one of our guys was keeping it under surveillance from the other side of Killdeer Pond.

Trevor was essentially in charge now, and once the crowd at Jolinda's place was more or less settled I approached him and asked where we stood.

"We need a little more time," he said. "Maybe an hour, not more than two. Shannon's headed to downtown Schuyler, she's probably in place by now, and once everything else is set up we alert her by walkie-talkie and set this thing in motion. Plus we need to allow for travel time from Schuyler to here. But once our ducks are in a row I give it half an hour from first alert to showtime."

Which was more time than I would have liked, but good work, considering.

Trevor's radio crackled again. Since the majority of us were right here, the call could only have been from Shannon or the guy watching the Het house from the other side of Killdeer Pond.

Either way, it might be bad news: a delay, a unexpected hitch in the plan.

We stood on the damp porch of Jolinda's place, rain ticking on the eaves and sluicing down a drainpipe. The walkie-talkie was enormous by comparison with a phone, but it looked small in Trevor's hand. He put it to his ear and listened for about ten seconds, an unreadable expression on his face. Then he lowered it again.

"I don't know who the fuck it is," he said. "But he's asking for you. For Adam Fisk."

I took the handset and clicked the send button and said, "This is Adam Fisk."

A male voice said, "You've gone to a lot of trouble there, Adam. Don't you think we should talk this over first?"

"Who is this?"

"One of the folks playing host to your stepbrother. We've been listening to your radio chatter for the last few hours. And we think you're all needlessly upset. You're a negotiator, I understand. A kind of diplomat. Well, maybe some negotiation is in order today."

"What are you suggesting?"

"Just that you might want to come knock on our door before you break it down. You're a little ways south on Spindevil, right? So come up the road and stop by for a chat. Just you."

"And why would I want to do that?"

"To avoid unnecessary violence. Maybe get your stepbrother out of here in one piece, if we come to an agreement. You have our guarantee of safe passage, in and out. But this isn't an unlimited offer. I figure you're, what, five minutes from here by car? Plus a little time to sort this all out with your Tau buddies. So we'll expect you in fifteen minutes, or not at all."

I said, "Why should I believe you?"

But there was no answer.

Trevor was against it.

It was Trevor who drove me up Spindevil to the Het house, with Jolinda in the backseat to make sure we reached the right property. We took the Toyota: the disposable vehicle. He said, "You'll be giving them another hostage—you know that, right?"

We had talked this through once already, though not to Trevor's satisfaction. "They don't need another hostage. That's not what this is about."

The Toyota's rattletrap suspension was no match for the potholes on Spindevil. Trev kept his eyes on the road, though he spared the occasional sidelong glance in my direction. The rain had stopped, suddenly and finally, but a chilly wind bowed the roadside oaks and beeches. The clouds had thinned to show a disk of sunlight the color of milk.

I repeated what I had already said to him. Since the Hets were aware of our presence, they could put Geddy in a vehicle and leave the farmhouse, and once they were in motion there was little we could do to stop them. Any kind of direct intervention would endanger Geddy and risk the kind of law-enforcement attention we couldn't afford. But as long as I was in the farmhouse talking, they would stay put until we were ready to intervene. And if everything went according to plan, it wouldn't matter whether I was inside or out.

"That's a huge fuckin' *if*," Trevor said. "We're talking about the people who put four Taus in the hospital. They'll do whatever they think they can get away with."

"Just up around the bend ahead," Jolinda said. "You'll see the house once we pass that stand of oaks."

"They're Hets," I said. "They won't do anything violent unless they've cleared it with their bosses."

"That might be true of most Hets," Trevor said. "On a statistical basis. But you'll be dealing with, like, one guy. Maybe somebody on the far end of the Het curve. Somebody willing to take action on his own hook."

"There!" Jolinda exclaimed. "See it?"

Trev slowed down as the farmhouse came into view. From this distance it looked like any of a half dozen other properties we had passed. A two-story wood-frame house maybe fifty or sixty years old, painted a bilious, weathered green. Gaps on top where shingles had fallen from the roof. Sagging front porch. Wild oaks on the south side of it; on the north, a few acres of patchy scrub that someone might have tried to farm, once, long ago, in a fit of unjustified optimism. Surrounding all this, a chain-link fence on which signs had been posted:

NO TRESPASSING OR LOITERING
VIOLATORS WILL BE PROSECUTED

"It's also possible I can talk Geddy out of there. Maybe they reconsidered the whole thing. Maybe they got a call when the telecom was up, telling them things had changed, they don't need him anymore."

"Like the way you talked to Amanda," Trevor said.

"Right."

The car came to a stop at the end of the laneway that led to the farmhouse, tires crunching on gravel. I took a long look down the laneway to the house, five dark windows facing us: two on the ground floor, two above, and a tiny dormer window in what must have been the attic. Probably a Het guy in each one, watching. Trev said, "There are three vehicles parked in back of it, four Het SUVs and the car Geddy was driving when they took him. We figure at least eight potential hostiles inside. You might not see all of them, so don't make assumptions. You have the radio?"

One of Shannon's walkie-talkies, strapped to my belt. We had arranged this before we got in the car. Fifteen minutes after I gained admission to the farmhouse, Trevor would make contact by radio. I would say certain words, or I would not; and as a result certain things would happen, or they wouldn't.

"Best get on down there if you're going," Jolinda said from the backseat.

I opened the door and got out and closed the door behind me. I felt the wind on my face, moist from the morning's rain. I heard the branches of the oaks groaning in the wind, the spastic idle of the car's engine. My legs felt too heavy to move but I moved them anyway. I began to walk down the graveled drive to the sagging farmhouse porch, thinking about the people watching me from the lightless mirrors of the windows, wondering which of those rooms Geddy was in.

The porch was in even worse shape than it had looked from the road. The plank steps bowed under my feet, elastic with rot. A naked lightbulb above the door was half filled with rainwater and rust. The door itself was subtly askew on its hinges, and it opened as I raised my fist to knock. A man stood in the shadows behind it. "Come on in, Mr. Fisk," he said.

I recognized the voice: it was the man I had spoken to over the radio.

And as I stepped inside, I recognized the face.

CHAPTER 23

At least I thought I recognized him. The face was familiar, but I couldn't connect it with a name or a concrete memory. He was a tall man, white, probably in his forties, with a gym-rat body, bald head, and angular cheekbones that made him look faintly Slavic. He wore jeans and a black sweatshirt, plain but clean. His lips were compressed in a smile that verged on a sneer. He stood back and waved me in.

Where had I seen his face before?

Inside the farmhouse was a large square room, stairs leading to the second story, an arch opening into what appeared to be a kitchen. The floor was wood, floorboards scuffed and muddied to a smoky black. The walls were covered in scabbed green utility paint. The furniture consisted of a worn sofa, six plastic kitchen chairs, and a woodstove ticking away in one corner of the room.

Assuming the tall guy was the boss, three of his subordinates were also present in the room: one next to the window, one blocking the way to the kitchen, and a third (a woman) perched on the stairs. They all carried holstered handguns, and they looked at me with expressions ranging from contempt to indifference.

"Sit down, Adam," the tall guy said. "Might as well make yourself comfortable while we discuss things."

"There's nothing to discuss until I know Geddy is safe."

"Okay, that's understandable. Maggie? Want to bring our guest on down?"

The woman nodded and stood and trudged upstairs.

"I'd offer you refreshments but we're on slightly short rations here. So who's waiting for you in the car? Your friend Trevor? That local woman who runs Gizmos on Main Street? Smart of her to dole out radios like that. Working the tranche, right? But we have friends in town, too. People who might notice something like a local Tau and some strange man hauling armloads of walkie-talkies out the back door of an electronics store."

I said nothing. He shrugged. "Go on," he said, "sit down," waving his hand at a chair, and under the cuff of his sweatshirt I caught sight of a Het tattoo, small and black. A bisected rectangle, like a cartoon drawing of a sash window.

And then I realized: No, I hadn't *seen* his face before.

I had *drawn* it.

The woman came back downstairs with Geddy behind her and another Het guy taking up the rear, as if they were afraid he'd make a run for it. Not that he seemed likely to do any such thing.

Geddy wore the clothes he'd had on when he left the house a day ago: linen slacks, khaki-green cotton shirt, a pair of ratty sneakers. He looked as grim as a prisoner on his way to the gallows. But he stopped moving the moment he spotted me. His face went through serial evolutions: he grinned; then he looked confused; then he looked frightened.

"Hey, Geddy," I said.

"Hey," he said tentatively.

"You all right? Did these folks hurt you in any way?"

He gave it a moment's thought. "They won't let me leave. They didn't hurt me. But they threatened to."

"We'll get you out of here," I said.

"Hold your horses," the guy with the Het tattoo said. "That's not an established fact just yet. That's what we need to talk about. Sit over there on the sofa, Geddy." He turned to me. "So did his mother name him after Geddy Lee? From that old-time Canadian band, Rush? Because we asked, but he wouldn't tell us."

"The name's from his mother's side of the family. Long line of Geddys. How about you? Do you have a name?"

"Call me Tom."

"Is that your real name?"

"Of course not. And you really need to sit down."

I sat in the chair next to the woodstove. I crossed my legs and put my left hand on my thigh so I could see my watch without obviously checking it. Five minutes had passed since I had left the car. Ten to go. I said, "There's no point dancing around. Just tell me what you want."

Tom pulled a chair away from the wall and put it in front of me and sat in it so that our knees were almost touching. When he spoke I could smell his breath, sour and pungent, as if he'd been living on black coffee and brie. "No offense, but you people must be pretty stupid if you don't know what we want."

"Who's *we* in this case? You? Your tranche? Your sodality? Your Affinity?"

"Come on, Adam. We want your brother Aaron to vote on the Griggs-Haskell bill without interference. We know Tau has a different preference, and we know Tau is in possession of some video footage that might embarrass Aaron right out of the House of Representatives. We suspected something like that before we picked up Geddy, though he was kind enough to confirm it—right, Geddy?"

Geddy inspected the floorboards and said nothing.

"If you're making a threat," I said, "you need to be explicit about it."

"You're the folks making a threat. In your case, Adam, a threat against your own brother! We're just responding in kind. So don't talk like you have the moral high ground here."

I had drawn this man's face, years ago, in Vancouver, working from Rachel Ragland's description of the men who had come to question her. (*Bald as a bottle cap,* she had said, *head like a bread loaf, mouth that opens like a puppet's jaw.*) If this wasn't the same man, it was at least someone who matched both the description and the drawing. Rachel had also mentioned the Het tattoo: same size, same place. So it was no surprise the guy seemed to know me. He worked for Het security, and he could have been keeping a file on me (and Amanda and Damian) ever since the disastrous Vancouver potlatch. He might even have been involved in the murder of Meir Klein.

I said, "You're still not telling me what you want, *Tom.*"

"What we want is a guarantee that Aaron will be allowed to cast his vote unmolested, as God and the electorate intended."

"God and the electorate and the Het lobby."

"Sure, if you like. And let me emphasize, we have no interest in harming Geddy. But if you were to walk out that door with him, both Het and Aaron would be hanging in the wind. He's our leverage against Jenny, and without Jenny you have no acceptable case to make. The video by itself won't convince anybody. Jenny's the key. So we need to be in a position to bargain. We need Jenny to know something bad might happen if she joins this conspiracy of yours."

What this told me was that he didn't know Tau had secured a second affidavit from one of Aaron's recent girlfriends. As far as Tau was concerned, his threat was meaningless. Amanda had made it clear: the video would be released whether or not Jenny consented . . . and whether or not Geddy was still being held captive.

But I couldn't tell him that. In all likelihood he wouldn't believe me. He certainly wouldn't consider it grounds to give up Geddy. And if, miraculously, he *did* believe me—or if he successfully communicated the news to some higher echelon of the Het command chain—I would have betrayed my own Affinity by revealing the secret.

Of course I had *already* betrayed Tau by lying to Trevor. But I hoped I could be forgiven for that once Geddy was safe. I figured I could make Trevor and Amanda and maybe even Damian understand why I had done what I was doing.

"So," I said, "what are you proposing? Or do you have to wait for instructions before you can answer that question?"

He smirked. There was a twinkle in his eye: he actually looked *merry*. "That's such a tired stereotype—hierarchical Hets, always need a boss to tell them what to do. Some truth in it, of course. When it comes to collective action, yeah, we make sure we're all on the same page and doing the right thing. Situations like this, field operations? It's not brain surgery. You send along someone who can assume the authority to issue orders. Pending the end of the blackout, I'm that person. If you think we're paralyzed until the phones work, you're not just wrong, you're stupid."

I looked at my watch. Twelve minutes had passed.

"So," he said, "all I want to do here is lay out the terms. We can't give you Geddy. Not today. You understand that, right? There's no promise you can make that will secure his release. We need Aaron to vote as intended, and we need to hang on to Geddy until then. What I want to say is, that doesn't have to be a hardship. The vote's scheduled for next week, unless the crisis postpones it, and we can make Geddy perfectly comfortable until then. At an undisclosed location, of course, but somewhere comfortable and private." He turned to give Geddy a puppet-jawed grin. "Think of it as a vacation. Eat, drink, relax, watch videos until this mess gets resolved. Het picks up the tab, and then you go free."

Geddy continued inspecting the patch of floor between his sneakers.

I said, "And in exchange?"

"Isn't it obvious? You have people down the road contemplating some kind of rescue attempt. Which, excuse me for saying so, is a truly idiotic idea. Which I imagine you hatched precisely because you're out of contact with the, uh, Tau consensus, or whatever you call it. We both have *so* much to lose from a move like that. Somebody gets hurt. Or there's police involvement, which neither of us wants. Or the conflict escalates out of control. A ridiculous risk."

"You're asking us to give up everything we've worked for since Klein was killed."

"What, because of that bill before Congress? I won't kid you; we want Aaron's vote. But we've got our hands on lots of other levers. And even if this vote goes against us, what the fuck does that buy *you*?"

Fifteen minutes. The radio on my belt crackled. I said, "I need to check in with my people."

The Het guy shrugged and said, "Keep it brief."

Trev and I had arranged a kind of code. When I answered his call he said, "You've been in there a while—everything okay?"

Which meant the initial stage of the rescue plan had been set into motion and was evolving smoothly. Had there been a problem, he would have asked me what was taking so long. If the plan had been cancelled altogether, he would have told me he was getting impatient.

And I said, "We're still talking."

Which meant: *Come get us ASAP.*

Radio silence followed.

Tom said, "We need to wrap this up. I'm sure you know we have our vehicles behind the house. What's going to happen is, my people will put Geddy in one of those vehicles and we'll convoy down Spindevil to the highway. Nobody gets in the way. Nobody follows us. No contact until Aaron casts his vote, at which time we get in touch and tell you where to find Geddy. The video footage stays locked up in the meantime, or, if it *does* get released, Jenny Fisk tells the press it's not authentic. That's a win-win situation."

"It might be," I said. "Except we have no reason to believe you. You say you won't hurt Geddy—"

"As long as Aaron isn't interfered with, you can count on it."

"History doesn't bear out that assertion."

"No idea what you're talking about."

"I was on Pender Island a few years ago when one of your guys shot Amanda Mehta. Maybe you remember that. You'd been trying to squeeze information out of Rachel Ragland, looking to find something you could pin on me or Amanda or Damian Levay. Then you sent some asshole with a rifle to intimidate us. Unfortunately he was also an *incompetent* asshole."

The Het guy seemed less surprised than I had hoped, though he sat in silence for a moment. Then he sighed. "That 'incompetent asshole' was the father of three kids, did you know that?"

"Then he shouldn't have come hunting us."

"Father of three kids. His body was dumped into Georgia Strait from a height, according to the coroner, though he was dead twice over even before he was dropped—a drug overdose *and* a gunshot wound. You people are thorough, I'll give you that. As for Rachel Ragland, all we did was ask her some questions. We didn't hurt her. Harmed not a hair on her head. Hell, Adam, we didn't even *fuck* her, unlike you. And unlike you, we keep track of the people we come into contact with."

"Spy on them, you mean."

"Whatever you care to call it. And according to our research,

Rachel fell on some hard times after you left Vancouver. Moved in with a guy who had a pill and alcohol problem, which he was happy to share with her. Courts eventually took away that kid of hers—"

"Suze," I said, involuntarily.

"Suze, who I guess was fostered out, but I don't know, our records aren't complete on that. The point is, you're in no position to be claiming the moral high ground. You don't trust us with Geddy? How about this: I promise not to shoot him, overdose him with narcotics, or push him out of a helicopter. So help me God."

"At least," I said, "we didn't kill Meir Klein."

He laughed. "It was InterAlia that killed Klein, not Het. But yeah, we knew they were concerned about him going public. InterAlia's management trusted us with that knowledge, because we shared their concern. Het was thinking about the future long before you idiots started selling Affinity home-test kits, you know. The Affinities need real governance. If not InterAlia, then Het. If not Het, the government will step in and regulate us out of existence. We—"

A bare bulb in a ceiling fixture flickered to life. Everyone in the room paused to stare at it. Moments later there was a chorus of ringtones, including one from the phone in my pocket.

I ignored my phone, and the Het guy ignored his, but he waved permission at his people: *Go ahead, pick up.*

A bad situation. But maybe not hopeless. Behind the buzz and tinkle of phones I heard another sound, one I liked a lot better: the wail of a distant siren.

That would be a truck from the Onenia County Fire Department, hurrying up Spindevil Road.

Part of our plan. By now some of the local Taus would have gathered just a few yards down the road, hidden from the farmhouse by the stand of oaks. The disposable Toyota would be there, too, with Trev at the wheel and a canister of gasoline in the passenger seat.

Dangerous as these Het enforcers were, they would have been instructed not to take any action that involved witnesses or would attract the attention of law enforcement. So what we needed was a way to take Geddy out of the farmhouse under civilian observation and without guns drawn. We needed a cat's paw, and it had been Shannon who suggested the local fire department.

The most dangerous part of this plan was the setup, which required Trev to drive the rattletrap Ford up to the farmhouse and exit the vehicle after spilling and igniting enough gasoline to generate a vigorous blaze. The arrival of the Onenia County fire truck would block the road, leaving the Hets nowhere to go, and Jolinda would tell the firefighters there were squatters living inside the farmhouse. Best-case outcome: firefighters would evacuate the house, including Geddy and me, and civilian scrutiny would prevent any violent interference by frustrated Hets.

The Hets *weren't* squatters, of course, and the owner of the farmhouse could testify to that, but by the time it was all sorted out Geddy and I would be safely elsewhere. The blazing Toyota would have to be explained, but the local tranche figured they could finesse that one. All good, then . . . assuming Trev could get the car close enough to the house to pose a plausible fire hazard.

The next thing we should have seen was the Toyota barreling down the lane. *Soon,* or the bluff wouldn't work. The fire truck couldn't be more than a mile or two away. We needed to make smoke.

But: nothing.

Radio silence.

And my phone had stopped ringing.

But the Het guy's phone buzzed again, and this time he took it out of his pocket and looked at the display and put it to his ear. He said, "Yeah." He listened intently. Looked at me. Looked at Geddy. Listened some more. Then, "Yeah, okay." He turned to the woman on the stairs. "Rev up the cars," he said. "Time to go."

The sound of the siren came lofting across scrubland and groves of wild oak and maple on rain-damp air, too loud to ignore. The Het guy frowned and told one of his people to stay on the window until the convoy was ready to go. "Everybody else, *move*." He stood up and looked down at me. "*You*. Unless you want to come with us, tell me what that noise is all about."

I couldn't help casting a glance at the dusty front window. No sign of the Toyota. "I don't know."

He slapped me. Open palm, but a hard physical blow. My head rocked back. The pain was as sudden and astonishing. For a moment I couldn't see anything.

"Tell us what's happening out there," he said, "unless you want to come along with us."

I tasted blood, like salty copper. "Fuck you," I said. *"I don't know."* Which, at this point, was absolutely true.

"Fire truck," the guy at the window said.

Tom turned. "What?"

"Looks like a fire truck up at the road."

I could see it now from where I sat, a big fire-and-rescue vehicle, guys in yellow slickers climbing out of it. But no Toyota, no actual fire.

It wasn't hard to imagine what had gone wrong. As soon as the phones came to life, Trev must have called Damian or taken a call from him. Trev would have said the rescue was underway. And Damian would have told him there *was* no rescue, that I had been told to drop it, that the entire thing was a completely unauthorized clusterfuck, to be cancelled immediately, full stop.

"Help," Geddy said.

I guess it was the sight of the fire truck that set him off. Or the sight of the blood on my face. His voice was small at first, as if he couldn't collect enough breath to squeeze out the word. His second try was better, more like a bark: "Help!" Then the panic welled up in him and took a grip on his lungs: "HELP! *HELP!*"

Not that anyone outside could hear him.

He leaped off the sofa. The nearest Het tried to put a hand on him, but Geddy bulled past him. He was halfway to the door when the guard by the window tackled him and pinned him to the floor. Geddy kept shouting, though the sound was strangled now by the pressure of the guard's forearm on his throat.

I considered the window. Murky old glass. Maybe I could break it. And maybe that would attract the attention of the firefighters up the lane. But Tom had taken his pistol from under his belt, and he put it to my head. "Sit," he said crisply. "Everybody else, out back and into the cars *now*. And secure that hostage!"

Three more Hets came down the stairs and headed for the rear of the house where the back door opened through the kitchen. The guard from the front window rolled Geddy over and tried to haul him to his feet. They were too busy to see what I saw:

The Toyota, at last, fishtailing around the rear of the Onenia fire truck, kicking up a plume of gravel as it steered wildly for the farmhouse.

"*Two* hostages," the Het guy said. "Not your lucky day, Adam. Stand up."

I stood up.

The car gained speed. I couldn't make out who was behind the wheel, but it wasn't Trevor Holst. Somebody smaller, somebody without the swirl of facial tattoos. The Het guy saw me looking and followed my gaze. "Shit!" he said.

The Toyota sped up as if the driver had no intention of stopping. And maybe she didn't. The car was close enough now that I recognized the halo of curled hair behind the steering wheel. It was Geddy's girlfriend, Rebecca.

The Het guy raised his pistol as if he meant to shoot through the window, and I grabbed his arm and put my weight on it, and we both fell to the floor. I felt more than saw what happened next. The car struck the farmhouse's ancient porch, bounced up the wooden risers, and toppled a wooden pillar; the roof of the porch collapsed around it, shattering the front window and filling the room with billows of plaster dust and shards of rotted wood.

The Het guy struggled under me, eyes wide with rage and frustration. I felt him trying to raise his right arm and I let my knee bear down on his elbow until he screamed. Through the dust I saw Geddy break free of his captor and lunge toward the gap where the window had popped out of its jambs. Glass crunched under his feet. The farmhouse groaned as if the rafters had been stressed to their breaking point, as if the roof might come down around us.

I managed to stand up just as Geddy pushed himself through the empty window frame into the tumbled ruins of the porch. The Toyota was obscured by dust and debris, but Geddy had recognized Rebecca behind the driver's-side window. He shouted her name. He used his hands to shovel away raw boards and broken lathing.

I looked down at the Het guy, who was trying to get up, but his injured arm wouldn't cooperate. His face was white with plaster dust, a clown's face. He met my eyes.

"You dumb fuck," he said.

Then the room was full of Onenia County paramedics.

CHAPTER 24

Rebecca spent a night in the county hospital, under observation for the mild concussion she suffered when she drove the car up the farmhouse steps. The detonation of the airbag had left her with a pair of black eyes and a swollen nose worthy of a prize-fighter, but she was basically okay. Geddy stayed at her bedside, apart from a brief interview with local police and a few hours' sleep at my father's house, until she was released.

I spent the night at the Motel 6. Telecommunications had been fully restored, but no one was returning my calls. Not Amanda, not Damian, not even Trevor Holst. By now, of course, they knew I had lied to them in order to get Geddy released, and I assumed they were working out some kind of appropriate response—whatever that might be. I did manage to get hold of Shannon Handy, but when I identified myself she said, "Uh, sorry, Adam—it's complicated, I can't talk," and hung up.

So I watched the news, local and international. The end of the telecom blackout had produced a flood of footage from India and Pakistan, much of it terrifying. Mumbai had been hit by drone-delivered conventional weapons, not a nuclear device, but the destruction had been brutally widespread. No significant government building had been left untouched. A firestorm that began in the Dharavi slums had killed tens of thousands: the full accounting of the dead would eventually top one million.

Here in Schuyler, there was nothing about the events at the house on Spindevil Road. I guessed the local Taus, or Hets, or both, were well connected enough to shut down any real investigation. Rebecca had told the paramedics she couldn't remember how she had "lost control" of the car, and the Het owner of the property would have been instructed not to press charges.

In the morning I took a cab to the hospital, shortly before Rebecca was discharged. Geddy told me it was no use calling Mama Laura—neither she nor my father was in a mood to speak to me right now.

In other words, I had no reason to stay in Schuyler. I also had no ride home. The hospital rolled Rebecca to the curb in a completely unnecessary wheelchair, and Geddy helped her into their car. They were driving straight back to Boston. I asked Geddy whether he could drop me at the regional airport.

Rebecca leaned out of the passenger-side seat and said, "You'll need to take a puddle-jumper to some bigger airport. Why not come with us? Fly out of Logan?"

Geddy nodded vigorously: "Yes, come with us! Come with us, Adam."

So I said yes. In part because I craved their company, in part because I didn't want to face the other big question: when I went home, would I have a home to go to?

Rebecca was intermittently groggy from the pain meds she had been given, and Geddy had never been especially happy behind the wheel of a car, so I did most of the driving, which was easy enough, the New York State Thruway to the Massachusetts Turnpike, clear skies and cool weather all the way. Driving pro-

vided an excuse for my lapses into silence, during which I con-
templated and then tried not to contemplate what I had done.

Geddy chatted with Rebecca whenever she was awake. I had
been afraid the events of the weekend had traumatized Geddy,
but he spoke about them freely, and though he tensed up when
he described how the Hets had surrounded his car and forced
him into one of their vehicles, it seemed to have affected him
no more or less profoundly than the bullying he had occasionally suffered at the hands of my father. Geddy had always seemed
to shrug off those episodes . . . at least by daylight, though they
came back, weightier and more terrifying, in his dreams. Rebecca
might have to learn how to deal with his nightmares.

Or maybe that was something she had already learned. She
was as solicitous of Geddy as he was of her, and I began to recognize their relationship for the small miracle it was. In her presence Geddy was calm, relaxed, engaged. There were moments
when they almost seemed to forget I was in the car with them,
to forget what they had so recently endured, and their talk grew
soft and murmuring, confident as the sunlight that glittered from
the pavement of I-90 East.

We reached their tiny Allston Village apartment after dark.
I made repeated but futile attempts to reach Damian or Amanda
or Trevor by phone, and I thought about calling the tranche house
in Toronto, but in the end I didn't: I was afraid of what Lisa might
say. I was still awake well past midnight, sitting in the kitchen
reading the news and watching moonlight inch across the linoleum counter, when Geddy joined me, in shorts and a white
t-shirt with a wry, sleepy smile. He said he'd heard me moving
around. I apologized for keeping him up. "It's okay," he said.
"I'm a light sleeper."

He poured himself a glass of milk and sat at the table with
me. The window was open, and a sudden breeze lifted the
curtain and made him shiver. "You're going home tomorrow,"
he said.

"If I have a home to go to."

He nodded. "I want to thank you for what you did for me."

I shrugged.

"Seriously. I mean, you risked a lot. And now nobody will talk to you."

"Seems like. But I'm a Tau, Geddy. Sooner or later, they'll understand why I did what I did back in Schuyler. And they'll forgive me."

He blinked twice and said, "Is it really something you need to be *forgiven* for?"

We sat a while longer. He finished his milk and belched spectacularly. "I ought to go back to bed," he said. "It's late."

But something, maybe nothing more than the cool spring air and the sound of a dog barking in the distance, had put me in a philosophical mood. "So what do you think," I asked him, "is the world *old* or is it *young?*"

He looked startled. Then he smiled. "You remember!"

"Long time ago, huh?"

"Long time," he agreed. "*Long* time."

"So what's the verdict, kiddo? Just between us grownups. Is the world old or young?"

He took the question seriously. "Well, Rebecca helped me figure that out. It's about how it *seems*, right? How the world *seems* to people. Back in the dark ages the world must have seemed really old, like it was all, you know, Roman ruins and fallen empires. Like nothing big or good could ever happen again. Like you could stare at some crumbling aqueduct in the French countryside and wonder how it ever came to be built. But then there was the Renaissance and the Enlightenment and suddenly there were whole new ways of answering questions, and it made people feel like, no, they were at the *beginning* of something, a whole new world being born. Right?"

"I guess."

"And when you and I were kids, I guess what worried me was, it was like people thought everything was over—religion was empty, science was useless, progress was phony: if you thought about the future it was like, you know, global warming and over-population and wars over food and water. Like the world was old, finished, used up."

I said, "Those things are worth worrying about."

"Sure, of course. But no one could *do* anything about them. No single person could make a difference or ever hope to, nobody with money wanted to risk it, nobody with real power cared to exercise it. It seemed like it was just . . . too late."

"Isn't it?"

"That's what I learned from Rebecca. And New Socionome. When Meir Klein discovered social teleodynamics? That was a whole new way of looking at things. Like the Affinities—"

"To be honest," I said, "I'm not sure that's working out the way Klein hoped."

"No, but it was only the *beginning*. The Affinities proved how powerful social algorithms could be. But the Affinities were, like, the Model T of socionomic structures. We're building better ones! Evolutionary algorithms to enhance non-zero-sum exchanges of all kinds! A way to *address* the big problems!" He was starting to shout, the way he used to, years ago, when he talked about his enthusiasm-*du-jour*; but he caught himself and gave me a sheepish grin. "I don't want to wake Rebecca. But it's *young*, Adam. That's the point. The world's young! We're at the beginning of something, and it's big, and it's scary, but in the end it might be—" He flung his arms wide, as if to embrace the whole spring night. *"Beautiful!"*

The next day I managed to secure a seat on a flight to Toronto. The woman who settled into the seat next to me asked whether

I was beginning a trip or going home. "Going home," I said, because it was the easiest answer.

And arguably true. Or not. Depending on how you defined "home." After I cleared customs I took a cab to a downtown hotel and checked in for the night. My home address, of course, was the tranche house in Rosedale—it was where I lived when I wasn't on the road—but I wasn't sure I would be welcome there. So I spent another night alone, listening to the sound of the hotel elevators pushing air up and down their concrete shafts.

And in the morning I screwed my courage to the sticking point and called the house. When Lisa answered, I said, "It's me. I'm back in town."

A silence.

"Adam," she said.

"Yeah. I wanted—" But what *did* I want? To pretend nothing had changed? Not possible. "Wanted to let you know I'll be there soon."

"You're coming to the house?"

"Well, yeah. Of course."

Which produced a more protracted silence. Then, "What time will you be here?"

"I don't know. In an hour, say?"

"I suppose that would be all right. An hour."

"Lisa," I began. But she had hung up.

They say you never forget your first tranche house. In my case I had never really left it.

It looked as welcoming as ever, drowsing in the gentle heat of a spring afternoon. The lawn had been recently cut, the hedges trimmed. The big maple in the front yard was already putting out seed pods—years ago, Amanda had told me they were called *samaras*—and they fluttered around me as the wind shook the branches. Every step I took, I had taken a thousand or ten thousand times before. Along the paved walk, up the stairs to the porch. Fumbling in my pocket for the key. Needlessly, because the door opened before I reached it.

"Come in," Lisa said from the cool darkness inside.

I stepped into the smell of baked bread, of wood polish, of the fresh flowers she had cut for the dining room table. Any other day, any other homecoming, Lisa would have taken me into her frail arms. Today she did not. She stood well back, cautiously, as if I had become radioactive. The house was quiet. Unusually quiet, even for a weekday afternoon. As if there had been some communal act of avoidance, a collective absence, perhaps orchestrated by Tau telepathy. "You can't stay, of course," she said.

If I did not find those words shocking, maybe it was because I had unconsciously anticipated them. "But I live here," I said.

"No, not any longer," she said. "I'm sorry."

I had no compelling argument to make. I stood in the entrance hall, neither defiant nor penitent, as Lisa explained what would happen. I would arrange to have my possessions removed from my room. I could return once more, for that purpose. Today, I could take away anything I cared to carry. Otherwise, the tranche house was closed to me.

The afternoon had become unreal, as vague and unfocused as a dream. I went up the stairs to my room, which had become a dream of a room, all memory, no substance, all past, no present. The double bed, the desk, the shelf of books. The window, its bottom sash held open by an empty wine bottle. The lace curtains Lisa had installed years ago, before my time. The sound of the maple tree turning its branches in the fitful breeze, a sound that had lulled me to sleep on hot summer nights.

Most of what I owned was in this room. None of it felt like it belonged to me.

She was waiting when I came back downstairs, empty-handed. Her blank expression made me a little angry. "I'm still a Tau," I said. "Despite all this. That doesn't change."

"But it does," she said, and something that resembled sympathy finally came into her eyes. "It has. Poor Adam. This is our fault as much as yours. You were never curious about your numbers, were you? Meir Klein's arithmetic was always a little beyond you."

"What are you talking about?"

"Drift," she said mournfully. "Just—drift. It's what made you useful to us, these last few months. You were always good at talking to outsiders. You could see the world the way they did. You had that knack. Almost a sort of double vision, yes? Tau and non-Tau. The reason for that is simple. You've been on the edge for many years—a Tau by the skin of a decimal point, so to speak. But at your last requalification, you simply failed. No, Adam, you are not a Tau. Not any longer."

I could not speak.

"Poor Adam," she said again. "But you see, it's not entirely your fault that you betrayed us. We should have anticipated it."

"You *knew* this about me? And you said nothing?"

"Damian and Amanda knew. I was told. No one else. Trevor didn't know, not until after you did what you did in Schuyler. We would have told you as soon as your sister-in-law's video was released, of course. Until then . . . we thought it was better to postpone the revelation."

"Because I was useful."

"Bluntly, yes. We're not proud of that. It was always a gamble. But we did it for the sake of the Affinity, Adam. You would have done the same, once, in our place."

"Once. But not anymore."

"No, not anymore. Because you used *us*, too, didn't you? Lied

to us so you could rescue your stepbrother. We failed to anticipate that. But we don't blame you—it was the drift that made
it possible."

Because there was no way to process what she had told me, I
tried to pretend she hadn't said it. I told her I would arrange to
have my things moved out as soon as I had a place to put them.
Then I said good-bye, for the last time. Walked out the front
door, for the last time. Passed under the maple tree with its pa-
pery rain of samaras, for the last time. I felt as if even my grief
and anger had been stolen from me. I wasn't entitled to them: I
wasn't a Tau. I was, in effect, no longer anything at all.

Jenny's video was released to the Internet a few days later, along
with an affidavit from Aaron's most recent ex-girlfriend, who
turned out to be a skinny forty-year-old with unconvincing red
hair and a taste for leopard-skin-patterned clothing accessories.
Maybe her testimony wasn't as convincing as Damian had
hoped—in the end Aaron was forced to resign his congressional
seat, but serial denials kept him in office until after the vote on
the Griggs-Haskell bill.

Which passed. Worse, it passed with a suite of draconian but
bipartisan amendments that Het had lobbied hard to suppress.
The law applied only to the American sodality, but it was a model
for subsequent legislation in Canada and Europe and, ultimately, around the world.

In other words, it was the beginning of the end of the brief
age of the Affinities. I told myself I didn't care. But I continued
to carry my Tau identity with me like a second skin, a name I
could no longer call myself, a raft of memories too essential to
be extinguished, though they became, with time, a collation of
orphaned moments. A lighted window on a winter night, footsteps on a hidden stairway, the sound of distant voices.

EPILOGUE

The Sound of Voices

The arc of history is long, but our algorithms
bend toward justice.

—REBECCA DRABINSKY

The invitation arrived as a text message. A handful of names,
the address of a downtown café, a date and time.

The first six months after I left the tranche house had been the
most difficult. I was alone and unemployed, though I had a savings account with a balance big enough to keep me in groceries
and pay the rent on a one-bedroom basement apartment in a
seedy but not actually dangerous part of town. My savings would
have been exhausted by the end of winter, but for a stroke of
luck: I ran into a woman I had known slightly when I was a student at Sheridan College. She had recently quit a lucrative advertising job to open her own start-up agency, and she needed
a graphic artist with professional skills who would work at an
entry-level salary. I was honest: I told her I was years out of date
on digital graphics platforms, but I was a fast learner and salary
wouldn't be a problem. It was the last clause that sealed the deal,
I suspect. But it was work and it was honest and it filled my
otherwise empty days.

I didn't talk to my family again until my father died. It was Mama Laura who called with the news. "I cannot say he didn't suffer, but the hospital was generous about painkillers, so it wasn't as bad as it might have been. Aaron came to see him at the last. Aaron's drinking pretty heavily these days, I'm sorry to say. But he was sober for his father's sake."

A funeral and memorial service had been arranged. My father's business acquaintances would all be there, including the leading lights of the Onenia County Republican Committee. I would not be turned away, she said, if I chose to attend. But it might be awkward, under the circumstances.

"Did he ask about me at all, before he died?"

It was a stupid question, and I should have known better than to ask.

"Adam . . . no. But I'm sure he thought of you."

I didn't attend the funeral.

Geddy and Rebecca were in India at the time, doing volunteer work for an NGO, helping to assemble modular housing for the legions of Mumbai's poor made homeless by the Short War. They came back shortly before the funeral, and I began to hear from them every week or two. Their calls became absurdly important to me.

Rebecca talked a great deal about New Socionome. She wasn't evangelical about it, but her enthusiasm would have been hard to conceal, and she wasn't interested in concealing it. She blogged on the subject, and I read some of her posts. I liked her idealism, except when it grated on me. She called from Boston one winter evening when I was home from a day's work, facing unwashed laundry and maybe an hour of pointless television before bed. She was eager to tell me about some fresh iteration of a New Socionome algorithm, the words spilling out of her until I said, more cruelly than I had intended, "Does it matter? I mean, Jesus, what does it change? Eight billion people on the planet, weather disasters, war—what does it matter than somebody invented a new way to *make friends*?"

She was surprised but not deterred. "I think you *know* it matters," she said. "I think that's why you're so scared of it."

They called it the Klein test now. It had been simplified and streamlined since we introduced the first crude Affinity home-test kits eight years ago. A headband sensor array, software to interpret eye movement and skin conductivity, a secure link to a New Socionome test site, and a few hours spent looking at generated images and answering apparently simple questions.

Plus, of course, the final and decisive keystroke, the one that entered your data into the global calculus.

In this case, *my* data. The suite of numbers that defined me. My one and only true name.

Weeks passed. Nothing happened.

I figured I must be unique, a totally insular human being, no useful social valency at all, nothing to contribute to the centuries-long project of making the world a better place.

Then I received the text message. A terse invitation. Date, place, time. The names of certain strangers.

"It takes real courage," Geddy had warned me, "not to hit DELETE."

So I found myself on a crowded sidewalk on an early summer evening, heading for an unfamiliar address.

The world was as shitty and imperfect as it had ever been, but lately I had been wondering if Geddy and Rebecca might be right: maybe there was something (as Rebecca had said in her blog) "a little Renaissancey" in the air. Some shared intuition, unspoken but felt, a verdict of the heart, a suspicion, too fragile to be called optimism, that the world was not old and exhausted but young and undiscovered. Something that passed between strangers in the twilight like a knowing smile.

A wind came up from the west, raising dust from the summer-hot street, and I turned a corner and saw the address I had been given. A small café, its windows spilling yellow light onto the pavement. And yes, I *was* afraid. But it felt good to be in motion, to be for that moment no one and nothing but myself, stepping through another door into the sound of human voices.

AUTHOR'S NOTE

Science fiction is a genre that famously generates new words. Readers may have noticed the word "teleodynamics" in *The Affinities* and assumed it was another such science-fictional neologism. But I didn't invent the term; I borrowed it from Terrence W. Deacon's fascinating *Incomplete Nature: How Mind Emerged from Matter* (W. W. Norton & Company, 2011). In Deacon's book the word refers to the kinds of thermodynamic processes that are intrinsic to living things, and by extension to human consciousness. And while at one point Deacon hints that teleodynamics might eventually help us understand social interactions, he nowhere suggests anything even remotely similar to what I describe in *The Affinities*. In other words, I thank him for the loan of a useful word and a fascinating concept, and I apologize for extrapolating it far beyond anything he ever intended.